DAYZEE DAZZLE
AND HER
MANIC MANSION

Other Books by Edward Allen Karr

SERIES: Thrills N Kills in the Hills
(Racy, Comical Horror in Beverly Hills)
Dayzee Dazzle and the Kildare Killers – Book One
Dayzee Dazzle and the On-Set Onslaught – Book Three
Dayzee Dazzle and the Cadaver Collectors – Book Four
* * * * *

SERIES: Socrates Lewis Stories
(Psychological/Religious Fiction)
Crosswinds – Book One
Crossovers – Book Two
* * * * *

SERIES: Fringes Of Infinity
(Contemporary Fantasy Fiction)
Lin Finity and her Mayhem Rising – Book One
Lin Finity in Holding On – A Novella
Lin Finity and the Words Unspoken – Book Two
Lin Finity and the Islands of Time – Book Three
Lin Finity and the Flights to Forever – Book Four
Tayo Tersoo and the Hunter of Souls – Book Five
* * * * *

SERIES: A World So Close
(Middle-grade Fantasy Adventure & Coming of Age)
Jayden Blue and the Gift to Imagine – A Prequel
Jayden Blue and the Sword in his Shadow – Book One
Jayden Blue and the Call of the Wings – Book Two
Jayden Blue and the Lair of the Iron Lions – Book Three
Jayden Blue and the Journey to Val ka'Yoom – Book Four
Jayden Blue and the Forest of Night Fallen – Book Five
Jayden Blue and the Wait of the Sun – Book Six
* * * * *

DAYZEE DAZZLE

AND HER

MANIC MANSION

Thrills N Kills in the Hills
Book Two

Edward Allen Karr

LAKESIDE LETTERS, LLC

Lakeside Letters, LLC
30628 Detroit Road, #247
Westlake, OH 44145

Dayzee Dazzle and her Manic Mansion
Thrills N Kills in the Hills Book Two

First Edition, 2021
www.LakesideLetters.com

Cover design by JD Smith Design
Editing by Preferred Proofreading, LLC

ISBN-13: 978-1-950886-21-0

"Oh, good," said Marilyn. "Kind of like playing matchmaker."

"God, Sis. Some kind of One-Eighty thing living in Kenzie like she's a puppet, and Carlos the yard guy, called here to remove a burnt, headless body from under the bed? You call that 'matchmaking?'"

"Girls," said Dayzee, "this is Beverly Hills. Things like that happen all the time."

From Chapter 2 – Sexy Prison Guard

Table of Contents

Chapter 1 – Anything It Wants

"Ooh, is that you, Kozy?"

Dayzee Dazzle resisted opening her eyes and smiled at the tender touch on her left arm. She lay on her back in the middle of her massive four-poster bed, caressed by the silk sheets and covered by a thick quilt. Her bare arms were up with her fingers laced behind her head and covered by her long, wavy blond hair. Everything beneath the covers was bare too.

"Mm . . . I was hoping you'd sneak in and wake me up. I'm curious how worked up you are right now. Let's just pretend there's all kinds of danger everywhere, alright?"

The soft touch began on her right arm, too, and when both touches became weightier, Dayzee snapped open her steel blue eyes.

"Oh, God no. Stop it!"

She saw that the two thick wooden posts at the head of the bed had leaned over and pressed down on her forearms, pinning them there and keeping her hands trapped beneath her head. A touch to her legs caused her to glance down, and she saw the posts at the foot of the bed leaning low and squeezing her thighs into the mattress, the big, polished balls at the ends feeling strong and unyielding.

Unable to kick her legs around under the covers, she screamed for their protector, the one that had been sent by the Guild and had arrived through the portal at the Prism Bar and Grill just the day before. No one had seen its arrival, but they'd marveled at its effects after it took over their new friend, Kenzie, a barmaid at the Prism.

"Kozy! Kozy, help!"

She heard no answer, no sound of feet running down the hall of her mansion in The Flats of Beverly Hills, and she thought of burning her way out of the trap her bed had become. Before heating up, she realized that if she sent the heat to her hands, she'd only burn her own hair first and then her head. If she sent her overpowering heat to any other part of her body, she'd only ignite her bed, and then the entire house would light up.

"Kozy! Mare! Fia! Anyone?"

No one answered, and she felt the post pinning her right thigh relax and withdraw until it touched her softly, just like how the nightmare had begun. She stared in shock as the large ball slid smoothly along her thigh until it rested on her hip. Then, it began to move closer to her middle.

"No! Oh, don't you dare! Kozy! Girls! Get in here already!"

The heavy ball hesitated, then moved quickly toward her face, causing her to wince, but it stopped at the edge of the quilt. It wiggled under it and snapped it to one side, leaving her covered by only the thin sheet, which conformed to every detail beneath it. The post then slid down between her breasts, gently gliding over her belly until it rested at an area below her navel.

"Oh, no, no, no!"

With eyes stretched wide open, Dayzee listened and heard nothing, even as she watched and felt the ball moving into just the position it wanted.

"No, don't! There's no way—"

It began a pleasant pressure, a soft rubbing up and down, lingering higher up to trace out tight, gentle circles, and Dayzee paused her pleas for help.

"Oh, you know, this is weird as hell, but . . . I mean . . . that's just . . . so . . ."

The post continued its amorous activities, and Dayzee closed her eyes and said, "Oh, that's . . . wow, that's . . ."

She let out a deep sigh and whispered, "Kozy, for the record, I'm still calling for help. Maybe you . . . you should . . ."

Seconds later, she felt the large wooden balls holding her arms down begin to press against the sides of her head, even while they still locked her arms in place. At first, it was a soft touch, but they zeroed in on her temples and began to imitate a vise.

"Kozy! Girls! I need help!"

She felt the pressure growing against her head, and the post between her legs began to show more enthusiasm. Dayzee strained against the parts pressing her arms into the mattress, then let them relax. She angled her eyes down to spy the large wooden ball moving more rapidly, dragging the soft sheet across her, bunching it up, then smoothing it back out. She closed her eyes and grinned until the squeezing of her head grew more intense.

"Kozy!"

Rapid footsteps in the hall preceded a crash against the closed bedroom door. It got snapped off of its hinges, and it danced upright for a second before falling to the floor. Kozy stood in the doorway, assessing the situation while wearing only baggy pajama pants. In an instant, he was sitting on Dayzee's lap, close enough that the romantic post bumped into his pants with each steady motion. From there, he reached for the two posts threatening to smash Dayzee's head.

"Hurry, Kozy! It's killing me!"

"We must avoid that, Dayzee."

He grabbed each of the two posts just under the balls at the ends, pulled them away from Dayzee's head, snapped the ends off, and tossed them to the floor. The shattered, splintered ends hesitated only a second, then they both lunged back at Dayzee's head, but he was too quick and got an iron grip on both of them again.

He broke the twisting, stabbing posts again, this time so low that they could no longer reach Dayzee's head. Still, they writhed in every direction, doing their best to poke their prey.

"You saved me, Kozy—my bed's trying to kill me!"

"Yes, I should have anticipated this possibility. It is constructed of wood. You were in great danger."

Dayzee looked down at Kozy's large bulge threatening to break free of his plaid pants.

"Well, look at you—you seem to have more wood than this crazy bed right now!"

"It is the danger. That is how we One-Eighties react. Do not let it trouble you."

"Oh, my—no trouble at all. Looks like you need a shave all of a sudden too. And your voice . . . it's gotten so much more—"

"Yes, I am very much reacting to the situation at the moment. I must hurry to save you from that other post."

Kozy started to turn, and Dayzee reached down and held both of his arms.

"You know . . . maybe there's not such a hurry for that one. I mean, with all this danger, you sure are . . . I mean . . . and you're sitting right there . . . and that bad post sure knows what it's doing down there."

"Dayzee, you still face considerable hazards."

"Yeah, and I like what that's doing to you. Maybe you should, you know, move a little closer, and—"

"What on Earth is going on in here?" Sophia said from the doorway as her eyes darted around at every detail.

"Oh, Sissy, what are those two up to?" said her twin sister, Marilyn.

Both wore short white robes and stared at the scene on the bed. Marilyn's wavy blond hair fell softly around her shoulders, and Sophia's straight black hair fell neatly far down her back. Two pairs of blue eyes stared at Dayzee and Kozy.

"I'm in great danger, girls," said Dayzee, "and you know what that does to Kozy. Oh, my goodness, girls!"

Dayzee closed her eyes and laid her head back on the pillow. Her hands moved to Kozy's thighs.

"What exactly is your bed doing to you?"

"Anything it wants, Fia. I never knew my bed could . . . oh, you know . . . that's so—"

In the blink of an eye, Kozy had spun around but still sat on Dayzee. Several snaps later, both posts that had trapped and caressed her were short, jagged serpents, still attacking with blinding speed.

"Oh, Kozy," said Marilyn, "you really are our hero!"

"Very impressive," said Sophia. "How could you be so strong and so fast? You look really hot in just pants too. Hey, check out the whiskers, Sis."

"Well, Kozy sure is taking care of business," said Marilyn. "I kind of wish my bed would attack me next."

Dayzee's hands again held Kozy by the thighs, which were muscular and straining against the thin cloth, and she said, "Girls, his legs are amazing. Wow, that's some serious muscle tone."

"That's not all that's really toned up and ready to go, Sissy," said Marilyn.

"Well, Sis, this is a crazy amount of danger. What did Kozy say One-Eighties do? They spring up?"

"Yes, Sophia," said Kozy. "My male characteristics amplify during times of strife. It will not last now that the danger has passed."

"But, Kozy," said Dayzee, "before all that's gone, maybe you could, I don't know, show us?"

"I'm thinking of more than just showing," said Marilyn. "We should hurry before it's all gone."

"It will never be all gone, but it has retreated. The danger has been neutralized," said Kozy.

"You still look damn good, especially without a shirt," said Sophia.

"It's true, Sissy," said Marilyn. "Wow, I think his muscles are still growing."

Before Kozy could get up, Sophia said, "Dayzee, is he wearing anything under those pants?"

"Nope. Not a thing. I can tell you for sure that Kozy was at attention and had my attention."

He climbed down off of Dayzee and the bed and stood at the side looking down on her.

"Are you intact? Did the assassin succeed in injuring you?"

"No, I'm fine. You got in here just in time. It was about to crush my head, though."

"It was doing something else to you, too, Dayzee," said Marilyn. "I think you liked that part of it."

"It did feel pretty good, Mare. Too good. I almost didn't care that it was trying to kill me. Kozy, what was that all about? What kind of thing is trying to kill us now?"

"I do not have an exact answer for you, Dayzee, but I have heard that the laboratories run by the Guild are an affront to all morals and ethics."

"What does that mean?" said Marilyn. "Bet it's not anything good."

"It means that they do not just mix chemicals or modify existing life forms. They recognize no limits, and they often operate outside of strictly scientific realities."

"Huh? Kozy, in English, alright?" said Dayzee.

"They have been known to mix science with sorcery. They—"

"What sorcery?" said Sophia.

"A recent Guild expedition to a passing asteroid uncovered a cache of sorcery crystals. They are rare in the universe and very unstable. When mixed with science, there are virtually no limits, and it seems they have created something especially diabolical in their attempts to terminate the three of you."

"Diabolical, huh? How diabolical?" said Sophia.

"They call it sorsciencery. It appears that they have sent an entity which seeks to seduce you even as it kills you."

Dayzee sat up, and she and Marilyn and Sophia looked at each other for several seconds with no one uttering a word.

"It did that, girls," said Dayzee. "It really knew what it was doing too. More than most others that have been through here. I almost didn't care that it was smashing my head."

"It felt that good, Dayzee?" said Marilyn. "Just the post from your bed?"

"Really, it did. In the end, though—"

"That's where it was probably headed next," Sophia said with a smirk.

"Good one, Sissy," said Marilyn. "I bet it was too. Who wouldn't?"

Sophia grinned and said, "Now, that's something I'd like to watch because—"

"Alright, you two. I'm just glad it wasn't enough to completely make me not care about my skull."

"It is still learning," said Kozy. "It will soon know how to take you to the highest point of your pleasure, and when—"

"I bet Kozy could do that too," said Marilyn.

"Ditto that, Sis," said Sophia. "Especially after he gets used to this planet and gets horny."

"I hope it doesn't take too long because I—"

"Girls! Let Kozy finish."

"—yes, and when you are there at your highest point, then it will kill you."

"That sure is diabolical," said Dayzee.

"Well," said Marilyn, "if I'm in my bed, which is made of wood, wouldn't I be in terrible danger?"

"Yes," said Kozy. "You would. We are sure of that now."

"Why don't you come see, just to make sure I'm tucked in all nice and safe?"

"I can inspect your room for potential dangers if you wish."

"How about my room?" said Sophia. "My bed isn't wood, but the dresser sure is. Oh, and those boards going around the windows. Those might get me. Maybe you should come and check on me first?"

"Oh, you girls are really too much."

"We just get awful itchy," said Marilyn.

"Sis is right," said Sophia. "Watching Kozy all worked up sure didn't help."

"Let's try to make it through the night, and we'll figure it all out tomorrow."

Chapter 2 – Sexy Prison Guard

Even though she'd barely been able to pry her eyes open, Dayzee had put on a tight red skirt with black heels and a black blouse. She'd managed to brush back most of her thick blond hair, and she'd left the blouse mostly unbuttoned.

After shuffling across her kitchen, she stopped near the refrigerator to rub her eyes and yawn. When she opened them again, she focused on the coffee maker, stared at it a few seconds, then took short steps in its direction.

Several minutes later, the smell of fresh brewing filled the room and wafted up the stairway to her sleeping companions. A short walk to the freezer yielded a box of waffles, and after fumbling with the package, she ripped the end apart, removed four of them, and got them started toasting. Soon after, the scent of blueberries joined the coffee on its journey to the mansion's upper levels.

She found her phone on the counter, punched a few numbers, waited for the message to wrap up, then said, "This is Dayzee. Monday isn't happening. I've had a ridiculous couple of days, and I'm going to need more than a Sunday off to rest up. Let's shoot for a Tuesday shoot. Hey, that's kind of funny. Later."

She ended the call and set the phone back where she'd found it. Leaning against the counter, she closed her eyes, took a deep breath, and stretched her arms straight up while arching her back. The two buttons holding her blouse closed loosened, and she shook her head with a soft laugh and fastened them again.

At the sound of footsteps on the staircase leading into her kitchen, she opened her eyes to see Kozy dressed in jeans and sneakers and a light gray t-shirt. He still had Kenzie's long, straight brown hair, and it had all been brushed and fell far past his muscular shoulders and down over his V-shaped back. A few wisps fell to the front and lay across a chest that threatened to split the t-shirt open.

"Good, you have nutritional resources."

"Good morning, Kozy. Yes, there's food. Thanks again for saving me last night. I guess I'm surprised the bed didn't keep attacking me after you splintered it. Why is that? It let me sleep the rest of the night."

"I have only a preliminary theory at this stage of its evolution."

"Huh? Kozy, it's kind of early. How about keeping it simple?"

"Such creations often evolve and gain strength and capabilities. I believe we tired it out."

"Huh. *You* tired it out. You're saying that it needed to recuperate?"

"Yes, that is likely."

"Thank God, because I needed some rest. I still need some rest. You're hungry?"

"More than this simplistic Earth language can describe. I am operating Kenzie's physical form at a very demanding metabolic speed."

"How? You're not doing all that much."

"Look at these," Kozy said and held up both arms and flexed his biceps. One hand dropped down to point at the thighs packed tightly into the denim, and he said, "and these ambulatory limbs. It requires energy to manifest and maintain such alterations."

"Oh, well, let's make sure you have plenty to eat, then," Dayzee said with a big grin. "What about Kenzie?"

"She is here, too, and she is starving as well."

"Can she say hi?"

"No."

"Alrighty, then. Got it. Here, take these," Dayzee said and handed her own plate to Kozy, who tore into them, packing his cheeks and snarling noticeably.

"Whoa, slow down—there's more of them in the freezer. You can eat all you want."

"These warm, brittle disks are surprisingly satisfying. I would like to consume several additional stacks of them."

"Sure thing. Just be sure to leave a decent figure for Kenzie when you're done here."

He set the plate on the counter and held the last waffle, taking big bites, and reached down for the t-shirt's bottom hem. After pulling it up high enough to show his lean, bare abdomen, he said, "Kenzie is remarkably fit. That is unusual on this planet, is it not? I only added some muscle."

Dayzee stared.

"Wow, Kenzie sure was in good shape. I love what you did with that too."

Dayzee walked up and stood in front of him. She reached out and held his waist with both hands, squeezing it and smiling.

"Solid as heck. How did she manage that?"

"I do not know, but she will not gain weight from my eating. I need copious quantities of food."

Dayzee shook her head, smiled, and said, "Heck, eat all you want," and kept looking down at Kozy's bare abs. She poked at his navel with one finger and smiled.

"What's going on with you two now?" said Sophia. She'd dressed herself in a short black skirt with black heels, and her light blue blouse was tight, largely unbuttoned, and matched her eyes. Her long black hair fell far down her back.

"Oh, good morning, Fia. Kozy and I were just admiring how fit Kenzie was. I guess he would have ended up a lot different if Kenzie wasn't built so well. Come see."

Sophia walked over to stand behind him, reached around with both hands, and said, "Oh, that's really something, Kozy. Even Kenzie would like what you've done. When you leave, she'll be back to the way she was?"

"Yes. I will not leave a trace of my displacing her."

"Good. I bet she worked hard for that."

"If anything, she's in even better shape now," said Dayzee.

"No one invited me to the party?" said Marilyn as she navigated down the stairs while rubbing her eyes with one hand and sliding the other along the rail. She'd found one of Dayzee's short white dresses, and the blue high heels fit too.

"Oh, Mare, it's not a party. Although, I guess it could be," said Dayzee. "We're just checking out Kozy. I was groggy starting my day, but this is waking me up."

Marilyn walked over, joined the group, and said, "Um, you could probably let go of him now, Dayzee."

"Oh. Yeah, you're right. I'll get some more waffles going."

"You too, Sissy."

Sophia let go and said, "Do you have any spaghetti? You could watch me inhale it like one of those cleaner machine things."

"Good one, Sissy."

"Oh, Fia, you mean a vacuum? You're just being silly. Waffles are better."

Dayzee filled the toaster and pushed the levers down. Kozy and the twins took seats at the kitchen table, and Kozy finished chewing and swallowed the last bite of his waffle.

"I barely slept last night, girls. That bed was still scary after Kozy beat it up, and I kept thinking it was going to get me again."

"Hmm . . . from what I saw, maybe you wished it would get you again," said Marilyn.

"That's what I was thinking, Sis," said Sophia. "Dayzee and that post really had something sweet going on."

"It only felt that way at that moment, Fia. Right now, that just seems creepy, nothing more."

"You're lucky Kozy came to your rescue," said Marilyn. "Hey, is that bed thing still alive?"

All eyes looked to Kozy for an answer.

"I do not believe the bed is still animated. Its attempts at attacking through that article have failed. It will seek another way."

"That's pretty ominous," said Sophia. "It can take over anything made of wood?"

"Wood," said Marilyn before giggling. "Can it take you, Kozy?"

"Yes, it appears most in tune with wooden items," he said to Sophia before turning toward Marilyn. "No, the assassin cannot take me."

"Can *we*?" said Sophia.

"All of us?" said Marilyn.

"Girls, this is serious."

"You're right, Dayzee," said Marilyn. "We'll try to behave. For a while anyway."

"Good. Now, here's something I just thought of."

She walked over and set a full plate of waffles in front of Kozy.

"What about us?" said Sophia.

"Yours is on the way. What I'm thinking is that since Kozy is our bodyguard, wouldn't some kind of uniform make more sense?"

"I love that idea!" said Marilyn. "Let's get Kozy all dressed up!"

"Those jeans are filled out really nice," said Sophia, "but yeah, some kind of hot uniform would be so much better."

"Girls, I never said a 'hot' uniform."

"Oh, come on, Dayzee," said Sophia. "Just because it wasn't your idea."

"Alright, it is a good idea. Let's finish breakfast and take a look in my costume storage."

"Wait," said Marilyn, "you have a stash of costumes?"

"I sure do. A couple of cabinets full, way up on the third floor."

"Wait again," said Marilyn, "you have clothes for Kozy too?"

"They might not fit perfectly, but yeah, I think we can find something. Let's take the elevator up."

"Since when do you have an elevator? I haven't seen an elevator," said Sophia.

"I haven't seen it in a while myself," said Dayzee. "It's here somewhere, though. Let's eat, then we can try to find the blasted thing."

*　　*　　*

They all took in their fill of waffles and coffee, and Dayzee led them up the stairs and down the hall.

"Why didn't we take the elevator up from the first floor?" said Sophia.

"Oh, Fia, I just thought it'd be easier to find on this floor."

They walked down a long hall past several bedrooms on each side.

"You led us right to it," said Marilyn. "You knew where it was."

"Sure, this one."

"What? There's more than one?"

"I think so, Mare. We can look later."

Sophia pressed the button, and the door opened to a wood-paneled cab with a polished wood plank floor.

"Uh-oh," said Marilyn. "Lots of wood. Kozy, are we in danger?"

"It is possible, but the assassin is not as adaptable yet as it will be soon."

Marilyn looked down lower on Kenzie and said, "Still, shouldn't you be ready for that?"

Kozy responded as she'd suggested, and Marilyn clapped her hands and said, "That's better!"

"Sis, we can't play with Kozy like some kind of wind-up toy."

"Why not, Sissy, especially since I'm always wound-up? If we're really in danger, we'll need Kozy ready, and I mean *really* ready to—"

"Oh, Mare. Let's get Kozy dressed up nice and then see about that. Hit '3,' will you?"

"Sure, Dayzee."

*　　*　　*

The elevator door opened to a lengthy room with a steep, peaked ceiling. Large windows at each end let in the bright Beverly Hills morning daylight, and several ceiling fans spun slowly.

"What do you think?" said Dayzee.

"I see many wooden cabinets and chests. The seating assemblies are wood also," said Kozy.

"Always looking out for us," said Sophia. "That's pretty hot too."

"Kozy will be even hotter with the right outfit," said Marilyn. "Those wardrobes are all full of costumes, Dayzee?"

"Yeah, from all the films and shows I've been in. I insisted in all my contracts that I keep everything I wore. Are you alright with this, Kozy? Gosh, we never even asked you."

"There is no need to ask, Dayzee. Dress me as you wish."

"One-Eighties are so much fun," said Marilyn.

"I am here to serve and protect."

"Oh, that sounds like a police officer," said Sophia. "How about it, Dayzee? Anything around here like that?"

"You know," said Dayzee, "in one of my favorite films, I played a sexy prison guard."

"Were you abusive too?"

"Oh yeah, Mare. Mean, horny, and out of control. It was wonderful—I barely had to act."

"But Kenzie isn't a girl anymore—she's Kozy now," said Marilyn.

"Let's just say I wasn't all that feminine in this flick," said Dayzee.

"Point us in the right direction," said Sophia, "and we'll turn Kozy into our own sadistic prison guard."

"Ooh, I like the sound of that!" said Marilyn.

"Girls, settle down. Remember that Kenzie is still in there somewhere too."

"Kenzie will love it. She likes playing dress-up," said Sophia.

"That's funny, Sissy, because we mostly saw her undressed when we used her to kill the last assassin. You were naked, too, except for your heels. Neither of you wanted anything to do with dressing up."

"That was just a weird night, alright, Sis? It was Halloween, remember?"

"Uh-huh. Sure, Sissy."

"Let's look in this one, I think," Dayzee said as she swung open the heavy wooden doors. "Yeah, there it is."

She reached in and pulled her hand back out just in time as both doors slammed shut.

"Oh, that was close," said Marilyn. "I think it tried to bite you."

"It almost did bite her, Sis. Kozy, this stupid furniture just attacked Dayzee. Is it that killer again? You're not going to put up with that, are you?"

Kozy swept back his long brown hair and faced the wardrobe with his fists on his hips.

"I will handle this for you should it exhibit more violent behavior."

"You'll have to because we need to get in there. You want a hot outfit, don't you?" said Marilyn.

"If it pleases all of you, yes."

One by one the doors ripped themselves away from the cabinet, sending screws and hinge parts rattling across the wood floor. The doors stood a moment on their own, rotating slowly, as if looking around the room. They'd just risen up and started to fly at Dayzee when Kozy grabbed both of them, slammed them flat on the floor, and stood with one clean white sneaker on each.

"Kozy, you did it!" said Marilyn.

"Not yet," he said as each of the doors shook and bent themselves up and away from the floor.

He gave each one several hard stomps, cracking one of them, and they quieted down and lay flat.

"It has retreated."

"Well, that's very impressive," said Marilyn.

"Yep, Sis, but those sneakers have to go. The jeans too. Kozy is way too sexy for those clothes."

Dayzee reached in and took out hangers with black khaki pants, a crisp white shirt with lace in the front, and a short black jacket with shiny brass buttons and wide padded shoulders.

"Oh, I think this is it, girls."

"I love it," said Marilyn. "Except for the shirt, of course."

"Sis is right. He'll just have to get by without a shirt."

"I agree, girls. We just need to find the right pair of boots."

"What kind of boots, Dayzee?" said Sophia. "There's no way any of your boots will fit him."

"No, Fia, not any of mine. Not long ago, one romantic encounter ended with him running for his life. He never came back for his boots, and I kept them."

"Probably tossed them in the basement, right?" said Sophia.

"Nope. Right here," said Dayzee, and she held a pair of shiny black boots with raised, thick treads. The toes had brass covers, and heavy brass buckles covered the outsides.

"Perfect," said Sophia.

"How about a hat too?" said Marilyn. "This is fun!"

"I know just the one. It's in the closet in that bedroom where—"

Dayzee stopped herself, and Sophia said, "What's wrong?"

"God, I just remembered something, Fia. Come on, let's ride back down and let Kozy change. I have to make a phone call."

*   *   *

Alone in the elevator with the Kildare Killers, Dayzee said, "Girls, we never got rid of that body under the bed. Remember that?"

"Oh yeah, I remember," said Sophia. "You and Sis wrapped it up and stuffed it under there when I was—"

"Getting to know Kenzie better," said Marilyn. "Well, at least until that first assassin took control of her."

"Well, Sis, I still got to know her. Remember how that headless dead guy was going at her?"

"Yes, I sure do remember, Sissy. Kenzie was dead, too, and naked and lying right there between your legs. Oh, I remember that well!"

"That's right, girls. That was a crazy time, but the more I think about it, I think I can trust Carlos to help out with that dead guy too."

"You're calling Carlos?" said Marilyn. "Sissy, let's get our teeny robes on. He won't even see Kenzie because Kenzie is really Kozy now, and—"

"Oh, you know what, Sis? I think Carlos would like Kozy better than Kenzie. You know what I mean?"

"Oh, you're saying that Carlos prefers—"

"Yep, I think so. Nothing happened between him and Kenzie. Maybe he'd like—"

"Who wouldn't like Kozy? Well, we'll just have to get them upstairs, then push them both in a room, then—"

"Girls, stop! Fia, hit '1,' please. We need Carlos to get rid of the headless body under the bed, remember? That's why I'm calling him. Not so you can set him up with the One-Eighty version of Kenzie."

"She's right, Sissy. That dead body has to go. Besides, I want the One-Eighty version of Kozy to myself."

"What about me?" said Dayzee. "Come on, this is my house."

"Oh, okay," said Marilyn. "I bet there's plenty to go around."

"Good. Thank you."

The elevator landed, and all three began walking toward the kitchen until Dayzee stopped and turned around.

"What's the matter, Dayzee?"

"Nothing, Mare. I just want to remember how to find that thing on this floor."

Dayzee studied the sight, then turned back around, and they continued walking through the halls and large rooms until they got back to the kitchen.

"Will Kozy know how to find us?" said Sophia. "We should have left a map."

"Good idea, Sissy. Dayzee, we can draw a map sometime, okay?"

Dayzee shook her head, smiled, and sat at the table.

"Sure, Mare," she said with a grin. "It's not like we have anything else to do."

She took out her phone and hit a few numbers.

"Carlos, it's Dayzee. Thanks again for all your help with the yard. Sweet of you to not ask any questions too."

She listened quietly for a few seconds.

"Are you blackmailing me, Carlos? It sounds like you are. I always pay you extra anyway because—"

More silent seconds passed. Dayzee looked from one twin to the other with a grin.

"Okay, fine. Come out one more time for some special work, and we'll find a way to make it worth your while. We think we know exactly what you might like. How does that sound?"

Dayzee examined several of the diamond rings she wore, smiled, and listened.

"Perfect. Just text me before you're about to show up, alright? Okay, talk to you soon. Thanks, Carlos."

She ended the call and set her phone on the table.

"Girls, what you were just talking about . . . let's give it a go. I have no idea how we could make that work, but I think you might be right about what Carlos wants."

"Oh, good," said Marilyn. "Kind of like playing matchmaker."

"God, Sis. Some kind of One-Eighty thing living in Kenzie like she's a puppet, and Carlos the yard guy, called here to remove a burnt, headless body from under the bed? You call that 'matchmaking?'"

"Girls," said Dayzee, "this is Beverly Hills. Things like that happen all the time."

*   *   *

Sophia had volunteered to toast more waffles, and she and Dayzee and Marilyn sat at the table eating and drinking hot coffee. All crunching stopped, and all heads turned at the sound of footsteps in the hallway leading to the kitchen.

"Oh my God," said Marilyn, "now that's hot!"

Kozy walked in wearing the uniform they'd chosen: black boots with brass buckles, black khaki pants that were tight and showed off his muscular legs, and a crisp black jacket that came down only an inch or two below his waist. The jacket couldn't come close to closing, and

Kozy's bare abs and chest showed bulging muscles like they were cut into granite.

"What is your assessment of this appearance?"

"Wow," said Sophia. "You *really* know how to play dress-up."

"Here," said Dayzee as she tossed a black cap over. "That'll finish it off."

Kozy put on the hat with a short brim and a shiny badge on the front and let out a deep sigh.

"Oh, Kozy likes it," said Marilyn. "Do you like that outfit, Kozy?"

"Yes, Marilyn, but that was Kenzie that expressed some relief and acceptance with the new clothing. She is occasionally able to manifest insignificant gestures and expressions."

"Told you, Sis. Kenzie likes dressing up," said Sophia.

"Only until someone undresses her, right, Sissy?"

"Girls, the important thing is that we now have a proper protector in a stylish uniform. I'm ready to be attacked by anything wooden now."

"Or something with wood," said Marilyn.

"Huh. Save that for Carlos, Sis. We owe him."

"I guess I'll have to, Sissy. That was the deal for him to get rid of the dead guy. Still, I'm hoping that I get a turn to—"

Marilyn's phone rang, and she picked it up off of the table. Kozy came closer, and all three waited quietly.

"Hello, this is Marilyn."

Twenty seconds of silence passed.

"That sounds amazing! Yes, I'm sure we'd all like to hear about it!"

Ten more quiet seconds passed.

"Today? Well, I guess that would be okay. Yes, I'm sure it'll be fine. I'll call you back if they say no, okay?"

She waited a few seconds, then said, "Wonderful! See you in an hour!"

Marilyn put her phone away and smiled from face to face.

"What, Sis? What's going on?"

"Oh, Sissy, that was our special admirer. You know . . . *that* guy. He said he has an idea for a reality show—starring all three of us!"

"No way, Sis! You're serious?"

"Uh-huh. Yes, he's serious. He wants all three of us as stars."

"What guy are you two talking about?" said Dayzee.

"A secret admirer," said Marilyn. "He'll be here in an hour to explain the whole deal. Dayzee, it's okay, isn't it? He wants to use your mansion. Come on, say it's okay!"

"Hey, why not? That could be fun. We'd have to mix it in with all of our other projects, but we could work it out."

"Did he say the name of the show, Sis?"

"Yes, he sure did. He said it's 'Kildare in the Hills.'"

Chapter 3 – Even Bigger Stars

"'Kildare in the Hills,' huh? That's what he said?"

"That's right, Dayzee. He said it's because we came from Kildare," said Marilyn.

"Why the heck did he call you? He wants to use my house, but he calls you?"

"Well, he doesn't have your number for one thing. Besides, I think he might have some special feelings for me, that's all."

"No way, Sis. I'm sure he likes me better."

"I didn't mean to exclude you, Sissy. I think he has special feelings for both of us."

"Who exactly is this guy?" said Dayzee.

"We never told you," said Sophia, "but he's given us some pretty nice gifts over the years."

"Like what?"

"Cash. Lots of it!" said Marilyn. "He says it's because he wants to help us with our careers, but we know better. He just digs us."

"He really does, Dayzee."

"Does he know you're the 'Kildare Killers?' Does he know where you're really from?"

"That's silly, Dayzee. No, of course, he doesn't know any of that."

"Ah, this shouldn't surprise me, Mare. You and your sister are so hot, and—"

"So are you, Dayzee."

"Thanks, Fia. Alright, the big question is: have either of you ever, you know, with him?"

"Mm . . . we sure do think about it, don't we, Sissy?"

"Yep, but we haven't. We've never even met him. Besides, we don't want to risk losing all that cash."

"We might burn him up by mistake, Dayzee."

"I'm proud of you girls. Very smart. You said he's coming over in an hour?"

"Yes, that's what he said. He wants to propose—"

"Propose? Really?"

"No, Dayzee, not like that. He wants to give us his proposal about the show. He said he has producers lined up and ready, and we just need to go over the details."

"You said he wants all three of us?" said Dayzee. "What about Kozy?"

"Oh, I know—he could be a houseguest."

"A really hot houseguest, Sis. If Kenzie ever comes back, she could be a houseguest too."

"Hey, we could say they were brother and sister, Sissy. He's a weightlifting freak with all kinds of muscles, and she's just a hot barmaid."

"This could work, girls. Kozy, are you okay with that? Do you want to be part of the show too?"

"If that is required for me to continue protecting you, then yes. Sign me up."

"That's funny, Kozy," said Marilyn. "'Sign me up.'"

"It's nowhere near as fun as dressing you up," said Sophia.

"Undressing, too, right, Sissy?"

"That was Halloween, and it was part of the plan, remember? Kenzie and I didn't really do—"

"Girls! We need to get ready. Marilyn, what's the guy's name?"

"You're not going to believe it. I hope it's an alias."

"Go ahead and tell us, already, Sis."

"Sutcliffe Gutsquid."

"Lovely," said Dayzee. "What the hell kind of a name is that?"

"Did you say 'Gutsquid,' Marilyn?" said Kozy.

"I sure did, Kozy. Why, do you know him?"

"No, I am sure I do not. The name sounds familiar, that is all. It reminds me of an entity rumored to inhabit a nearby asteroid."

"Entity?" said Dayzee. "What kind of entity?"

"It is supposedly a fish-like, parasitic life form that thrives in the digestive tracts of other living things, eventually consuming them from the inside out."

"Sheesh," said Sophia.

"You didn't know his name, Fia?"

"No, Dayzee, I just took the cash. We've never met him. Sis is the only one that has dealt with him."

"Well, whatever his name is, if he's for real, this could be fun."

"You sure do have the house for it, Dayzee. We're going to be even bigger stars!"

"I think you're right, Mare. We're going to be even more—"

Dayzee froze.

"What's the matter, Dayzee?"

"Oh, Fia. This isn't going to be easy. First of all, we have a dead body upstairs. Carlos could show up at any time to deal with that, and don't forget why Kozy is here. Anything inside or outside this house that's made of wood can attack us when we least expect it. We can't always be together, so Kozy might not be around for all of us all the time."

"Yep, especially when Carlos finishes his dirty work," said Sophia. "If we get Carlos alone with Kozy, no one will be around to protect any of us."

"We'll manage, girls. This is show business—things are always crazy."

A clatter near the sink quieted everyone, and they all turned to look. A rack of knives on the counter started bouncing around, tipping from side to side and rattling each knife until they all fell out. One at a time, each knife floated up and drifted toward the staircase, where they sailed in an orderly line up and out of sight.

They all listened to the silence. Dayzee looked away from the staircase and toward Kozy.

"What the hell?" said Dayzee. "Knives?"

"With wood handles," said Kozy.

"Kozy, what's that all about?"

"It appears to be gathering weapons. Or maybe it . . ."

"Go on, Kozy. What else?"

"Maybe it is trying to scare all of you."

"It worked," said Marilyn.

"Me too, Sis."

"It wants to kill us, doesn't it?" said Dayzee. "Why would it want to scare us?"

"It will play with your emotions. Three of the four posts on your bed were determined to damage you."

"Damage is right," said Dayzee.

"The fourth had a different objective. It sought to distract you with pleasure."

"You're right about that, Kozy," said Sophia. "That thing was giving Dayzee some sweet kind of treatment."

"I liked it too," said Dayzee. "I really did."

"Fear. Lust. Death. Anything is fair game to it."

"That's especially crazy," said Marilyn. "How will we ever pull off this show? Can we do the show somewhere else?"

"No, Sis. That thing will try to kill us wherever we are. Scare us too."

"You might all be safer, at least for a while," said Kozy, "if you were to leave this mansion. It has settled in, and this has become its preferred playground. Is that the appropriate word?"

"Close enough," said Dayzee. "Well, I'm not running. Let it try to scare us."

Marilyn said, "Nothing scary about that empty knife rack, Dayzee. It looks stupid just sitting there all by itself."

The block of wood began vibrating and rattled around on the counter.

"Uh-oh," said Marilyn.

All any of them saw was the briefest of blurs as it raced toward the table. No one saw Kozy move to a new place sitting on Marilyn's lap.

"Oh, my!" said Marilyn. "Did you catch it?"

She peeked around Kozy to see that he held the flying block securely in both hands. She let out a deep sigh, hugged him tightly around his waist, and laid her head against his black jacket.

"You saved me!"

Her hands dropped down farther, and she said, "Oh, wow, that sure was some danger, wasn't it? My goodness!"

Dayzee said, "Well, Kozy did tell us."

"Pretty good, huh, Sis?"

"Oh, yes, Sissy. I better make extra sure, though."

"You're really helping yourself there, Sis."

"I really am. It's not going away either. Why is that, Kozy?"

Kozy brushed back his long brown hair, and Marilyn still held on tightly.

"Have you located the knives?"

"Well, no, we don't know where they are," said Dayzec. "Oh, I get it. We're still in danger. That's it, isn't it, Kozy?"

"Yes. It could strike at any time. You are all in peril."

"I'm kind of liking the peril right now," Marilyn said as she moved her left hand up to Kozy's abs and her right slipped inside his khakis. "I'm not even looking for those silly knives."

"But if we found them," said Sophia. "If we somehow put them all back where they belong, what then?"

"Then, I will revert to a more relaxed form."

"All the way relaxed?" said Sophia.

"Yes."

"Don't you dare go find those knives, Sissy," said Marilyn. "Not yet, at least."

"Hey, why would I spoil your fun? It would be different if, you know, my hands were in—"

"Alright, you two. We have to figure out—"

The doorbell rang out like a giant gong, and they all sat silent and stared at each other except for Marilyn, who still rested her cheek on Kozy's back and held on tight.

* * *

"I hope it's Carlos," said Dayzee. "There's a headless corpse rotting up there that we need to get out of here before your friend—"

"Sutcliffe?" said Marilyn.

"Yeah, that guy. Before he gets here. Even with the dead guy gone, we still have a ton of problems. Like those knives. Where the hell are those knives?"

"Don't ask me to find them, Dayzee," said Sophia. "Sis is having too much fun."

"Me neither," said Marilyn. "I could sit here all day and—"

"Fine, I'll just answer my own door," said Dayzee, and she rose from her seat and began walking toward the front door. "I really should get a butler."

Marilyn still held Kozy on her lap, and Sophia walked over and gazed up the stairway with her hands on her hips.

* * *

"Hello, I'm Dayzee. Dayzee Dazzle. I was expecting a young man named Carlos, but you're obviously not him."

A middle-aged man with lightly graying hair stood with a ball cap in his hand. He wore jeans and a polo shirt, and under his arm, he carried a leather portfolio.

"And you are obviously stunning. Sutcliffe. Sutcliffe Gutsquid at your service. Please, just call me Cliff."

Dayzee held out her hand, and he took it for a quick kiss, all the while looking into her eyes with a smile.

"Oh my, aren't you sweet, Cliff? Pleased to meet you. Please, come in."

Once they both had entered the expansive foyer, Dayzee closed the door behind them and leaned her back into it.

"I was surprised to hear from Mare just this morning about your proposal. I'm intrigued!"

Cliff looked around at the tasteful architecture and expensive furnishings. He shook his head with a grin and said, "This is magnificent. It's more luxurious than I'd even imagined it to be."

Dayzee walked farther inside and turned to face him.

"Well, thanks. I call it home."

Marilyn and Kozy walked in side-by-side, and Marilyn said, "Wow, it's you—we finally meet."

"Marilyn, you're even more beautiful in person."

She left Kozy to walk up to Cliff for a quick hug.

"Your twin sister is here too?"

"She sure is."

Sophia gave up on the stairs and walked into the foyer.

"Ah, the gorgeous Sophia. I'm Cliff. It's an absolute pleasure to meet you too."

"Likewise. Thanks for everything. Sis and I have appreciated all you've done for us."

"That was *my* pleasure. I only hope that it helped you in some small ways. Which is why I'm here today—a proposition that could catapult you all even higher into the stratosphere, where only the brightest stars can be found and adored."

"Oh," said Marilyn, "he does have a way with words, doesn't he?"

"I'll say," said Dayzee. "Cliff, you should be a writer or something."

"Well, Dayzee, I am. I've been lucky to have most of my books sell very well."

"What do you write?"

"Novels. I write in the obscure but profitable genre of Alien Romance. I guess all of my readers like to fantasize about affairs with aliens. Imagine that."

"Hey," said Marilyn, "are you sure your readers aren't aliens fantasizing about getting it on with a human?"

"Sis, that's crazy talk. Everyone knows there are no—"

"Now, Sophia," said Cliff, "your sister might be onto something. I get some fan mail asking me if I'm really from some other planet. I dodge and weave enough that they're never really sure."

"But you're not, right?" said Dayzee. "You're not from another planet, are you?"

"Oh, Dayzee, you're a treasure. You even looked concerned, or maybe fearful, when you asked me. I love it."

Dayzee turned to look at the twins. Marilyn sighed deeply and shook her head, and Sophia shrugged. Cliff continued to grin at all three before he turned to look at Kozy.

"And who might you be? I must say, that's a dashing outfit you have on."

"I am Kozy. I am here only to help them with any problems that might arise."

Sophia elbowed her sister and said, "Arise. That's never a problem, huh, Sis?"

"Stop it, Sissy."

"I'm Cliff. I'm very happy to meet you as well."

"Mr. Cliff, did you originate on a planet other than Earth?"

Cliff lost his smile and stared into Kozy's eyes. Dayzee and the twins stayed silent and waited. After five quiet seconds, he shook a pointing finger at Kozy and grinned.

"I like that—a direct question. No chance for me to sneak around it, right? Okay, Mr. Kozy, I will tell you flat out that I am *not* from a *planet* other than Earth. How about that, huh?"

"That is a relief. I already have my hands full, as it is sometimes said in this world."

"Kozy means in Beverly Hills," said Dayzee. "First trip here."

"What do you have your hands full of?" said Cliff.

"I have been assigned the role of security specialist."

"Oh, I see. That's your uniform? I like it."

"We do too," said Marilyn. "We just got him into that outfit a short while ago."

"Excellent choice. Well, I promise not to add to anyone's problems here. What I have is a proposal for you three and maybe Kozy too."

He held his hands out together to mimic a camera lens, which he looked through as he pointed it at Dayzee, then Sophia, then Marilyn, then Kozy.

"Let's put three—or maybe four?—gigantic, bright, blazing new stars up in the sky. Ladies and Kozy, let's get real!"

"I can assure you," said Kozy, "that I am real. I am able to take any form that—"

"Kozy will gladly take and fill out any forms you need, Cliff," said Dayzee.

Chapter 4 – Just Toss It Out

At the sound of rapid pounding, Cliff jerked his head around to look at the front door. Four pairs of eyes stared past him, and Dayzee walked up to the wall to hold steady the small painting that vibrated from the knocking.

"It must be . . . what was his name? Carlos?" said Cliff.

"Let's hope," said Sophia. "It's still close to Halloween, so maybe it's some wannabe scary guy without a head."

Marilyn elbowed her sister and said, "Sissy, Cliff doesn't want to hear—"

Cliff turned and said, "Oh no, Sophia, I sure do. It's that kind of spontaneous, off-the-wall banter that will make this show a hit."

He turned back to the door.

"You know what? I'd welcome a headless guy at the door. That's great stuff, girls."

Dayzee reached for the doorknob, let out a deep sigh, and pulled the door in.

"Carlos! I'm so glad you could make it on such short notice. Please, come in."

"Happy to help, Dayzee. I'm only a call or text away. What do you need?"

"Oh, um, that's something that . . . I mean . . ."

"It's the kitchen sink," said Sophia. "Come on, I'll show you."

She took Carlos by his hand and led him toward the kitchen. Before they got too far, she turned and said, "Sis, how about if you and Kozy tag along too?"

"Sure, Sissy."

Marilyn took Kozy's hand, and they followed Carlos and Sophia into the kitchen.

"That must happen all the time, huh?"

"What, them holding hands? Oh, I think it will, but they're just—"

"No, I mean a plumbing repair. This house is immense, and it's good that you have someone you can call."

"Oh yeah, of course. Yeah, Carlos is the best. Before we take a tour of the house, why don't you have a seat right here in the living room, and I'll be right back."

"This furniture looks custom made. Very nice."

"Oh, well, thanks. Yeah, custom and imported. Let's hope it behaves."

"What's that?"

"Nothing. Can I bring you a drink? What would you prefer?"

"Double scotch, please."

"Whatever you want. It's not too early for that?"

"It's five o'clock on some planet somewhere," he said with half of a smile, and he sat and gazed up at Dayzee.

Dayzee shook her head and stared for a few seconds before saying, "Um, yeah. I guess you're right about that."

She grinned and shook a finger at him.

"Hang on. I'll be right back."

*　　*　　*

Dayzee walked into the kitchen to find Carlos leaning over the sink, with a twin on each side and Kozy looking over his shoulder.

"I'm looking right in there, and I don't see anything wrong. Look,"—he turned the water on and off, then he switched on the disposer—"everything works."

Dayzee crowded in with them and peered over his other shoulder.

"The sink is fine, Carlos," she said. "We just didn't want to discuss the real problem with you in front of our guest."

"Discuss what?"

"There's been an accident. I'll owe you big if you could help out."

"Dayzee, you've been very good to me. I was kidding before about calling the cops. What is it?"

"Um, there's . . ."

"She's trying to say," said Sophia, "that there's a, um, a—"

"Sis is almost saying," said Marilyn, "that upstairs, we have a . . . there's a—"

"There is a headless human body lodged under a bed on the next level up," said Kozy, causing him to turn his head enough to lock eyes. Kozy didn't smile.

"A what? There's a dead guy up there?"

"It was a horrible, freak accident," said Dayzee, and he spun his head to look at her.

"No foul play, we promise," said Marilyn. "Can you help us out?"

"Where's his head?"

Dayzee hesitated, so Sophia said, "We have no idea. It's not in the house; we know that much."

Carlos looked from face to face, then he turned his back to the sink and looked up at Kozy, then he looked all the way down and back up.

"Hey, you look a lot like Kenzie, except for the muscles and whiskers and stuff."

"Love that stuff," said Marilyn.

"I am Kozy. Kenzie is still—"

"Kenzie is still on vacation," said Dayzee. "This is her brother, Kozy. See the similarity? Kozy works out like a lunatic, though."

"Oh, I get it. You sure look like Kenzie. The hair's the same. I mean it's exactly the same. How do—"

"About that body, Carlos," said Dayzee as she stood with her arms crossed and tapping a toe on the kitchen floor.

"Oh, sure, Dayzee. Where's it at?"

"The girls can show you. Don't you need some bags or buckets or something?"

"Is it that messy?"

"No, not really. It's wrapped up in a blanket."

"Cool. That's easy. I'll just carry it down and—"

"No, Carlos!" Dayzee said and pushed on his chest, leaning him back over the sink. "You can't just stroll out of here with a body slung over your shoulder. We can't let our guest see any of that."

Marilyn grabbed his arm and began urging him free of Dayzee and toward the stairway.

"Come on, Carlos. We'll figure it out."

"That's right," said Sophia. "You go keep squid guts company, and—"

"His name is Cliff, Sissy. Try to remember how much he's done for us already."

"Sure, Sis. Kozy, you're with us because, you know, there are things still on the loose. Let's get going on our little project."

All four walked to the base of the staircase, and Kozy said, "Do not worry. I will watch for the knives."

"What knives?" said Carlos.

"Oh, nothing," said Sophia. "We've just misplaced a few, that's all."

"Yes, let's go," said Marilyn. "It'll be fun!"

*   *   *

"Here's your drink, Cliff. Is the furniture giving you any problems?"

"No, Dayzee, it's quite comfortable. Is everything under control in the kitchen?"

He took a deep swig.

"Between the girls and Kozy and Carlos, it'll be fine."

"As much as I enjoy the sight of your legs, Dayzee—I mean, they're breathtaking—why don't you have a seat? We can chat awhile before the twins and Kozy return."

"Oh, of course. Why am I just standing around?"

She held the polished wood arm of the chair that faced Cliff on the couch and lowered herself onto the soft cushion. She held both of the arms and looked from side to side, then she sighed and leaned back into it.

"You're quite the actress, Dayzee. You just convinced me that that chair was anything but comfortable, but I'm sure it is."

"You don't miss much, do you, Cliff?"

"I guess it comes with writing. I tend to focus on as many parts of a scene as I can. This, right here, is a memorable scene. Your company is enchanting."

"Oh, why, Cliff . . . that's so sweet. You're right, of course—this chair is just fine. I'm just having some fun, that's all."

"I'll tell you something fun, Dayzee: hardly anyone knows my real name. Sutcliffe Gutsquid is my pen name."

"Wait. Hold up. You could pick anything, and you picked that? What on Earth is your real name?"

He laughed and said, "Without even trying, you've just put together a very amusing question that's impossible to answer!"

"Huh? What do you—"

"It's Dirk. Dirk Diamond."

"Your real name is Dirk Diamond? Why would you call yourself that other name? What's wrong with your real name?"

"It goes with the genre. It makes my readers see me as a bit more quirky. Less approachable, too, maybe. Less like an Earth inhabitant."

"Oh, there you go again. We all know aliens aren't a real thing."

Dayzee held her breath and stared at him. Seconds passed.

"Hmm. Well, all I know is that this scotch is out of this world."

He tipped his glass all the way back. Dayzee tipped her head to one side and gazed at him without smiling.

He grinned and said, "Could I trouble you for another?"

*　　*　　*

Sophia led them down the hallway to the room she'd shared, if only briefly, with Kenzie two days earlier—the bedroom where they'd left a headless body crammed under the bed. She switched on a light, and they all walked in.

"It's there," said Sophia. "Around the other side."

Marilyn said, "Dayzee and I shoved it under there. We had to hide it because Sissy and—"

"Alright, Sis, I don't think Carlos needs a complete history of the whole thing. Carlos, it was just a tragic accident, that's all. It was very upsetting for everyone."

"Especially the dead guy," said Marilyn. "No, wait, I think he might have been happy for a while because he was really—"

"Sis! We need to hurry. Carlos, can you get that thing?"

"Yeah, but then what? Dayzee doesn't want me dragging it through the house."

"Hey," said Marilyn, "just throw it out the window."

"I can wait below to catch it," said Kozy in a monotone voice.

"Huh?"

"Kozy's just messing with you," said Sophia. "Such a joker. I say you just toss it out. Not like he's going to get hurt."

"Sure, I could do that."

Carlos walked over and looked down from the window, seeing only lush backyard landscaping and a pool a good distance from the house.

"Does this window open?"

He unlatched it and tried to raise it up, but it was jammed. Kozy walked over and lifted it with one hand.

"Okay. Weightlifting pays off. Thanks, Kozy."

"You are welcome, but I did not wait to lift it."

"What?"

"Never mind that. Now that the window's open, Carlos," said Sophia, "we're good to go."

"Right. I just need the body."

Carlos stood by the side of the bed for several seconds, let out a deep breath, and dropped to his hands and knees. He lifted up the bed skirt and stared. Several seconds crawled by. He reached in and grabbed the blanket. He braced himself for a strong pull and dragged out nothing but a blanket.

"It's just a blanket. Is this some Halloween joke?"

"Pretty funny, huh, Carlos?" said Sophia. "Dayzee put us up to it. I didn't want to jerk you around like that, and neither did my sister, but Dayzee, she—"

"Wait," said Carlos. "This blanket is all bloody and stuff. What the hell."

"Yes, *fake* blood," said Marilyn. "That's Dayzee, for you. Funny stuff."

"So, I guess I just get rid of the blanket then, huh?"

"Could you?" said Sophia. "Forget about throwing it out the window, though. Just take it out to the trash for us?"

"Sure, Sophia. I'm not sure this is such a funny joke, though."

"We do try to tell Dayzee when she goes off the deep end. She doesn't listen."

"Sissy's right about that," said Marilyn.

He yanked the rolled-up blanket all the way out, picked it up, and tossed it up and over his right shoulder.

"Lead the way, Carlos," said Marilyn. "You're our hero."

As Carlos walked toward the door, the twins looked at each other and shrugged. Kozy looked at them both and said softly, "As I stated earlier: anything with wood, which I believe is an appropriate term. You said the dead man was happy. How happy?"

"Sheesh. Happy enough," said Sophia. "This gets better all the time."

"It is only a theory and subject to revision," said Kozy.

*　*　*

Dayzee returned with a fresh drink and handed it to him. This time, she brought one for herself too.

"Ah, very good. Thank you, Dayzee. Your house really is spectacular. How many bedrooms do you have?"

"I think there are ten, Cliff."

"You think?"

"Yeah, probably ten. They're all suites too. It's kind of like a hotel up there."

"That grand staircase in the foyer certainly is grand. I take it you have another stairway somewhere?"

"Yeah, there's one off of the kitchen. I think there's another one too."

"You're pulling my leg, aren't you? You don't know?"

"Well, Cliff, or Dirk, I'm usually so busy with shoots and parties that I rarely have time to explore. When I'm not here, I'm usually in France."

"France?"

"Or Ireland."

Cliff stared.

"You've definitely had a stellar career so far. How about if we try to jack that up even higher?"

Dayzee raised her glass, and they clinked them together.

"I'm all for that. I'm eager to hear what you have in mind."

She looked over Cliff's head toward the kitchen.

"All we need is for—"

She froze at the sight of Carlos walking to the front door with a blood-soaked bundle over his shoulder.

"Carlos! Out with the garbage, remember? Not through the—"

"Sorry, Dayzee. It's just a blanket. I thought this would be the easiest way to toss it in my truck."

"Oh, just a blanket, of course. I knew that. I did. Go ahead. Thanks, Carlos."

Carlos continued out onto the porch and pulled the door shut behind him.

"Dayzee, you look like you've seen a ghost. Are you alright?"

"I'm fine. It's just that the work never ends around here. Thank God for Carlos."

"He seems like quite a handy fellow."

The twins and Kozy turned the corner and joined them in the living room.

"Good. Everyone's here. If you'd like, I could get started."

"You girls look like you could use a drink too," said Dayzee.

"Oh, yeah," said Sophia. "Things are not what we thought. The problem was gone."

"Gone?"

"Yes," said Marilyn. "No problem, or we don't know where the problem is, at least."

"But that's not possible. Kozy, is everything okay?"

"No, Dayzee, but Marilyn and Sophia are correct: we have not yet located what we are now calling a problem."

Kozy and the twins left for the bar. Dayzee sighed deeply and finished her drink before again looking at Cliff.

"Alright, let's not worry about that for now. When the girls get back, give us your very best pitch."

Chapter 5 – Quite an Attitude

Cliff sat with Sophia to his left and Marilyn on his right, and Dayzee and Kozy sat across the wide coffee table in the two well-cushioned chairs. All held cocktails, and Cliff put his down and unzipped his portfolio.

"I have handouts for three of you. Sorry, Kozy, but I didn't know you existed until just a short while ago."

"In some ways, I did not."

"Oh, Kozy is just being funny," said Dayzee. "Such a comic. It's fine, Cliff. We'll manage."

She turned to her left and said, "Kozy, pull your chair closer, and we can share."

Kozy picked up the heavy chair with one hand and set it closer to Dayzee's left. Everyone watched, but no one made any comments.

"Alright, I think we're ready. We're very excited, Cliff. Marilyn said you have an idea for a reality show?"

"Yes, that's exactly right. I plan to call it 'Kildare in the Hills.' Kildare, because that's where you two are from"—he turned to glance at Marilyn, then Sophia—"and the Hills, because this is lovely Beverly Hills."

"I'm from Kildare too," said Dayzee. "I came to the Hills a while ago to seek fame and fortune. These beautiful twins spend a lot of time here, too, but they like to call Ireland home."

"Oh, that's even better—all three of you are from Kildare. Kozy, if you don't mind my asking . . . where are you from?"

"Far away. You would not be able to pronounce it. It is in a location speculated to have resulted from the consolidation of neighboring—"

"It's so far away," said Dayzee, "that it doesn't even seem real anymore. This is Kozy's home now too."

"Okay. Sounds good. First of all, I'd like the show to be based right here, in this fabulous house. I hope you'd consider that, Dayzee? I'd rather not have to buy a house just special for the show."

"You'd do that?"

"Don't dare me. Are you daring me?" he said with a big smile. "I'd do it, Dayzee."

"No need for that. We can use this house."

"Good, because this house is perfect for what I have in mind. The architecture and landscaping appear mostly modern. The reason we'll call the show 'Kildare in the Hills' is because one of the main themes will be that the three of you slowly change the place into more of an Irish property. Nothing big, Dayzee, like knocking out walls and adding rooms or even tearing out extra stairways that no one can find anyway. But how about some new decorating more reminiscent of Ireland?"

"We could do that," said Marilyn. "I love Ireland."

"We all do, Cliff. I really like this idea," said Dayzee.

"Fantastic. The outside could be a big part of the show too. Any one of you, or all of you at different times, could design and oversee landscaping changes, such as new gardens, flower beds . . . even new trees. How about an orchard too? Statues, maybe?"

"I love the idea," said Sophia. "It makes such good sense too—we'd really be bringing Kildare to the Hills."

"Exactly," said Cliff. "I'm so glad you like that foundational theme, but there's more. We'll need to spice it up with drama, maybe some danger and, of course, romance."

"We certainly attract all of that," said Dayzee. "Just in our daily lives, we—"

Dayzee felt the wooden left arm of her chair fracture without a sound, and it began to move around under her own arm, which rested on it.

"I mean, we—"

She leaned over and grabbed a thin blanket from its place beneath the coffee table and draped it over her left arm, and it covered her legs too.

"Dayzee, are you okay?"

"I . . . I just caught a chill, that's all."

She fluffed up the blanket and felt the chair's arm snaking around hers, stretching itself out, getting thinner, and coiling around her forearm. She froze, staring down at her arm hidden under the blanket.

"Kozy, I think maybe—"

Kozy looked down, saw the problem, and began reaching for Dayzee's arm.

Dayzee looked up, past the three pairs of staring eyes on the couch, and saw the headless body approaching aimlessly and moving slowly, hands quietly opening and closing in front of it.

"Kozy, can you get me a glass of water from the kitchen?"

Dayzee gestured with her head toward the kitchen, and Kozy looked up and saw the approaching monster.

"Yes, of course. I will attempt to hurry back with your drink while resolving any problems I might find."

Cliff frowned while staring at Kozy, who rose, left Dayzee to fend for herself, and hurried toward the body. Sophia turned to watch Kozy walking away and gasped at the sight.

Cliff turned to her and said, "Is everything okay, Sophia? If you'd like a glass of water, too, I wouldn't mind getting it for you."

He shifted forward to stand, and Sophia turned toward him, held his shoulder in her right hand and his leg in her left, and forced him back into the couch.

"No! I mean, no, I'm fine. This cocktail is good enough."

Cliff looked toward Dayzee, and Sophia gave her sister a gesture toward the kitchen. Marilyn turned briefly and saw Kozy approaching the roaming thing without a head. She grabbed Cliff too.

"We're both fine, Cliff. There's no need for you to leave. Just sit back, and tell us more about your brilliant idea."

"Well, okay, Marilyn. Sure."

Dayzee tried to free her arm and found that it was held like in a vise. Then, the front right leg of her chair began to curl up, sneaking along her calf, caressing her all the way until it reached her knee. Like a thick worm, it wiggled along her bare skin, and she hurried to hold the blanket up to conceal its twisting around under it.

"I think maybe Kozy is having trouble, Sissy. I'll go take a look."

"No, Sis. Stay here, alright?"

Marilyn chuckled and said, "Who knows, maybe Kozy is in some kind of danger. I better go see. That's something I'm sure I can help with."

She got up and left for the kitchen. Sophia shrugged at a curious Cliff and said, "Oh, that Sis of mine. Always a big help."

"See? This is why you're all perfect for a reality show—already, I have no idea what to expect. Am I right, Dayzee?"

They both turned to Dayzee and saw her eyes darting between each of them, then above them and toward the kitchen.

"Dayzee, are you okay?"

"Yeah, Cliff. Of course. Just—"

She felt the animated chair leg slide between her thighs, bunching up and pinching her skin, so she spread her legs and fluffed the blanket again with her right hand. Her left was still held prisoner. She tried to lean forward to be sure everything was hidden, and the chair started to tip from its right front leg being busy with something else. She snapped herself back, sending her blond mane flying over the chair back.

"Well, that's certainly dramatic," said Cliff.

"Dayzee?" said Sophia. "Are you alright?"

"Yeah, I think,"—the tip of the sneaky leg reached its destination and paused with a gentle pressure—"oh, oh my. I mean—"

"Maybe you'd like another cocktail?" said Cliff, and he shifted forward on the couch, causing Sophia to grab his shoulder and force him back down.

"No! I mean, look, she still has her drink."

"My drink. Yes, I really need my drink!"

Dayzee picked up her glass and raised it to her lips. She tipped it back and focused her eyes on the kitchen. Marilyn had her back to the wall, and the headless guy was ambling toward her. At the last moment, Kozy came up from behind and grabbed it in a tight hug.

The leg between Dayzee's legs didn't stop with a touch—it traveled just a bit farther.

"Ah!" she said into her drink, sending trails of it to each side, out of the glass, and down her chin.

"Dayzee Dazzle, perhaps you really *don't* need another drink," said Cliff. "You can barely handle that one."

Dayzee's invading wooden leg traveled a little farther. Dayzee gasped.

"Are you okay?"

"Oh, no, that's just . . . oh, it's a good drink . . . I mean . . ."

Dayzee struggled to move her left arm, but she couldn't. The polished end of the wooden chair leg held its position as she watched the scene behind Cliff and Sophia.

*   *   *

"Oh, Kozy," said Marilyn too softly to be heard in the living room. "You're my hero!"

The dead guy was grasping at Marilyn, its hands reaching toward her breasts as Kozy held it just out of reach.

"It is surprisingly strong, Marilyn. You still face a significant menace. Remain stationary."

"Oh, I think I like menace now. I'm glad you're so strong because—"

Marilyn looked past Kozy and saw the five truant knives floating in a neat line above the landing of the staircase, their pointy ends aimed straight at them.

"Uh-oh, Kozy. The danger just went up a big notch."

"Please, describe in more detail."

"The knives. They're behind you. They're planning their attack."

"Hold on tight, and do not let go."

Kozy whipped around and backed into Marilyn, holding the dead guy between them and the knives. Marilyn hugged Kozy, with one hand on his bare abs and the other a bit lower.

"Oh my, Kozy. Tsk, tsk, tsk. You are such a One-Eighty!"

*　　*　　*

Dayzee stopped attempting to free her left arm, and the drink in her hand shook around, so she set it back down. The extra leg beneath the blanket began moving, and it couldn't decide whether to stay in or out.

"When they get back, Dayzee, we can—"

Dayzee let out a short scream at the sight of Marilyn fondling Kozy, who still held the dead guy tight while pressing Marilyn into the wall. A second later, five knives, one after the other and evenly spaced, flew toward the two living bodies and the dead one. Kozy appeared to dance the dead guy around, and Marilyn followed his lead. Each knife found the dead thing's chest, even though Kozy seemed to lift it off the ground for the second and fifth knives.

"Dayzee, what's wrong?"

Cliff tried to turn his head to see where Dayzee was looking, but Sophia held his face with both hands and turned him toward her. She squeezed her red lips into his and said, "That's just for all the good things you've done for Sis and me. We really appreciate it."

He tried to turn again, and she pulled him in for another kiss.

"There, now you've been properly thanked."

She still held him and turned him to face Dayzee.

*　　*　　*

"Now what, Kozy? I'm still holding on, and I'm so impressed!"

"You have chosen a very specific attribute to hold."

"Uh-huh. I sure did."

"I believe the danger is now—"

"Oh, no it's not. There are all kinds of dangers everywhere in this crazy mansion."

"Still, we must remove this body. It seems to have lost its life. And Marilyn?"

"Yes?"

"All five knives have been recovered. You can release me now."

"I suppose I could."

Ten seconds passed.

"If you let me go, I can transfer this refuse to the garage."

"Oh, okay. I'll come with you. Hey, that sounds like the best idea yet."

* * *

"Well, Sophia, that's not necessary. I really am happy to contribute to you two beautiful twins. I'm sure not complaining about how you thank me, though."

"Good. I bet my sister is grateful too. She'll be back in a minute, I predict. Kozy too."

"You look tired or something," Cliff said after glancing at Dayzee. "Maybe that drink was too strong for you?"

The chair leg kept up its business, not too slowly and not too quickly, and Dayzee said, "Oh, maybe that's it. I'm just a little … distracted."

"Get yourself together," said Sophia. "We're going to talk business in a minute. Show business."

"Yeah, that's … yeah. Good. Good."

She closed her eyes and let out a deep breath.

"So good . . ."

"Dayzee?"

* * *

"Just dump it anywhere," said Marilyn. "It'll have to go out with the trash on the next garbage day."

45

"Perhaps you could call Carlos?"

"Brilliant. Yes, I'll have Dayzee call him. He snuck out of here too quick anyway. We had plans for him."

"The plan was to bring Dayzee a glass of water."

"Yes, we can do that."

"You can let go of me now."

Marilyn held on for a few more seconds, then said, "Oh, okay. Let's get back to the party."

*　　*　　*

Kozy took the seat next to Dayzee, and Marilyn returned to her seat next to Cliff.

"Everything okay?" said Cliff. "How far away was that water?"

"Things get complicated sometimes," Marilyn said as she reached over to give it to Dayzee.

Dayzee reached with her right hand, but she found that, even though she braced the chair to keep it from tipping, she couldn't lean forward from the steady action beneath the blanket.

"Meet me halfway, Dayzee," said Marilyn.

"I . . . I think—"

Kozy rose up faster than anyone should be able to move and took the glass from Marilyn. Dayzee accepted it with a shaking hand and set it on the end table to her right. While the activity hidden from view continued, Kozy began to reach under the blanket to free Dayzee's left wrist, but a glance behind her demanded a different plan.

Sophia watched them across the coffee table and saw Kozy studying the back of Dayzee's neck.

"Hey, Sis, while you were gone, I gave Cliff a great big kiss to thank him for everything."

"Oh, good idea, Sissy."

Kozy saw that a part of the chair's frame had wiggled loose and was weaving its way up to the back of Dayzee's head. The very end of it was shifting and throbbing until it had fashioned itself into a sharp point.

"So, go ahead and thank him, too, Sis."

"Glad to."

She touched his cheek and turned him to accept her kiss. Dayzee let out a soft moan. Cliff pulled away from Marilyn's lips, and all three gazed at Dayzee. They saw Kozy reaching behind the chair, heard a loud snap, and watched as he held up a sharpened piece of wood. Kozy looked from Marilyn to Sophia and back again.

"Cliff," said Sophia, "let's let Dayzee catch her breath, and the three of us can take a peek out back, alright?"

"That's a great idea, Sissy. Come on, Cliff, let's take a look at the pool."

"Well, sure. Okay. You're both very sweet—there's never any need to thank me."

"You just never know when the urge will strike us, right, Sis?"

"Exactly, Sissy. Expect surprises in this house."

Each of the twins took one of Cliff's arms and guided him up off of the couch and out of the room.

As soon as the three had turned and began walking toward the kitchen, Kozy pushed the blanket down onto Dayzee's lap and snapped off the chair part pinning down her left arm.

"There. Your arm is free, and the part behind you is now damaged too badly to be a threat. You are safe now."

Dayzee didn't respond. She only laid her head back on the chair and closed her eyes.

"Are you traumatized, Dayzee?"

"No, it's just that thing. That assassin. It really knows what it wants. It's got talent."

"What do you mean?"

Dayzee felt the indecision of the chair leg between her legs—it didn't know if it liked inside or outside better. It kept trying both, over and over.

"Okay, this is good, but it's kind of creepy at the same time."

She folded the blanket off of her, and Kozy saw the guilty piece of wood in action.

"You wish it to continue?"

Dayzee paused for several seconds, then said, "Maybe just a second or two."

They could hear the twins speaking and laughing with Cliff in the kitchen as they looked out the back door. Other than an occasional sigh from Dayzee, the living room was silent.

"The chair is still animated, Dayzee. I would like you to be a safe distance away from it. You are still in danger."

Without opening her eyes, Dayzee reached her left hand over to be sure Kozy was right about the danger.

"Oh, you're not kidding. Wow."

She reached up and caressed his stubbly cheek with the back of her hand.

"One-Eighties are amazing. Just another second or two."

Ten seconds passed in the quiet room as Kozy waited for the go-ahead command.

Dayzee let out a deep sigh and said, "Alright, Kozy. I guess that's enough."

He reached down, gently retrieved the chair leg, and held it away from Dayzee. It immediately sharpened itself to a fine point, and he strained to hold it in place as it made lunging motions for Dayzee.

"God. Talk about Yin and Yang!"

"Who are they?"

"Nobody I want to know. Just kill it if you can."

He snapped it off at its base and tossed it to the floor.

"This mansion, Kozy. It's developed quite an attitude. God, only in Beverly Hills."

Chapter 6 – Little White Boxes

Sophia yelled from somewhere out of sight in the kitchen.

"Dayzee! Hey, Dayzee, we're coming back, if it's okay?"

"Sure, Fia. Come on back. I can't wait to hear about Cliff's reality show."

The twins led Cliff back in, and they took their seats on the couch.

"Your backyard is perfect for this, Dayzee. I see beyond the pool you have two guesthouses too?"

"Oh yeah, I kind of forgot about those. I haven't been in them in a while, but I remember they're pretty nice."

"Splendid. I have plans for those too. Okay, is everyone ready? Nobody needs to jump up for a drink, do they?"

Marilyn laughed, and Sophia said, "Yep, I think we're good. Dayzee? Kozy? Everything alright?"

"I feel much better," said Dayzee. "I think I just needed a minute. Another minute might have been good,"—she turned to grin at Kozy—"but sure, I'm good. Kozy is too."

"Fantastic. So, some of this is written on your handouts, but that's just for your reference. I'll try to go through all the details. Basically, we—the interested producers and I—would like to shoot a reality series here, starring all three of you."

"What about Kozy?" said Marilyn. "Can't forget him."

"Of course, we can't. Yes, Kozy will be a star too."

"Which star?" said Kozy. "All known stars possess far too much mass—I would become severely diluted. Perhaps if a very small one can be found nearby, then—"

"No, silly," said Marilyn. "It's just a slang name for being famous on TV or in the movies."

"Oh. I could accomplish that."

"And you will," said Cliff. "From what I've seen of the backyard so far, it's perfect. We'll make sure to have lots of scenes of all of you in and around the pool. I think even when you're supervising yard work and landscaping, you should all wear bikinis," he said while looking at each of them. "Well, Kozy, I don't know about you. Something minimal."

"Or nothing at all," said Sophia. "Depends on the weather."

"Oh, I like that. You're thinking ahead to a movie about your lives here. But for TV, we might have to keep you all dressed. Not dressed with much, though."

"That all sounds good, Cliff," said Dayzee. "What ideas do you have for those guesthouses?"

"Here's what will really heat things up: we'll have different celebrities stay in one of the houses for a week or two, and we can see if any romances develop. At the very least, our camera might catch part of a midnight rendezvous."

"How will we find these celebrities?" said Marilyn. "Do you have anyone in mind?"

"No, that will be up to you three. I mean, you four."

"I do not know any humans," said Kozy.

Cliff stopped and stared at him.

"That's just silly. Of course, you do. You probably have a lot of friends."

"Not here. Everyone I know is back on—"

"Back on that island Kozy came from," said Dayzee. "Yeah, of course, he knows people. But what were you thinking, Cliff?"

"Here's the plan: we'll run the show for a couple of weeks before we take on a guest. That'll get the word out because having a guest will be a topic of conversation between all of you. I think people will be begging to get in the show. Part of the draw will be that they get to meet all of you. I believe all of you have more fans than you can imagine that would die to get close to you."

"Well, in this house," said Sophia with a smirk.

"What? What about the house? Is it haunted?"

"No, Cliff," said Dayzee. "The place is so big that it can spook you at night sometimes. We're all perfectly safe here, right, Kozy?"

"I will do my best to ensure your safety."

"Now see, that's kind of funny the way you said that. Just the way you all carry on is going to make this a hit. Just be yourselves, all of you."

He turned to Kozy and said, "You can be yourself in front of a camera, can't you, Kozy?"

"I can be Kozy, and if it enhances my mission, I can also be any other—"

"Any other character you might need—that's our Kozy!" said Marilyn.

"Kozy can change real quick, depending on how things go," said Sophia. "Kozy is a natural."

"Perfect. This is going to work out great. Okay, there's a career angle to this whole thing too. You three are actresses, and Kozy, I'm not sure what you are, but—"

"It is difficult to explain. I can be—"

"Kozy can be on time. Don't ever doubt it," said Dayzee. "What about us all being actresses?"

"I'd like the show to follow your careers too. Talking about roles you'd like and ones you'd never take. How you find them—do you seek them out, or do they come to you? You could share your experiences with tryouts, the roles you accept, and the ones you reject … all of that. I think the viewers would like an inside look at what life is like for film stars."

"We could do that," said Marilyn. "Sissy and I just got an offer two days ago."

"We really did," said Sophia. "We're just waiting to hear from our agent, and Dayzee was supposed to start a new shoot tomorrow."

"I called in sick to the first day of my new project," said Dayzee. "Sometimes, I'm juggling a few gigs all at once. It gets complicated."

"I believe that," said Cliff. "I have no idea what the life of an actress must be like since all I do is sit in a corner and write."

"Oh, you must do more than that," said Marilyn.

"Well, maybe. I do think about reality shows, don't I?"

"Yes, you do!"

"Okay, one thing I believe about pursuing an acting career is that it takes cash. That's part of the reason I've 'donated' to your careers in the past."

"And because he digs us," Marilyn whispered to her sister.

Sophia laughed softly and said, "He sure does, Sis."

"Okay, you two," said Dayzee. "Let the man finish."

"So, what I'm proposing is that you'll each receive a monthly payment too. This will be aside from any salaries you negotiate from the producers. This will just come out of my pocket. It will be a substantial sum, and my hope is that you use it for clothes and manicures and travel and whatever else you want. Just walking around money."

"That's awfully generous, Cliff," said Dayzee. "Are you sure about all that?"

"Dayzee, don't talk him out of it," said Sophia. "He's made up his mind, I can tell."

"He sure has, Sissy."

"Yes, I have. Oh, and when we get an idea of when the show will start, those extra payments will start six months beforehand. It couldn't hurt to have more clothes and stuff for the show, could it?"

"I like the way you think," said Dayzee. "Anything else?"

"Cars. You'll each need a car, too, and a driver for each of you. We'll set you up however you want."

"You really *are* from another planet, aren't you?" said Sophia.

"Sissy, don't scare him away!"

"Girls, he's going to get rich off of this show too. Aren't you, Cliff?"

"If I break even, that'll be fine with me. The adventure and the memories would be compensation enough. But for now, how about a tour of the house?"

"Uh-oh," said Marilyn.

"What's wrong?" said Dayzee.

"I just remembered something. You should call Carlos back. There's some more cleanup for him to do."

"Oh, you're right. Alright, I will. Why don't you two beautiful twins show him the great room, both offices, maybe a peek into the guest suite, the butler's pantry, the caterer's kitchen, the wine vault, the gym, the—"

"Alright, we get it," said Sophia. "We'll try to make it through the entire first floor. Won't be easy."

"Thanks, Fia. Kozy can sit with me while I call Carlos."

"Shouldn't we stay together?" said Marilyn. "Because . . . I mean—"

"So that we don't get lost, Sis? Is that what you mean?"

"Yes, that's it—Dayzee's house is gigantic!"

"Alright, I'll just send him a text, then."

Dayzee hit a few keys and put her phone away.

"Done. He'll be here soon. Let's take a stroll around the place."

*   *   *

The tour of the first floor ended in the kitchen, and Cliff looked down the hallway toward the door to the garage.

"Not to be nosy, but I would like to see the garage too. We'll be putting all of your shiny new cars in there, and I bet it's as nice as the rest of the house."

"Oh, about that," said Sophia. "It's a little messy right now. That's why we needed Carlos again."

"Sissy's right about that," said Marilyn. "There's some trash for him to get rid of."

"Nonsense, I'm sure it looks fine. It'll just be a quick—"

A slow, steady pounding on the door interrupted them and froze Cliff in his tracks. Kozy slipped through the staring group and began a purposeful walk toward the garage.

"Wait, Kozy," said Sophia. "Don't open that door yet."

"Oh, *that* trash," said Dayzee.

"I don't understand. Is that Carlos, your helper? Let's let him in. Maybe we can negotiate him into a quick appearance on an episode."

"No! I mean . . . these three can handle that," said Dayzee. "How about if you and I get a head start on the backyard?"

"Head start," said Marilyn before giggling.

"That's funny, Sis."

"I don't get it," said Cliff. "There's something funny about the backyard?"

The soft pounding from the garage continued.

"Yeah. It's kind of an inside joke. Let's go, Cliff. Let me show you my fantastic pool."

*　*　*

While Dayzee led Cliff away from the garage and toward the door to the backyard, Kozy and the twins walked down the hall and stood at the door.

"Why is it still alive, Kozy?" said Marilyn. "It had five knives in its chest."

"Sis, you know it's not really alive. Did you see that chair and what it was doing to Dayzee?"

"I saw her fighting with it, Sissy. That was a mean chair."

"The same thing animates the chair and the dead body," said Kozy. "I am starting to suspect that this assassin is not as serious as the Guild would like it to be. It seems to be a, um, it is a—"

"A slacker?" said Sophia.

"A joker?" said Marilyn.

"Yes, a slacker joker," said Kozy.

The twins stared at each other silently, then looked back at Kozy.

"A horny slacker joker," said Kozy, causing laughter from the twins. "I believe 'horny' is a common Earth expression."

"Sure is common with Sissy and me. Dayzee too."

"You both saw Dayzee's bed," said Kozy. "Her chair in the living room took obscene liberties with her too."

"Oh, poor Dayzee," said Marilyn. "That must have been terrible."

"Yes. Sure. She hated it." Kozy coughed and continued. "This assassin might have been intent on killing in the beginning. Now, it appears it would like to enjoy itself at everyone's expense. Then, perhaps it will kill."

"Still, it sent those knives right at us, Kozy."

"It did seem that way, Marilyn, and it probably looked like I used the corpse as a shield. I did not. It mostly moved on its own to catch the flying knives. The assassin toys with us."

"What do you mean?" said Marilyn. "It wants to have sex with us?"

"I believe so. Then, when it has had its fill, it will kill you."

"Fill then kill," said Marilyn.

"Unless you're there to stop it?" said Sophia.

"Yes. That is why I am here."

"Let me get this right. That thing in the garage—that headless guy with knives stuck in him—if we let him in, he'll want to, you know, with us?"

"I do not know, Marilyn. I suggest you do not investigate its intentions."

"Hey, I don't want to. I sure am itchy but not for that dead thing."

"Me neither, Sis," said Sophia. "I can wait. You know, I'll drag Cliff into a closet if I have to."

"We could both drag him. Before he knew what was going on, we'd have most of our clothes off, and—"

"No, Sis, I was kidding. We can't. He's setting up a sweet gig for us. He's just a friend, remember? Promise?"

"Sure, Sissy. Okay."

"We still need to dispose of the thing beyond this door," said Kozy.

"Well, we can't ask Carlos to throw it out like that," said Sophia. "Not punching and kicking."

"Hey," said Marilyn, "is he still looking for head?"

"Oh, I think he is, Sis."

"Regardless of what it seeks," said Kozy, "we must learn a way to stop it."

"How can we kill it for sure?" said Marilyn. "Carlos is on his way, too, so we need to hurry."

"I believe dismembering it will at least cause it to be less effective."

"Sheesh," said Sophia. "If all that does is slow it down, what then? We ask Carlos to shovel up a bunch of bloody, squirming parts?"

"We need containers for all the pieces. Locate and gather suitable receptacles, ideally waterproof, to put the parts in while I begin."

Kozy pulled the door in, and they all gazed for a second at the headless dead guy with knives in his chest. One fist was out for knocking, and it paused there. Two seconds later, it started walking toward them, but Kozy kicked it, ripping into it with one shiny black boot and knocking it back onto the garage floor. Sophia and Marilyn still stared as Kozy stepped down to the floor and pulled the door shut.

"Well, that's pretty weird, Sis."

"We need to find things for the pieces, Sissy. I have no idea what to use."

"Let's go ask Dayzee. She'll know."

"You know what would work really well, Sissy? Those cool little white boxes from Chinese take-out."

"I am a little hungry, Sis. We'd have to order a whole lot, though, don't you think?"

"Yes, you're right. We couldn't eat that much either, so we better just go ask Dayzee."

They started walking back down the hall, and without warning, a door swung out and clunked Sophia's head, sending her stumbling into her sister. She reached out with both hands and shoved the door shut.

"No! Stay!"

She held it closed and stared at it, frowning and taking deep breaths. After a few seconds, she pulled her hands away from it but kept them close. The door stayed.

"This house is starting to piss me off, Sis."

"It's not the house, Sissy. It's that thing. The thing that's trying to kill us."

"It wants to seduce us too."

Sophia took a step back, and both sisters watched the door for a moment.

"Maybe we just need to convince it who's boss."

"So, we should go out to the garage and help Kozy rip the dead guy apart?"

"Um, no," said Sophia. "Just kidding. Let's go find Dayzee."

"It's either that or we order some tasty food. I really am kind of hungry, so I could—"

"Sis, no. That'll never work. Come on."

Chapter 7 – A Headless Monster

"Yeah, Cliff, we keep the pool water sparkling and heated year-round. It's especially fun to swim on a cold night."

"You have quite the lifestyle here, Dayzee. This is perfect. I like how it's accessible to the main house and both guesthouses too."

"Did you plan on having special guests in each of the houses? That could get pretty complicated."

"I haven't even thought about that yet, probably because who has two guesthouses? You know what might be good, though? How about a special, possibly romantic guest in one house and maybe a family member in the other?"

"Oh, like a mom or a dad or a brother or something?"

"Yes, what do you think? You might have to sneak around for a tryst, not knowing if your mother is—"

"My mother, huh? Well, I'm not sure—oh, look. The girls are coming out. Why don't you go take a look at one of the guesthouses, and we'll catch up with you?"

"Sure. I think I'll check out the big one first."

*　　*　　*

"Dayzee," said Marilyn. "That thing without a head is still dancing around. What the heck."

"He's not really dancing," said Sophia. "Trying to kill us? Sure, but not dancing."

"She already knew that, Sissy. No dead guy is about to—"

"If it *was* dancing, I bet it would want to slow dance with one of us."

"I'd let you go first. You'd have to pull those knives out of its chest, then you can dance with him all you—"

"Girls, please. We need to figure this out. Where's Kozy?"

"Taking care of that thing before Carlos gets here," said Sophia. "We figured we couldn't ask Carlos to cart it off to the dump the way it was."

"Yes, dancing," said Marilyn with a chuckle.

"Sis, just let it—"

"Stop, you two! How is Kozy taking care of it? Can it be killed?"

"He didn't know, but we all agreed that if it was in small pieces, it would be more manageable for Carlos."

"Pieces, Fia? Really?"

"With each piece in its own container," said Marilyn. "What do you have? Any luggage you don't want? Oh, how about hat boxes? I'm sure that other Marilyn had stacks of those. Do they still make those? I don't know if I've ever—"

"Mare, I don't have any hat boxes! How is Kozy going to cut it up into little pieces? I don't have any chain saws or cleavers or hatchets or anything."

"He's pretty strong, Dayzee," said Marilyn. "I think he's going to rip it apart. If it still had its head, we'd hear it scream every time Kozy—"

"Sheesh. That's gross, Sis."

"In my garage? Kozy is tearing it apart in my garage?"

"I guess so," said Sophia. "If you don't have any tools, then—"

"Wait, girls, there he comes. Maybe it's all done already?"

Kozy joined them and said, "That was unanticipated. I removed the knives first, then it collapsed. I watched it for several minutes, and it did not move."

"So, we're back to having a dead body to get rid of?"

"This is good," said Marilyn. "It'll be just like before: Carlos will haul it away. He was going to before anyway."

"I thought the same thing," said Kozy. "I wrapped it in a tarp and raised the garage door. It is ready for removal."

Marilyn looked toward the garage and said, "Uh-oh. Maybe it's looking for a dance partner, Sissy."

The headless guy was staggering toward them, and all five knives were back in its chest.

"What the hell!" said Dayzee. "I thought you said it was good and dead again. What's going on now?"

"The knives with wooden handles," said Kozy. "The assassin has replaced them. Once more, it walks."

"And dances."

"Sis, stop it—it's not dancing."

"Maybe it needs some music? Sing it a song, Sissy."

"Oh, you girls. Alright, Kozy, what do you recommend?"

"I need to learn how to stop it permanently. The method is still unknown."

"In the meantime, we can't let Cliff see it. Can you drag it back to the garage, at least?"

"Yes."

He hurried over to the walking corpse and circled around behind it. After getting it in a snug hug, they disappeared back into the garage, Kozy walking backward and dragging the body's feet, and the door went down.

"Kozy sure looks good without a shirt, doesn't he, Sissy?"

"Pretty amazing, Sis. What a chest, and did you notice what the danger did?"

"I sure did," said Marilyn. "I bet that dead guy is noticing right about now too."

"Oh, you know? I think you're right. He sure was in the right place for that."

"Do you think he liked it?" said Marilyn. "I would."

"Who knows, but I bet it took some of the fight out of him."

"Kenzie probably would have cried," said Marilyn, "but Kozy rose to the occasion. Get it?"

"Yep, but not the way you'd like to get it. Why don't you run along and help Kozy with all that danger?"

"Good idea, Sissy—I'm getting awful itchy!"

Sophia shook her head and grinned as she watched Marilyn run into the house to go find Kozy.

"Fia? Why do you encourage her?"

"I was joking, Dayzee. I didn't think she'd actually go."

"Go where?" said Cliff. "What happened to the other two?"

"Oh, Cliff! They just ran into the house for a few minutes. Why don't you let Fia and I give you a tour of the guesthouses?"

*　　*　　*

Marilyn ran through the house giggling until she got to the door to the garage. She stopped and put her ear against it and waited a few seconds. There was only silence, so she opened the door and looked in.

"Hello, Marilyn. I have not had time to pull those knives out yet. It is struggling more than before. I will hold its arms while you remove the knives from its torso."

"Oh, I don't know, Kozy. Is it dangerous? Won't I be in danger?"

"I have noticed that you like the danger."

"Hmm . . . maybe not the danger, so much. Just all the goodies that sprout up!"

She took a step closer and leaned to peek around the struggling dead guy. She smiled at seeing that Kozy was reacting in such a noticeable way to the situation.

"Okay, I'll help. I'll get behind you, Kozy. That's the best way."

Marilyn gave the monster plenty of room and circled around until she was behind Kozy. She held his hips with both hands and reached around.

"Oh, there we go—you're all dangered up!"

"Yes, as long as this thing is animated. If you remove the knives, I believe it will revert to a dead state."

"You'll revert to a less thrilling state too."

"Yes. I am a One-Eighty. Still, we should neutralize this threat. I assure you that there will be more."

"Oh, okay," she said and reached up with her right hand for one of the knives. Her other hand crept down to the top of Kozy's pants, reached inside, and Marilyn found what she wanted.

"That is not a knife, Marilyn."

"It's like a science experiment. Let's see what happens when I yank the knife out."

"That is still not a wise—"

"Oops! I yanked with the wrong hand!"

The wrong hand kept playing, and she pulled a knife out of the thing's chest with the other.

"No change. That's good. Let's try one more."

She pulled out the next knife and said, "Still no change. That's because there's still a lot of danger, right?"

"Yes. You seem to enjoy your experimentation."

"Oh, I really do."

She withdrew two more knives and let them clatter on Dayzee's garage floor.

"Only one more to go, Kozy."

Marilyn took the knife out slowly, didn't notice any change in him, and pulled the knife out altogether. The body started to collapse, and so did that part of Kozy, so Marilyn plunged it back in. The monster came back to life. So did Kozy.

"You were almost successful. The thing was dead. What are you doing?"

"Oh, I think just one knife is good. You hold onto that thing, and I'll hold onto you."

She let go of the knife and brought her hand lower to help her other one.

"So much danger, Kozy . . ."

*　　*　　*

"That's a great idea, Dayzee. Please, give me a thorough tour of the guesthouses. I believe they'll become an exciting part of 'Kildare in the Hills.'"

"Dayzee," said Sophia, "I think I better go look for Sis and Kozy."

"I think you're right. You better hurry, too, Fia. God knows what's going on in there."

"What might be going on, Dayzee?"

"Oh, nothing, Cliff. I, um, don't want them eating all my ice cream, that's all. Hurry, Fia."

Sophia took short, quick steps in her heels on the way to Dayzee's mansion.

"Now, Cliff, let's you and I check out the larger of the two guesthouses. I seem to remember that it has two bedrooms and maybe two baths? This will be an adventure for me too."

*　　*　　*

"Sis, what the hell are you doing?"

"I'm in real trouble, Sissy. I'm just hanging on for my life, here."

"I can see that. Kozy, can't you stop that thing?"

"Yes, I can. I need only remove the last knife from its chest. But—"

"But what?"

"I find that I like how Marilyn responds to my response to the danger. I am in no hurry to deactivate this dead body."

"Me neither, Sissy. I like his body just the way it is."

"This is creepy as hell. We need to kill that thing, Sis. Carlos is on his way."

"Hmm . . . I think Carlos might like it too. We can find out. All three of us could—"

"No, Sis, Carlos can't see a headless body dancing around like that."

"I knew it was dancing!"

"Sis, stop clowning around. Pull that knife out!"

"Oh, okay, but I'm going to make sure I get myself in some serious trouble soon."

Marilyn yanked the knife out and tossed it to the floor. The body folded over on itself, and Kozy let it crumble to the floor.

"The danger is gone."

"That isn't the only thing that's gone, Kozy."

Marilyn backed away, and Sophia took her place.

"Are you sure, Sis? I better check."

Sophia slipped both hands down into Kozy's khakis, frowned, and said, "Yep, all gone. Hey, Sis, do me a favor. Stick one of those knives back in."

"That doesn't sound fun, but I'll do it for you, Sissy."

Marilyn picked up the closest knife and dropped it point-down, and it stuck. The dead man's arms began to reach straight up.

"Oh, that's better!" said Sophia. "Just like that . . . it's back!"

The dead guy sat up.

"So is the dancing headless guy, Sissy!"

"Kozy," said Sophia, "you know that even if that knife is out, it can fly back into that body any time, right?"

"I believe you are correct."

"Perfect. Go ahead and remove the knife. Remember that there's still a whole lot of danger, alright?"

Kozy bent over and pulled the knife out, and the dead body slumped to the floor. Kozy straightened up.

"Oh, now, see? No change, Sis. We just need to keep reminding Kozy about how close we always are to trouble."

Sophia smiled and kept both hands where they were. Kozy stood still and looked up at the ceiling.

"Oh, Sissy, look at Kozy. Kozy, are you liking all the attention?"

He only said, "I do not find it . . . objectionable," and sighed deeply.

Marilyn began pulling her white dress up and said, "Sissy, I'm just so itchy . . ."

*　*　*

"You know what, Cliff? I better run and check on the girls too. Have a seat. Maybe watch some TV. I'll be back in a second."

Dayzee ran from the guesthouse, around the pool, into the house, down the hallway, and into the garage.

"Fia, what are you doing to Kozy?"

"When there's danger, there's so much of him!"

"Mare, pull your dress down!"

"Aw, do I have to? Kozy is really ready!"

One knife floated high in the air, stabbed the dead guy where his head should have been, and he sat up.

"See, girls?"

Dayzee jerked the knife out and threw it across the garage. The body collapsed. Marilyn pulled her dress higher. Sophia grinned and kept her hands busy.

"You really should stop it, you two! We have to get this cleaned up!"

Sophia let Kozy go and stood next to her sister, who dropped her dress and smoothed it down over her thighs.

"We're just getting so itchy, Dayzee. We need something soon."

"I know, girls. I promise you—we'll figure something out. Kozy, can you wrap that thing up?"

Kozy looked down at his bulge stretching his pants out.

"No, not that thing! The dead guy!"

"Yes, Dayzee. Of course."

"Good, then open the garage door again, and Carlos can take it to the dump or a compost pile somewhere. Wherever yard guys throw out yard waste. Mare and Fia, we need to get Cliff out of here. This mansion is out of control. So are you two!"

*　　*　　*

"Did you two eat all of Dayzee's ice cream?"

Cliff smiled and waited for an answer, but the twins only stared at each other, then back at him.

"They didn't mess with my ice cream, Cliff. Now, have you had a chance to walk around the guesthouse?"

"Yes, I did. It's quite nice. I'd really like to see the rest of the main house, but I have another appointment. I didn't think I'd spend this much time here. Can you all look over the handouts and give this all some thought? I'm going to talk to the producers and see if we can put this thing together."

Dayzee reached her hand out, and Cliff took it and kissed it.

"We will, Cliff. Sorry you have to go. Perhaps we can have that tour someday soon?"

"I sincerely hope so."

He let her hand go and turned to the twins.

"It's been wonderful spending time with you both. You're even more heavenly in person. All three of you are. Kozy is quite a sight too. Hey, what happened to Kozy?"

"Oh, Kozy's just helping out with a little cleanup. Come on, we'll walk you to your car."

Outside the guesthouse, Dayzee looked ahead and saw Cliff's car parked close to the open garage door.

"Oh!"

"What's wrong now, Dayzee?"

"Nothing, Cliff. It's just that the garage is a bit of a mess. Girls, can you run ahead and click the door closed?"

"I'm sure it's fine, Dayzee. It's probably just the usual stuff in there. Probably nothing I haven't seen before."

"Oh, I don't know about that. Girls, hurry, please."

Marilyn and Sophia took off and shuffled quickly in their heels and tight clothes to the garage. As the door rolled down, they stood outside and waited. When Dayzee and Cliff got to his car, she let out a deep sigh.

"Good. Everything's in order. I hope you have a safe—"

A truck horn blared behind them, and Dayzee turned to see Carlos in his red pickup pulling up next to Cliff's car.

"Yay, Carlos is here!" said Marilyn.

"Time to take out the trash," said a grinning and nodding Sophia.

Carlos shut off his engine and climbed down, slammed the door shut, and the passenger door opened. Another man stepped out and walked with Carlos toward Dayzee.

"I was already riding with my little brother, Ramon, so he's here to help too."

The second man looked a lot like Carlos with his clean white t-shirt stretched over his lean muscles. He nodded to all of them, but his eyes ended up fixed on Marilyn, who returned his smile.

"He's not so little, Carlos," said Marilyn.

"No, he's really not. He just turned twenty. Dayzee, I got here as quick as I could. I hear you still have some garbage to haul away?"

"Yeah, just like before. You remember? Well, we found that trash. A quick ride to the dump would be wonderful."

"Happy to help, Dayzee. Where is it?"

Before Dayzee could answer, they heard the front door open and saw Kozy walking toward them with five bloody knives in one hand.

"Oh, see that?" said Cliff. "That's the kind of thing that will keep the audiences tuned in."

"Kozy, what are you doing?" said Dayzee.

"I thought it best to remain close to all of you."

"We appreciate that, but what's with knives covered with fake blood? Those were left over from Halloween, so maybe you should just throw those out?"

"Must have been some kind of party," said Cliff.

"You have no idea," said Sophia with a smirk.

"Look," said Carlos, "We have to get going. How about if we grab your trash and make a run for it?"

Carlos and Ramon were already walking toward the garage, and Dayzee shouted to them.

"Hey, wait—we'll get it for you."

"That's okay," he said as he hit the keypad. "I remember the code. I'll just toss it in the truck and get out of your way."

Dayzee and Sophia and Marilyn stared in shock as the door rolled up and Carlos and his brother walked in.

"I don't see anything, Dayzee. Just this tarp. That's it? That's what you want gone?"

The three of them rushed over to stand by his side. They looked all around the garage but saw no sign of the headless dead man.

"Uh-oh. Look," Marilyn said as she pointed at the open door to the house.

"That's just great," said Sophia.

"I think we might have wasted your time, Carlos. Can we give you a call later?"

"No, no, no, Dayzee. I'm here to help. Let me help you."

He kicked the tarp out of his way and walked toward the door to the house with Ramon.

"Carlos, wait," said Dayzee. "Don't go in there!"

"It's fine, Dayzee. We'll find your problem and clear it out for you."

They disappeared into the house and slammed the door shut.

"Oh, boy," said Marilyn.

"This isn't good, Sis."

"Maybe not, but did you see his brother, Ramon? He's a little cutie."

"You can have him. I like Carlos better anyway."

"Oh, Sissy, you don't miss Kenzie anymore?"

"Sure I do, Sis, but in the meantime . . ."

"Kozy," said Dayzee, "can you go in with the girls and maybe try to keep those two young men out of trouble?"

"Yes, we will go inside. If you need me, scream."

"He said to scream," said Cliff. "I love it!"

"Yeah, that's something, alright," said Dayzee. "Kozy, I'm sure I will."

Marilyn, Sophia, and Kozy followed Carlos and Ramon into the mansion.

"Looks like you have everything under control, so I should get going," said Cliff. "I have a dinner date with a lovely actress, who is in no way as beautiful and talented as any of you," he said quickly.

"Alright, Cliff. It's been a real fun experience since you got here," she said before turning to look at the door again. "Let's catch up soon to finish that tour, alright?"

"Yes, of course, Dayzee. Please tell Marilyn and Sophia that I hope to see both of them real soon too."

"I will."

"You know, that was quite an intriguing sight: the way Kozy was dressed, packed with muscles, and holding those fake knives. Let's plan to do something with that during the show, okay?"

"Oh, that Kozy. Stuff like that happens all the time. Yeah, we'll make sure it'll be part of the show."

He opened his car door and got in. Before closing the door, he said, "See you real soon, Dayzee."

He slammed his door shut, put on his sunglasses, and burned his tires over the circular drive. After his car was through the gate, Dayzee ran through the garage, swung in the door, and stepped inside. She found Marilyn and Sophia waiting near the door.

"Well, what the hell," said Dayzee. "This morning has been the longest month of my life."

"Oh, Dayzee," said Marilyn, "it hasn't been that bad. Sissy and I had some fun."

"You were sure close to having even more fun, Sis."

"Kozy didn't seem to mind all that attention either."

"I noticed that, Sis. We need to see how far we can go with that. Kozy is really catching on."

"Oh, no. Not with Kozy too," said Dayzee. "Listen, both of you: there's still a headless monster roaming the halls of this mansion, and don't forget that anything wood can be dangerous."

"Yes, that's certainly true," said Marilyn, "but Sissy and I know exactly what to do next time."

"You're right, Sis. As long as something isn't trying to kill us, we'll see what Kozy is capable of."

"He's sure built for some good times!" said Marilyn.

"Alright, who's brave enough to go see what's going on?" said Dayzee. "We need to find Kozy, Carlos, Ramon, *and* that guy looking for his head."

"I still think he's just looking for head," said Marilyn.

"I'm with Sis, Dayzee. Just like a guy."

"Oh, you're probably right. Let's hope we find Kozy first. We're in real trouble all by ourselves."

"What then?" said Sophia.

"We get rid of Carlos and his brother first. We can't let them see that thing walking around."

"Then what?" said Marilyn. "We still don't know how to kill this new assassin thing."

"We find Kozy, then we all get on some hot outfits and head back to the Prism, girls. We need to figure this out."

"Drinks always help," said Sophia.

"Rock and roll too," said Dayzee.

"And pool table fun!" said Marilyn.

"I want another Popsicle," said Sophia. "Strawberry would be nice."

Chapter 8 – Anything Made of Wood

Dayzee gestured for the twins to stay quiet, and they all tilted their heads to listen for any signs of the others that had disappeared somewhere in Dayzee's house.

"I think they're upstairs," said Marilyn. "I thought I heard footsteps."

"Did it sound like dancing, Sis?"

"That's still funny, Sissy. No, I don't think so."

"Maybe we should just stay here and yell for Kozy. What do you think, Dayzee?"

"No, I don't think so, Fia. That might just attract that headless body that's roaming around somewhere."

"Hey," said Marilyn, "how can he hear anything without a head anyway?"

"Good question, Sis. This is creepy stuff, and it doesn't even make sense."

"Girls, that thing can't hear us or anything else. It's the assassin. That's the problem. It's sending that corpse after us, and it's throwing knives and who knows what else."

"Dayzee, it's sure going to hear my heels walking through your house," said Marilyn.

"Why don't you slip them off, then?"

Marilyn smiled, shook her head, and said, "You know I won't do that, Dayzee."

"Yeah, I figured. Alright, just walk carefully. Can you try that?"

"Dayzee," said Sophia, "Sis can't help but strut. Look at her legs—she could strut before she could walk."

"You too, Sissy—I love watching you strut around!"

"Thanks, Sis. How about if we just go ahead and take our chances, Dayzee?"

"Sure, Fia. Let's get going and hope for the best. I strut, too, you know."

"We know," said Marilyn. "You've got the sweetest strut of all!"

The three began the walk toward the kitchen, their heels clicking on the smooth tile floor. When they'd reached the kitchen, Dayzee held her arms out to stop them.

"Girls, I definitely heard footsteps upstairs. Let's go."

They walked across the kitchen to the mansion's second stairway, and they began taking the stairs, stopping every couple of steps to listen. During a quiet pause, they heard someone scream out, "Oh, what the fuck!"

"Uh-oh. I think that was Carlos," said Marilyn.

"It might have been Ramon, too, Sis."

"Girls, it was probably both of them. Are you still itchy, Mare?"

"I'm going crazy, Dayzee."

"And you, Fia?"

"At least as much as Sis. Ever since that fountain of youth, I'm losing my mind."

"Both of you have wanted to turn up the heat for a long time, haven't you?"

They nodded.

"This might be your chance. I like Carlos, but let's face it—yard guys are a dime a dozen. It sounds like he saw our headless dead friend that's still alive. We can't let him leave."

"His brother, too, Dayzee?"

"Neither of them. Their days of manicuring lush lawns under a hot Beverly Hills sun are over and done."

"I'll take Ramon, then," said Marilyn. "Sissy, you can have Carlos."

"I can't believe we're actually going to do it, Sis. God, we've been good for so long!"

"I can feel things heating up in just the right places already, Sissy!"

"Don't feel guilty about it either, girls. We really have no choice. Let's go."

They all ran up the remaining stairs as well as they could in their high heels. Looking to the left down the long hall, they saw Carlos and Ramon frozen and gazing into a bedroom. They hurried over to stand with them, and they stared at the scene unfolding in the room: Kozy held the dead man's arms behind his back, and all four legs of a small table were implanted in his chest.

Carlos turned quickly to see Dayzee, then turned back to Kozy and his corpse.

"Dayzee, what the hell is going on?"

"Well, I told you we had some trash to throw out. There,"—she pointed into the room—"that's the trash."

"Is he alive? Where the fuck is his head?"

"Oh, the head is long gone, Carlos," Sophia said with a chuckle. "I think it got kicked around like a football."

"Maybe a mountain lion got it, Sissy. Remember that fun story?"

"Oh yeah, maybe that's it. Damn lions . . . always stealing heads."

"What? I mean—"

"He's been looking for it," said Marilyn. "He's looking for head, just like any other guy."

"Mare, we need to focus here," said Dayzee.

"Car, what the hell?"

"I don't know, Ramon, but this ain't right. I'm gonna call for help or something. This is fucked up."

"Oh, Carlos, no, no, no," said Dayzee. "You can't call anyone. Here's what we're going to do: Kozy is going to cut that thing up into little pieces. We'll package it all up nice and neat, and you and your brother can haul it to—"

"Oh, no fucking way, Dayzee! I'm a yard guy, for God's sake!"

"Me too, lady. I can't be hauling bodies around."

"Well," said Dayzee, "it's just one body. Lots of pieces, though."

"That's worse!"

"Boys," said Dayzee, "it'll compost just like everything else, won't it? After a while out in the sunshine and weather, all the pieces will stop twitching, and then—"

"Oh, no fuckin' way, Dayzee!"

Carlos reached for his phone, and Dayzee poked Sophia with her elbow. She grabbed his wrist.

"Can you give it some thought, Carlos? For me?"

He shook his head and never looked at her, so she reached for his chin and turned him to face her. He looked into her blue eyes, and she said, "I've been told my eyes are beautiful. You might like the rest of me even better. Why don't you take a peek?"

Carlos looked down from her eyes and focused on her lips, which were big and red, then his eyes continued down to her large breasts, squeezed together in her tight blue blouse. She took a step back so that he could see her legs better, and he looked along every inch until he got to her black heels.

As his eyes came back to hers, he said, "I, um, I can think about it. I guess."

He continued to stare while he put his phone away.

She reached around his waist and pulled him in close for a kiss. He broke free after several seconds and tried to turn his head toward the struggle in the bedroom, but Sophia again held his cheek and kissed him.

"There, that's better. Why don't we take a little walk?"

"Yeah . . . yeah, alright."

"Sis, you coming?"

Marilyn only looked into Ramon's eyes, who'd been staring more at her than the corpse.

"I don't know, Sissy. Tell me, Ramon . . . will I be coming?"

"Uh . . . if you . . . I mean—"

"Let's make sure we both do. Kiss me, Ramon."

He did. Sophia kept kissing Carlos too. Dayzee saw that the twins had captivated both yard guys, and she walked into the bedroom, let out a deep breath, and closed the door behind her.

*　　*　　*

"Dayzee, I do not know how to permanently kill the Guild's assassin."

"Let's take that table out of its chest. Maybe that'll help?"

"No, we should wait. When I removed knives from the body earlier, it reverted to being completely dead, but that did not kill the assassin. Leaving the table like this might contain the assassin here in this body, at least for a while."

"Alright, so we leave the table there, jabbed into it. Then what?"

"I do not know. Bruno said you killed the first assassin. How was that done?"

"Oh, that was truly perverse. It had to do with sex between the headless guy and a human woman, and—"

"Perhaps this time, it will require *you* to—"

"Oh, no. No way! I'm not doing anything with that guy!"

"He was likely more attractive before he had been stabbed so many times."

"Yeah, way back when he had a head too. Damn lions."

"I do not understand the humor in references to lions."

"Gotta blame someone, right? Why not a lion?"

*　　*　　*

"Sis, I know just the room. Come on, boys. It's time you really met the Kildare . . . girls."

"Good one, Sissy."

Each took their guy by his hand, and Sophia led them down the hall. She passed two bedrooms on the right and brought them into the third.

"Ooh, Sissy, I like the floor!"

"Tile is unusual for a bedroom, huh, Sis? A good thing for us, though, right?"

"You two are sisters, for real?" said Carlos. "I thought you were just messin' with us."

"We haven't even begun to mess with you," said Sophia.

"She's right, you know," Marilyn said before she held Ramon close and kissed him.

She shifted her behind into the door to slam it shut, then reached back to lock it.

"Don't you think we're hot?" said Sophia, but she kissed him again and didn't let him answer.

*   *   *

"It appears that the assassin can use anything made of wood to kill you and Marilyn and Sophia."

"Yeah, Kozy, it sure can, but it also uses it to have some fun with us. At least, it did with me. Remember the bed? And the chair? It knew what it wanted, and you know what? If I could ignore how creepy it was, it really wasn't all that bad."

"Yes, Dayzee, but here is something I have noticed: it can kill a living thing with the wood that it controls, and it can also bring back to life something dead the same way."

"Oh, that's brilliant, Kozy. I think you're right, but how does that help us?"

"I do not know. Is there anyone else you can trust that might know?"

"I think the Boss might, but I'm not sure he'd help us. We really abused him the other day so much that we almost killed him. There wasn't much left of him when we kicked his ass back through the portal."

"I believe your best hope lies with your Boss. Maybe you should seek his counsel."

"It's hard enough even to contact him or get him back to Earth. You should have seen what we put ourselves through last time."

"However bad it was, you might—"

"Oh, you know what? I think Mare enjoyed it. I bet she'd want to give that another go."

"Then, we must return to the Prism."

"Alright, but that won't work again now that I know how much she truly enjoyed it."

"Still, I believe we must summon your Boss to find the answer."

"What about the dead guy?"

"If I render him into smaller pieces, no single piece will be able to—"

"Yuck. That sounds too messy. Can we leave the table stuck in him like that and tie him up?"

"I think we can. Where would you like to store it?"

"That's funny, Kozy. 'Store it.' How about in the garage?"

"Yes. Will Marilyn and Sophia be successful at eliminating your yard workers?"

"Hey, that sounds pretty harsh."

"I apologize. Will they be alright?"

"Oh, they sure will. Carlos and Ramon? Ashes to ashes, as they say here."

*   *   *

"You two, have a seat on the bed. We want to get each other undressed for you. How does that sound?"

"Yeah. Oh, yeah," said Carlos. "I'd like that."

"Me too," said Ramon. "Damn."

They both sat on the foot of the bed, and Sophia turned to her sister.

"No turning back, Sis. We have no choice now."

"Sissy, I can't wait. I can't believe we're finally turning up the heat again!"

"God, it's been so long."

While smiling at the two hypnotized yard guys, Marilyn undressed her sister, and Sophia undressed her sister, and within minutes, there were two naked twins, one blond and one brunette, wearing only their heels and smiling at the two human men.

"God," said Carlos. "You two are . . . I mean . . . damn."

"Yeah. Like he said," said Ramon.

They started to get undressed, but Sophia said, "Oh, we don't have time for that. Are you boys ready?"

They nodded.

Marilyn looked at their laps and said, "They're *really* ready, Sissy. It's funny how we always get that kind of reaction."

"Well, you're really hot, Sis."

"You too, Sissy. Are we really doing this? I just can't believe it!"

"Believe it, Sis. We have no choice, so let's enjoy the hell out of it."

*　　*　　*

"I will drag it by its feet. Its arms will wave around, but your hallways are wide enough that it will not be able to disturb the decor."

"Alright, I like that idea," said Dayzee. "That'll keep the table jammed in there too."

Kozy dragged the dead guy down onto his back and hurried to grab him by his ankles. The tabletop was nearly level, even while the thing thrashed around.

"Too bad I can't set something on there, just for fun," said Dayzee. "How funny would that be?"

"Like a tasteful floral arrangement?"

"Yeah, like that. That would make a funny photo. You're developing a nice sense of humor."

"I adapt as time progresses, but perhaps we should be more concerned with securing this thing safely."

"Yeah, you're right. Alright, let's get going."

Kozy began dragging the dead guy out of the room and down the hall while Dayzee followed and watched closely. When they passed the closed bedroom door, Dayzee stopped to listen.

"Oh, those girls are smart. They picked the right room. We'll need a broom and a dustpan pretty soon."

Kozy, Dayzee, the dead guy, and the table continued down the hall to the stairway.

"We have an elevator somewhere around here," said Dayzee.

"I can drag it down the stairs. I believe the table will remain embedded in it."

"Alright, sure. Let's give it a try. Not like we're going to hurt him."

*　　*　　*

Soon, the two yardmen had been coaxed to lie flat on their backs on the cool tile floor. They remained fully clothed, with only enough access to give the twins the seats they wanted and needed.

"Oh my, Sissy. Ramon sure is ready."

"You always get that, don't you? You're absolutely gorgeous, Sis."

"You too, Sissy. Look at Carlos—oh, my goodness!"

"Let's start them out easy, Sis. Just have a seat, for now. They're not going anywhere. Hell, they're already in a trance."

"Sometimes, I really love Earth. It's just so easy here."

Seconds later, after they'd found just where they'd wanted to sit themselves down, Marilyn said, "Oh, that's nice, Ramon. Good boy."

"You too, Carlos. Does that feel good when I move like this?"

Carlos could no longer speak, and he could barely nod his head.

"Sissy, you already know it feels good. It's like nothing they've ever felt before."

"Look at them smiling, Sis. Alright, it's time. Let's start out slow—just a little bit of heat."

"Mm . . . mine's going now. Just a little bit, but it feels oh, so good."

"Me too. Let's just enjoy it for a minute."

"Okay," said Marilyn, "but no longer than a minute. I can barely hold back!"

"You know what, Sis? Let's just give them all of it. We don't have time to drag this out anyway."

"Yes, if he can't handle me at my worst, then . . . well, hell, he'll still love me at my worst. Fire in the hole!"

"Good one, Sis! Yes, I'm going all the way right now."

Seconds later, after the two guys were nearly expired from the heat, Sophia said, "That smell. Ooh, this is like heaven."

"I know. I can't believe how good it feels. Sissy, we should do this all the time. They're just earthmen, after all."

"Yep, and we're the Kildare Killers. Why fight it, Sis?"

*   *   *

Down the stairs and all through the house, Kozy dragged the headless guy by his ankles until they'd reached the garage.

"Do you have rope, Dayzee, or something stronger?"

"Oh, I have some ropes, but they're in a special drawer in my bedroom."

"I am not surprised. There are many forms of recreation here on this planet."

"The way I'm living? Oh yeah, but I'd rather not get blood and goo on any of that. Hey, how about if you hold that thing still, and I'll drive one of my cars up onto its leg or arm? That should hold it down."

"That will do. It cannot even chew through its trapped limb to free itself."

"No, because it doesn't have a head," said Dayzee.

"Damn lions."

"Good one, Kozy!"

*   *   *

The twins continued at their highest temperatures until nothing remained of either yardman except two piles of smoldering dust.

"Oh, Sissy, now I'm starting to feel bad. I know they're just earthmen, but still . . . we killed them."

"They were going to rat us out, Sis. We gave them a chance. You and I could have just shown them the best times they ever would have had. Maybe they could have even been part of our gang."

"They did make that choice. Now that it's over, I'm not sure I want to keep burning men up like that."

"Yep, me neither, but I sure didn't want to stop when we were in the heat of the moment."

"Good one, Sissy. Yes, me too. We'll still be the Kildare Killers, won't we?"

"Always, Sis."

"Hey, look."

Marilyn fingered through her pile of ashes and pulled out a shiny gold chain with a simple cross.

"Souvenir, Sis?"

"Why not? More like a trophy, Sissy."

Marilyn put on the necklace, and they left for the garage.

*   *   *

With the dead man pinned to the garage floor by one of Dayzee's cars, she and Kozy returned to the kitchen. The twins had gotten dressed and came down the stairs to join them. Sophia held a metal waste can with a thin wisp of smoke rising from it.

"Good job, girls," said Dayzee.

She saw the lack of smiles and said, "Hey, don't feel bad, alright? They saw way too much. There was no other way."

"We know," said Sophia. "Right now, we're not happy about killing them."

"But a few minutes ago?" said Marilyn. "I couldn't have stopped."

"God, Dayzee, that's the best," said Sophia. "Sis and I will never get tired of using our heat. I even thought of using my barbs, but I didn't."

"I thought of that too, Sissy. Even without the barbs, though, that was incredible. Ramon sure enjoyed it, even while it was killing him."

"Carlos too. That's a funny thing about earthmen: as long as it feels good, they don't care that they're being destroyed."

"Maybe that's the best an earthman can ever have, girls: to be burned to dust by the unbelievably hot Kildare Killers."

"That's us," said Marilyn, "but what's next, Dayzee?"

"We need to figure out a way to kill the assassin. Kozy suggested we try to get the Boss back here and ask him. What do you two think?"

"We were pretty rough on him, Dayzee," said Sophia. "Do you really think he'd tell us, even if he knew?"

"It might be our only shot. Hey, what if we promise to give him the same treatment, but maybe without the barbs? He seemed damn happy up to that point."

"We were too," said Marilyn. "The Boss is actually kind of hot. I mean 'attractive' hot, and he can take the heat, not like these weak earthmen."

"Alright, so we're agreed: if the Boss tells us what we need to know, we'll show him a good time?"

"Sure, Dayzee, sounds good to me," said Sophia. "How do we get him back through the portal? Same as the first time?"

"Ooh, yeah, I liked that," said Marilyn. "This time, I'll wear just a bathrobe. Let's do it!"

"Oh, Sis, that'll be hot. I'll have to have Kozy roughing me up since Bruno isn't around."

"Hmm . . . I think you'll like that even more, Sissy. Dayzee, we need that photographer friend of yours."

"Girls, this isn't all fun and games. We have a dead guy trapped in the garage, and we have to figure out how to kill that thing once and for all."

"We can still have some fun, Dayzee," said Sophia.

"We're not about to stop," said Marilyn.

"You girls are too much."

"Wait a minute," said Marilyn. "I just thought of something. One of us will have to be in loads of danger while Kozy is threatening to kill the other. I think since there will be tons of danger, I'd rather be the one that Kozy is attacking. You know, because of what the danger will do to Kozy. Sissy, you'll have to wear the bathrobe."

"I can do that. Oh, you know I can wear a short bathrobe."

"Nobody wears a short robe like you, Sissy."

"Except you?"

"Well, we're twins, so—"

"Okay, we have a plan," said Dayzee. "It's Saturday, and it's still kind of early, but there should be enough men in that bar for you to work into a frenzy, Fia."

"That's what I'll do, while Sis is at the mercy of Kozy, all in the middle of a bunch of danger."

"Can't wait, Sissy."

"Why don't you set those two guys—"

"The ashes?" said Sophia.

"Yeah," said Dayzee. "Set their ashes up on the counter to cool down. Let's get changed and go. Fia, just pack your robe—you can change there."

"Can we go see what you did with the dead guy?" said Marilyn. "That sounds kind of fun."

"Fun?" said Dayzee. "You girls. Fine, we'll go out through the garage."

Chapter 9 – It Found a Good Spot

"He's not going anywhere," said Sophia. "Funny how he's just wiggling around on the concrete. He's sure not saying much either."

"Well, Sissy, he's got a table stuck in him, and he doesn't have a head. What would you do?"

"You do make a good point, Sis."

"Have you seen enough?" said Dayzee. "Let's get in the limo and head over."

"We should consider relocating the dead man's vehicle," said Kozy.

"The headless guy?" said Marilyn. "He didn't drive any—"

"No, I think Kozy means Carlos's pickup truck. Kozy's right—we need to move that anyway."

"Hey, is that head still somewhere in the Prism?" said Marilyn. "Maybe they're using it as a decoration or something."

"Who knows, Mare? I guess we'll see."

"Hey, Dayzee," said Sophia, "back away from that guy and see what happens."

"What? Why?"

"I'm just wondering. Go ahead. Let's see what happens if it's just me that's close by."

Dayzee retreated across the garage, and Sophia stood so close that she could touch him. He stopped moving.

"Huh. Look at that. Sis, now it's your turn."

Marilyn took her place, and the dead guy still lay there like a dead guy.

"Okay, Dayzee, you're up."

Dayzee replaced Marilyn, and the headless man began thrashing all around, tipping the table and trying to pull its leg out from under the tire of Dayzee's car.

"What the hell?" said Dayzee. "It looks like it only wants me."

"You *are* pretty hot," said Marilyn. "Why wouldn't he want you?"

"Girls, it's not a him or even an it. It's that assassin. What's going on with it?"

"It wants only you," said Kozy. "It appears to have lost interest in the other two."

"How did that happen?" said Dayzee.

"I think it might be because it got to know you well. Intimately. It has not had that experience with Marilyn or Sophia."

"Aw," said Sophia, "that's kind of sweet. The dead guy's got a thing for you."

"I know which thing, too, Sissy!"

The dead guy rolled from side to side, banging his table into the car while reaching for Dayzee.

"Just wonderful," said Dayzee. "Seriously, that's the most repulsive fan I've ever had, and boy, I've had some real winners."

"Even the dead ones are after you now," said Marilyn. "That means Sissy and I are off the hook."

"Yep, but we'll still help you, Dayzee," said Sophia. "We'll help you kill that thing."

"We still need the Boss. You have your robe, Fia? If we can't think of anything else, we'll have to try that again."

"I sure do."

"Then, let's go. We need to wrap this up so I can get going on my new film. I can't be on set and have a headless guy wander on camera during a scene."

"Oh, you know, if it's a horror movie, that might be pretty good," said Sophia. "Just keep the cameras rolling."

"Off-script with an assassin aiming a dead guy at me? Actually, that might be pretty good stuff, maybe even for Kildare in the Hills, but how about if we save that for the next monster? I just want to kill this one already."

"That is wise," said Kozy. "It will soon know just what you like. You might be helpless to its advances next time."

"That would be a sight," said Marilyn.

"Wouldn't it, Sis? I'll bring the popcorn."

"God, you two. Okay, let's just get to the Prism. First, Kozy, how about moving that truck around the side of the house where it can't be seen?"

"As you wish."

Kozy turned and began hiking out of the garage and toward Carlos's pickup on the driveway.

"Try swinging those arms a little more," said Sophia.

"Good idea, Sissy. Give it a try, Kozy. Show us some swagger."

Kozy didn't turn around, but he did start taking bolder steps and swinging his arms

Dayzee looked him up and down and said, "Gets better all the time, girls."

*   *   *

Kozy parked the limo in their usual spot across the street from the Prism. The afternoon sun beat down on them as they walked along Sunset Boulevard. Heads turned, and more than a few whistles and yells erupted from passing cars.

Dayzee wore her short black skirt with fishnet stockings, tall black boots, and a tight white blouse. Marilyn wore her customary white heels and dress, short enough to give a clear view of her long, bare legs. Sophia wore a tight black skirt and her standard black spike heels; her red lips matched the fiery red of her low-cut blouse. And Kozy still wore his uniform: black khaki pants and black boots, with no shirt under a short jacket reminiscent of a military official. A striking black hat completed the ensemble.

"They're all whistling at you, Sis. You look really hot in that white dress. You always do."

"Thanks, Sissy, but I'm sure that's all for you or Dayzee or Kozy. You're all hotter than any of these humans deserve!"

"Girls, I'd say it's mostly the women cheering for Kozy. That jacket can't begin to cover up his chest. And I must say, those tight pants are showing off some nice features."

"You're right—Kozy is gorgeous."

"That's for sure, Sissy. Even that hat makes a difference."

"Funny how nobody cares about dead bodies and heads and stuff, but they notice us," said Sophia.

"Good point," said Dayzee. "It's just a weird corner of the world. Let's go inside and have some fun."

Kozy held the door, and they all entered the dark lounge. Mack was taking care of the bar crowd, and he smiled and shook his head as they approached him.

"Well, what do we have here? You three ladies all look lovely as hell. Hey, for some reason, you look a lot like Kenzie."

"Yet, I am not Kenzie. I am her brother from far away."

"That's right, Mack," said Dayzee. "This is Kozy, who's visiting for a while. Kenzie wasn't feeling well, so she crashed back at my place."

"A brother? So, you're what . . . a bodybuilder or something?"

"'Something' is a broadly general term. To be more specific, I am a—"

"Personal trainer too," said Dayzee. "That's what Kozy is."

Mack stared into Kozy's eyes for a second, then he glanced up and down, lingering briefly on his exposed abs and chest.

"Well, whatever you're doing, keep it up."

"That's what I was thinking," said Marilyn.

"Sis, you're kind of obsessed. Shouldn't you be calmed down some after what we just did?"

"Oh, I don't know, Sissy. I think I'm even more worked up."

"Mack, Kozy just likes to stay in good shape, but we all want a drink. We're here on a mission to figure some things out."

"I can help with the drinks. The usual, girls?"

Three heads nodded, but Kozy only stared.

"Choose any representative sampling of alcohols for me."

"Uh, okay. Sure."

Mack turned and started fixing their orders.

"See what I see, Sis?"

"I sure do. A bunch of frat boys all around the pool table." She laughed and said, "I had bikers, but you might get these guys. Do you think you can get them riled up enough?"

"Have you seen me in a short robe and heels?"

"I have—really hot, Sissy! You're going to drive them wild. Go change—get that tiny robe on already."

"You're right. I was going to have that drink first, but I don't want to wait. This'll be like a fun little vacation for me. I try to always take a vacation."

"Vacation from what, Sis? Not from clothes because you always seem to end up naked."

"In a bar, though?"

"Not as often, no, but okay, I guess I see your point."

"Good. Watch me when I strut out from the lady's room, Sis."

"Oh, I can't wait!"

"We'll all be watching, Fia," said Dayzee. "I bet those young men will be staring the most. They've never seen anything like you and your beautiful twin sister."

"You'd think they'd guess we're not from Earth, huh? Silly human men. Alright, I'm off."

With that, Sophia turned and walked away to change, and most of the guys around the pool table stared intently, watching her long steps and shifting hips.

Mack set four drinks down on the bar and just started to speak, then he stopped himself and turned his head to watch Sophia. She wore only a short white robe and her black heels, and her long black hair fell straight behind her. Her lips were bright red, and her blue eyes shined as she walked back to her place at the bar.

"Wow," said Mack.

"That's my Sissy," said Marilyn. "Isn't she the hottest thing ever?"

"Fia, you're not wearing anything under that robe, are you?" said Dayzee.

Sophia snorted once with a smirk, shook her head, and picked up her drink. While taking a sip, she looked sideways at the pool table and all the eager faces. After drinking half of it, she set the glass back down.

"You know, ladies . . . oh, and Kozy too—guess I keep forgetting that you've changed."

"Yes, but I will return Kenzie to her natural form when my mission is complete."

"She'll be back to all her usual stuff, right?"

"Yes, Marilyn. The anatomy I have imposed on her will leave when I do."

"But right now, you sure look strong. Wow."

"I am here to lend assistance. That is my main focus."

"You're just plain gorgeous," said Sophia. "Alright, we're doing the same plan as before? Except this time, I'll be the one in trouble. Kozy, you'll be threatening to hurt Sis in some way, and—"

"With all that danger, Kozy will really get worked up again, and I can't imagine what kind of abuse I'll be receiving."

"You sound pretty eager, Mare," said Dayzee. "You're not supposed to be enjoying it, remember? I'm supposed to be upset about you being attacked by those guys, Fia, and you, Mare, by Kozy."

"What is the purpose of such a contrived plot?" said Kozy.

"Fia can't allow herself to fight back against whatever's going to happen to her because if she does, Kozy, you'll have orders to harm Mare. I won't be able to stop any of it once it gets started. All I can do is get more and more upset, and at some point, that will call the Boss, and he'll come through the portal. It's our only hope."

"If it doesn't work, there's no way to stop this, Kozy," said Sophia "You'll have instructions to hurt Sis if I resist the abuse from all those young men. So, once we get started, if the Boss doesn't show up, I'll have to take whatever they give me, and by the way they're looking over here, I'd say they're all getting some big ideas."

"Oh, like you'll mind, Sissy. I think you secretly hope the Boss doesn't show up. Actually, I hope so too. I get to watch you with that gang over there, and I'll have Kozy all over me. You know I'll like that."

"So, I'm supposed to just keep getting more and more upset?" said Dayzee. "How can I now? I'll know that you're both enjoying the hell out of all of it. I won't be upset at all."

"Can we do it anyway, Dayzee?" said Marilyn. "At least for a while? We'll worry about calling the Boss later."

"I'm ready," said Sophia. "Who cares if the Boss shows up or not? Look at all those impatient faces over there, and I'm wearing barely anything. All I need to do is strut over there, maybe bend over to pick up the chalk, and those guys will—"

"Oh, God!" said Dayzee.

She and her barstool tipped forward, and her arms flew out to catch her, spilling her drink and Marilyn's. She couldn't look down, but the other three saw that the front two legs of her stool had curled up and were coiling around her ankles. The stool rested on only its two back legs.

"Oh yeah, now I remember. We shouldn't be around anything with wood," said Sophia, and she reached for her drink.

"Well, except for Kozy, because Kozy is—"

"Not now, Mare! Help! The chair is attacking me!"

"Aw, all it's doing is holding your ankles. It looks like some kind of sexy bondage thing going on."

"Fia! You girls, I'm being attacked! The barstool is—"

"Shh . . ." said Sophia. "Mack is coming. We'll have to kill him if he sees what's going on."

"Another drink, ladies?"

"Yes, set us up, Mack," said Marilyn. "Doesn't Sis look like a dream in her short robe?"

Sophia stepped back so that he could see, and he grinned while looking her up and down, all the while the barstool was getting a tighter lock on Dayzee's legs.

"God, yeah. I've never seen anything like that. Sophia, you're—"

"A little cold, Mack. Yep, you're right. Can you bring me a blanket or something?"

"Yeah, sure. Of course."

He hurried off, and Sophia said, "Dayzee, we need to cover you up. We can't let Mack see what's going on."

"No, Fia! No blanket—get me away from this thing!"

"Uh-uh. Nope. Forget the pool table guys. Forget Kozy ravaging Sis while the danger causes—"

"Hey, Sissy, I want to be ravaged."

"I know, and I want the college guys all over me, too, but don't you see? This will work better. We need to let Dayzee get in a lot of trouble herself, and maybe that'll bring the Boss."

"You're a genius, Sissy!"

"I am not to intervene this time?"

"No, Kozy. Just let it happen."

"No, girls! I already feel it trying to pull my legs apart! I know what's coming next!"

"That's funny, Dayzee."

"No, I didn't mean it like that, Mare. I need you to—"

"Shh . . . Mack is back."

"Here's your blanket. Yell if you need anything else. I have to hit the kitchen for a few minutes."

He turned and left, and Sophia wrapped the blanket over Dayzee's shoulders, covering her legs too.

"What? You're just going to cover me up and let the damn barstool take advantage of me?"

"Yep. That's the plan now," said Sophia.

"You could still go have your fun with that gang over there, Sissy."

"Sure, and you could probably talk Kozy into doing whatever he wants to do to you, Sis."

"I will do as instructed," said Kozy. "I am here to provide whatever—"

"Girls . . . and Kozy! Come on, help me, alright?"

"Sorry, this is the only way," said Sophia. "We need the Boss. You said so yourself."

They all heard a snap as the wooden footrest split directly in front of Dayzee. They watched as one end started lengthening and thinning and circling around Dayzee's waist beneath the blanket.

"Wow, that's really something to see," said Marilyn.

"I guess it's tired of getting kicked around," Sophia said with a smirk.

"Payback time, Sissy?"

"Girls, this isn't funny!"

The very end traveled first around both of her wrists, which Sophia quickly covered with the blanket, then up between her breasts and wrapped around her neck under her long blond hair.

"Kozy, maybe you, please? Can you do something already?"

"We have all agreed that summoning the Boss is required. This is a logical plan, Dayzee."

"I never should have given you that hat!"

Dayzee shook her head and frowned as Kozy turned only his eyes up and tipped his hat forward, leaving only enough room to peek out from under it.

"Nice. That's just wonderful. Very dramatic. Thanks, Kozy."

Sophia pulled the blanket up higher and wrapped it more tightly so that Mack wouldn't see the thin wooden strap holding Dayzee around her throat.

"Girls. It's not done. The other end of that thing is crawling up my leg. Hey, it just passed my left knee."

"You're in real trouble, Dayzee," said Marilyn.

"I know, but it sure is smooth. It's not really hurting me either. It's just—oh no, it's moving along my thigh."

"On the inside?"

"Yeah, Fia. It's pulling my legs apart too. Oh no, not again!"

"This is big trouble," said Sophia. "No one's going to help you either. How does that make you feel?"

The very end between Dayzee's thighs wiggled its way closer until it found its destination.

"Oh, my," said Dayzee. "Girls, I think . . ."

"You think what?" said Marilyn.

"I think we should wait a minute or two. Just to be sure, you know?"

The twins looked at each other and shrugged.

"Oh, it found a good spot. There, that's it . . ."

"Dayzee? Are you still okay?" said Marilyn.

"Ah, such a sweet kid," Dayzee said with a smile. "Yeah, it's just—ooh, now it's trying to—ah, there we go."

"I can help if you clearly command it, Dayzee. I can—"

"No, Kozy, let's just see how things go. This thing, I don't think it's really an assassin, girls. It's—oh, wow. It's, you know, kind of a nice thing. Maybe we could be friends with it?"

Mack returned and said, "Another round, ladies and Kozy? How about you, Dayzee? You look kind of, uh, distracted or something."

Five silent seconds passed while Mack stared. He looked at Marilyn, then Sophia, then Kozy.

"Sure, Mack. Another . . . round. I might need a cigarette soon too."

"A what? You don't smoke, Dayzee."

"I might start."

Mack shrugged and turned to prepare their drinks.

"This isn't working, Sis. She's enjoying it too much."

"Should we ask Kozy to stop it, Sissy? What should we do?"

"Let's enjoy our drinks," said Sophia. "Frankly, I'm a little jealous. I never got that kind of treatment."

"Neither have I, Sissy," Marilyn said and reached over and felt around on Kozy's lap.

"Oh, but Dayzee's still in trouble. Kozy sure knows it. I have the proof right here in my hand."

"So, everyone's getting some kind of action except for me? That's it—I'm strutting over there, and you know what? I'm not just going to tease them and hope something happens. I'll take this robe all the way off, maybe even give a few lap dances, and then I'll—"

A gagging sound from Dayzee cut Sophia off, and Marilyn said, "Ooh, even more danger. Very impressive, Kozy!"

"Mare . . ." said Dayzee in a throttled voice. "Fia. It's . . . strangling . . . me!"

Sophia lifted the blanket up off of Dayzee's lap and saw what the slender, smooth wood was doing down there.

"You're still enjoying it, though, aren't you? How about if I go over and play naked pool with those boys? I think that's what I'll do. Let's see how far I get on that first lap dance."

"Good for you, Sissy. I'm going to ask Mack for another blanket, then I'm going to sit on Kozy's lap. I want to feel every bit of danger that Dayzee is in. Really, what else can I do?"

"The more danger, the better for you, Sis. While you're on his lap, you can watch me get bent over the pool table. Mm . . . it'll be even better knowing you're watching."

"Girls . . ." said a struggling voice. "This . . . thing . . . is . . . choking—"

"Mack, we need another blanket here!"

"Sure thing, Marilyn. Coming up."

"Yes, like you wouldn't believe!" Marilyn said with a big smile.

"Good one, Sis. Watch this."

Marilyn watched as her twin sister began untying the belt, ready to reveal nothing but her beneath the robe.

"I'll give them a good sight on my way over. They'll know right away that—"

"Kozy . . . I need help. I can't . . . barely—"

"You're in some real trouble there, Dayzee. Why isn't your helper helping you?" said the Boss.

Instantly, Kozy reached under the blanket and snapped the coiled wood strangling Dayzee. Its sharp end darted around to evade Kozy's grasp, but he got a grip on it and broke it again close to Dayzee's wrists. It gave up the fight but still had her wrists locked in place. The other branches still held Dayzee's legs, and the one between her thighs hadn't slowed down.

Kozy began reaching for it, but Dayzee shook her head and said, "No, wait. Save that one for last."

Kozy tried to get a hold on the thin boards around her wrists, and Dayzee again shook her head.

"No, don't. I like that too."

Kozy looked down at the boards spreading Dayzee's legs.

"Nope. Like those too."

"Oh, Dayzee," said the Boss. "You should let Kozy help you. That might feel very good right now, but that could change in a heartbeat."

Dayzee sobered up and said, "Oh yeah, like the chair at my house. It got real pointy! Kozy, help! Quick!"

He quickly pulled the single branch out of Dayzee—causing a loud laugh—leaned over, and ripped it loose where it grew from the footrest. Next, Kozy freed Dayzee's wrists, then her ankles. All of the wooden attackers remained still.

"I believe it suffers fatigue after reaching its capacity for exertion," said Kozy.

"I think you're right," said Dayzee. "Boss, don't ask us to apologize for what we did to you before. We thought—"

"Apologize? Why would I do that? My God, that was the single best experience of my life."

"Even the barbs?" said Marilyn. "I know that had to hurt like hell because it felt so good to me."

"Me too," said Sophia. "That was like heaven for us."

"But you didn't kill me, did you, girls? Now, if you would have killed me, then yeah, I might have been upset."

"No," said Dayzee. "You'd just be dead."

"Okay, yeah, but you didn't kill me. Somehow, knowing you were about to kill me only made it better."

Kozy took a drink, and the other three looked at each other.

"Alright," said Dayzee, "we can try to understand all that later. Whatever we just did, all of us, must have worked because here you are. We need your help."

"To kill the assassin? I don't know, girls. That lab is dabbling in sorsciencery, and it—"

"We know. Kozy sort of told us that. Look, either we kill it, or it kills us."

"Well, Dayzee, it seems to only want you," said Sophia.

"Sissy's right about that. I think it kind of got a taste of you, and now it wants to focus just on you."

"Wonderful. Yeah, you're right. So, Boss, we need your help. We'll make it worth your while."

The Boss got a big grin and looked from face to face.

"Heat?" he said.

"Like you can't imagine," said Dayzee.

"Barbs?"

"All the way, this time," said Marilyn.

"Just try to stop me," said Sophia.

The Boss grinned and said, "Let's get to work, girls!"

Chapter 10 – Rather Die on Earth

"Everyone okay back there?" Dayzee said as she turned to look at the back seat.

Marilyn sat on the left, then the Boss, then Sophia. All were squeezed together, and when Dayzee looked down at all the bare legs, except for the Boss's, she shook her head and smiled.

"Looking good, girls. Kozy too. Boss, how do you like sitting in there so tight between those beautiful twins? Are you thinking about what they did to you just two days ago?"

"Oh my God, yeah. I only hope I can help you somehow. That's the deal, right? If I can help you kill that thing, then—"

"Then, we'll mount you like a mechanical bull, one after another, all of us, over and over, with heat and barbs and—"

"Dayzee, don't forget what's waiting in your garage. We can't just leave that there like that, can we?"

"Well, Mare, we could always have Kozy rip it apart, and we can bury all the little pieces everywhere in the landscaping."

"Sheesh," said Sophia. "That doesn't sound fun. Hey, wait a minute. Are we sure that dead thing is still alive? If it is, what just attacked—I mean enjoyed—you at the Prism?"

"Good question. Let's see if it's still kicking, or maybe dancing, girls?"

"Good one, Dayzee," said Marilyn.

She turned to glance at Kozy piloting the limo down Dayzee's street in the Flats.

"That uniform is working out damn well, Kozy. You make a very attractive chauffeur."

"A damn sexy one," said Sophia.

"At some times more than others," said Marilyn.

"Thank you. I am beginning to understand the satisfaction of feeling visually appealing on this planet."

"Good for you," said Dayzee. "Glad you're catching on."

Kozy pulled through Dayzee's entrance gate and parked near the garage.

"Well, let's take a peek," said Dayzee, and she hit a few numbers on her phone, sending the garage door up.

"That's not good," said Sophia. "All I see is that stupid table."

"Sissy, the leg is there too. See it there under the tire?"

"What else should we be seeing?" said the Boss.

"A dead guy, pinned down by one of Dayzee's tires—not just its leg," said Sophia.

"Oh, and he was looking for head," Marilyn said with a giggle.

"I can relate," said the Boss, "but this is serious. We need to capture that thing. Do you think it's in the mansion?"

"Oh, Boss, probably. That mansion has turned into a crazy place."

They all got out of the limo and walked cautiously toward the garage. Once they were close enough, they stopped and studied the scene.

"Look—a puddle of blood. Why would a dead guy still bleed?"

"Because he was brought back to life?" said Marilyn. "Sort of?"

"Sure, but how did he—"

"Look at the knives," said Sophia. "It looks like the knives cut the leg off."

"So, where did the rest of him go? Now, he's missing a head *and* a leg."

"I guess he hopped into the house, girls. See, Boss? See what we're dealing with? It's creepy and hilarious at the same time."

Before he could answer, they watched all five bloody knives float up into the air, their deadly ends pointing right at them.

"Great," said Sophia. "One for each of us."

"That's funny, Sissy, but not really."

Dayzee let out a big sigh as they watched all five knives turn and float through the open door and into the house.

"Wonderful," said Dayzee. "Any advice, Boss?"

The Boss remained silent for a few seconds, then gave his answer.

"Kozy, you're here to protect Dayzee, right? Let's all go inside and see what's going on. If we all stay together, I'm confident that Kozy will disrupt any attacks the assassin might launch."

"I hope you're right, Boss," said Sophia. "Hell, even that bloody table there on the floor could attack us. There's no place safe for us in there."

"Yay," said Marilyn. "Full-time danger—I love what that does to Kozy."

"Oh, Mare, you're obsessed."

"I'm just itchy."

"Alright, let's go inside and hope for the best," said Dayzee.

"I'm actually starting to like the danger," said Marilyn.

"I'm looking forward to using my barbs again, Sis."

"Oh, yes, and our heat. Sissy, we win either way!"

"Well, I'd rather not be assaulted again, girls, so let's try to figure this out," said Dayzee.

"Huh. You didn't seem to mind all that much," said Sophia.

"She's right, Dayzee. You liked it. I think that assassin knows just what you like," said Marilyn.

"No, I was just, I mean—"

"Just remember that it can become deadly at any moment, Dayzee," said Kozy. "That might diminish its appeal."

"Fine. I'll try not to get turned on by an assassin that animates wooden objects and dead guys to molest and kill us."

"Hearing it like that just sounds weird, Dayzee," said Sophia.

"Well, it *is* weird, but you know what?"

"Yep, I sure do," said Sophia. "This is the Hills."

*　　*　　*

"I can sure use a drink, Dayzee," said the Boss. "I bet these beautiful girls could too."

"Drinks all around," Dayzee said as she began walking to the bar in the great room.

"I will accompany you," said Kozy. "It appears you are the only one being targeted now."

"Sure, come on along. Don't let a folding chair take advantage of me."

"Or a wooden spoon," said Sophia.

"That's funny, Sissy."

Dayzee and Kozy left the kitchen, and the Boss scanned the room until his eyes fixed on the can on the counter with a thin trail of white smoke rising from it.

"What the hell?"

He looked at Marilyn, then at Sophia.

"That's not . . . you didn't—"

"It's just garbage, Boss," said Sophia. "Nothing to worry about."

"What kind of garbage?"

"Um, yard waste?" said Marilyn.

"Good one, Sis. She's right—it's just yard waste. Never mind that. How are you feeling, Boss? Are you too far from the portal?"

"Now that you mention it, yeah, I'm not feeling so well. Let's try to figure out how to kill that thing quick before I get too tired to help."

"You still want the heat?" said Sophia.

"And barbs? I like using my barbs," said Marilyn.

He let out a deep breath, smiled, and said while nodding, "I'm not sure I'd survive that, girls."

He walked back over to the can of ashes that used to be Carlos and Ramon and said, "Girls, I know what this is, and it's fine. Do either of you even remember all the details of your mission here?"

"Well, sort of," said Marilyn. "We were supposed to study humans and learn what they find attractive."

"Do you remember why? What the purpose was?"

"I do," said Sophia. "That's how we'd launch the invasion—we'd use their weaknesses against them."

"Correct. You've both been ignoring the project, haven't you? Dayzee too?"

"Oh, yes, Boss, we sure have."

"Sis is right. All we're doing is having fun."

Dayzee and Kozy returned and handed out the drinks.

"Cheers, girls. And Kozy," said the Boss, and they all tasted their cocktails.

"What are you all talking about?" said Dayzee. "Sounded pretty serious."

"We were going over your instructions for the mission, which all of you have abandoned to pursue every selfish pleasure you can imagine."

"We sure did that, Boss. I did, too, not just these gorgeous twins."

"I need to remind you of something, and then I'll tell you about the latest development."

Everyone stared and waited, except for Kozy, who continued to watch every wooden object within sight, with an occasional glance at the stairs and the bloody knives that might appear there any second.

"Okay, the reminder first. You were told to use your considerable talents, your deadly talents, to avoid detection at all costs. You were told that humans are always expendable. Girls,"—he looked at Marilyn and Sophia and tapped his glass against the can—"I know what this is."

"Boss, we didn't mean—"

"It's okay, Sophia. This is what I'm talking about. Did you and your sister have to do it? Did you have to keep things secret?"

"Oh, yes, we really did," said Marilyn. "We didn't really have a choice."

"Sis is right, but we sure did enjoy it too."

"That's okay. All three of you are authorized to eliminate any problems. You're certainly free to enjoy it too."

"Whew, thanks, Boss," said Marilyn. "I wasn't so proud of myself after I burned him up."

"Me neither," said Sophia. "While I was burning him, though? Wow, I loved it."

"I'm glad we talked about this. None of you should feel bad about it. It's perfectly natural for you, and it's not your fault humans are so weak."

"Good," said Dayzee. "We don't have to torture you now. We can find anyone for that. We'll go back to the Prism, and the first—"

"No, Dayzee, you shouldn't just go around killing them either."

"Fine. We'll try to control ourselves. What else? What development were you talking about?"

"I've received word that this assassin that the Guild sent is the last one. They've decided to let all of you live. Really, though, it's because they can't control these things they create with that sorsciencery of theirs. Most of the things they hobble together roam around the lab trying to kill the researchers too. They've decided, instead, to close the portal and abandon you three here. There are plenty of other worlds to conquer."

"I'm okay with that," said Dayzee. "I have no desire to go back anyway. I doubt these twin beauties do either. We're having too much fun."

"We really are, Boss," said Marilyn. "Can you give us some advice before you have to leave?"

The Boss still leaned against the counter in Dayzee's kitchen, and his eyes closed as his head began to tip.

"Hey. Boss," said Dayzee. "You still with us?"

He snapped his eyes open and shook his head before looking at each of them.

"Yeah, I just . . . I'm kind of . . ."

"Tired?"

"Yeah, Dayzee. There's a theory going around the lab about how to fight an assassin like the one roaming around this mansion. You have to disrupt its normal attack methods. If you can do that, you might be able to incinerate it."

"I have no idea what you're talking about, Boss," said Dayzee. "We're used to reading scripts and screenplays and stuff, not science books."

"Or sorcery books," said Marilyn. "Remember? That thing is sorcery too."

"Sis is right, Dayzee, but I don't know what the Boss is talking about either."

"Okay, it's like this: that thing animates something made of wood, then it comes after you, Dayzee, and what does it do first?"

"It tries to have sex with me. God, this is creepy stuff."

"Yeah, and from what I hear, it has some notable skills."

"Yeah, it kind of does, but then it still tries to kill me."

"Right. So, you need to do something unexpected, and then maybe you can kill it."

"Unexpected how? What the heck are you—"

"Fake it out. Instead of resisting, try cooperating. Surprise it. Be a more willing participant. You need to feel like it's the kind of thrill you've always wanted. It won't know how to react to that."

"What . . . like try to believe a dresser is my hot lover tonight?"

"Or a wooden spoon," said Sophia with a smirk.

"Funny, Sissy."

"Hey, you two. Boss, you can't be serious."

"Sadly, I am. Once it gets going on you again, instead of fighting it, show it how willing you are. When something made of wood,"— Marilyn giggled and Sophia snickered— "attacks you, try showing it a good time. I think that would really confuse the hell out of it."

"Then I—"

"At that moment, when you're proving how willing you are, burn the hell out of it. Exactly."

"Could that work? Sounds damn dangerous to me."

"I don't know, Dayzee, but I think it's your best bet for killing it once and for all."

"I'm not sure that makes sense. If I do try something like that, can I keep Kozy close by? You know, to help if I need it?"

"Yes, I'd recommend that."

"I want to watch," said Marilyn.

"You want to watch Kozy, Sis. That's all."

"Of course, I do. All that danger!"

"Okay, girls. Thanks for the super creepy advice, Boss. You really believe that might work?"

"Eh . . . maybe. Hey, why don't you think of it as a part you're playing in one of those film things you're always doing? Just have some fun with it."

"Do I have to make it fun?"

"Yeah, that's the idea. Remember, you're trying to seduce whatever object it's using on you. You have to put it in the right mood too."

"This gets crazier all the time."

"Kill it, and you're all free to run wild on this planet. How does that sound?" said the Boss.

"Crazy. Really crazy."

"Oh, Dayzee, it'll be fun. Sissy and I will help."

"Fine. I'll give it a try. Boss, you look terrible. Are you going to make it?"

"No, I'm not. I'm younger than I look, you know that, Dayzee, but I'm dying."

"What? How?"

"Too many times through the portal. You can have your body diced and scrambled and slopped back together only so many times. I'm sure I'll be dead by suns down."

"There's only one."

"Sundown, then."

"So, there never will be a chance?" said Dayzee.

"What do you mean?" said Marilyn.

"Yeah, what are you talking about, Dayzee?" said Sophia.

"Nothing, girls. Boss, is this our fault? Did we drag you back here too many times?"

"No, I've been messed up a long time. I won't survive another blast through the portal. I'd rather die on Earth than get scattered all over the universe."

"Is there anything we can do for you?" said Marilyn.

"We'll help if we can," said Sophia.

The Boss's tired eyes found the energy to look up and down Marilyn's and Sophia's long bare legs, then he turned to look at Dayzee's shapely legs wrapped in fishnet, her tall black boots, and her generous cleavage barely held in place by her tight white blouse.

"I want to go out the best possible way."

"Heat?" said Marilyn.

"Barbs too," said Sophia. "You want barbs."

He looked from Marilyn to Sophia to Dayzee and said, "Would you?"

"I didn't know you'd want to honor the old traditions," said Dayzee.

"From the day I learned about that in school, I knew I wanted to go out that way. I can't imagine three lovelier ladies to send me on my way. So, you'll do it?"

Dayzee laughed and said, "Of course, we will, Boss—we'd love to help."

She took his hand and helped him stand, but before they started walking toward the garage, she said, "Fia, the Boss needs a drink. That *special* drink you gave him last time."

"Coming right up."

"That's doubly funny, Sissy!"

Marilyn went back to the bar with her sister, and Dayzee started walking with the Boss.

"We'll need the concrete floor, Boss. You understand, don't you?"

"Yeah, I know. There's no need to incinerate your mansion, even though it has become a nutty place."

"We need something else, Dayzee," said Sophia. "The ash can. I'll bring it."

"Are you ready, Boss?"

"Yeah, Dayzee. I want the last thing I know of life to be how hot all of you are, and all of you are so, so hot."

Chapter 11 – Hopping on One Leg

"Just throw that broom anywhere, Fia," said Dayzee.

Sophia finished sweeping and dumped the Boss's dust in with the warm remains of the yard guys.

"Kind of a shame, huh, Sissy?" said Marilyn. "He wasn't so bad."

"He died a good death, Sis. That potion sure worked him up. Wow . . . long after he was dead too."

"We all got our turns, girls. You saw the look on his face, didn't you? That was one happy guy. Then, he was a happy dead guy."

"We had to let you finish him off, Dayzee," said Sophia. "How did it feel to actually kill him with your barbs? I saw your face, and it looked like you might die from the pleasure too."

"Oh, Fia, I thought I might. Isn't it convenient we're made that way? It doesn't just stop us from ever being assaulted that way, but it—"

"No really means NO with us," said Marilyn. "Funny that earthwomen don't have anything like that."

"Yeah, but I was saying that it's not just protection—it feels so good too. If you girls ever have a guy that, you know, doesn't deserve to keep living, I'd say give it to him good."

"We will, won't we, Sissy?"

"Yep, we sure will."

"Good. Now that that's settled, I need a cigarette."

"You smoke, Dayzee?"

"After that? Oh, hell yeah. You would too. Let's go inside."

"There's still a headless, legless guy in there, Dayzee," said Sophia.

"Sissy, he's not completely legless. He does have one leg."

"Yeah, girls, he's hopping around somewhere in the mansion. I guess he has something made out of wood stabbed into him somewhere too. That's how the assassin gets him to move around and attack us."

"I guess pretty soon, you'll have something wooden stabbed into you too, Dayzee."

"That's funny, Sissy. She's right, though, Dayzee. When are we going to do that? I can't wait."

"Girls, one thing at a time, alright? Let's get inside. Kozy, I like the way you're watching over us. You haven't said anything, but I saw you looking all around for danger."

"I will never stop protecting you. We should get away from that broom."

"Oh, the broom, Dayzee," said Marilyn. "Maybe that could be your date tonight?"

"It could sweep you off your feet," Sophia said with a smirk.

"That's a really good one, Sissy. This is fun. I bet we can think up a lot more—"

"Girls! Oh, you're still riled up from your first fountain of youth, aren't you?"

"I'm just glad that I can grow older and never have to get one of those facelift things."

"Now, that one actually makes sense, Sis. Nice one."

"She's right, Mare. Well, maybe another drink will calm you both down. Come on, let's go inside."

*　　*　　*

Kozy lingered at the bottom of the stairway near the kitchen and studied the landing area halfway up to the second floor. Dayzee continued toward the great room with Marilyn and Sophia close behind. She looked back over her shoulder, then stopped and turned around.

"Kozy, do you see anything?"

"I did. A knife looked at me then fled."

"It looked at you?"

"I am attempting to insert more nuances into this local language. It appears the knives are waiting upstairs for you."

"Wonderful. Come on, you might as well have a drink too."

"When the danger has been eliminated, then Kenzie will have that drink."

Sophia stopped, too, and said, "Oh, that sounds like things being back to normal. Is Kenzie alright with all this?"

"Yes, Kenzie is enjoying it. She is fascinated by living the effects danger brings to me."

At that, Marilyn stopped too.

"Hey, I just thought of something. When there's a whole bunch of dangers, and you, you know, you respond to that, can you kind of let Kenzie take over for a while? Could that work?"

"Sis, that's crazy. That could never—"

"Yes. Kenzie can return at a time that is chosen carefully but only for a brief interval."

"Sissy, guess what I'm thinking."

"Oh, I don't know, Sis. That might be kind of a weird thing. I doubt Kenzie would—"

"It is true that Kenzie likes the novelty of that change. I believe she would like to surface at that time."

"Sissy, let's do it. We'll all say hi to Kenzie and see if she's okay. She's been through a lot with all of this."

"Alright. Sure, let's try it sometime."

"Very good," said Kozy. "I will determine a time when there is danger but it is safe enough for Kenzie to visit."

"Fun times coming up, Sissy."

"Speaking of fun times . . . Dayzee, are you having your little romance anytime soon? If not, and since Sis and I aren't in that thing's crosshairs, we need to do some shopping."

"Romance, Fia? God no, not with some wooden thing. You two might as well run along. Take one of the cars. The keys are hanging up near the intercom."

"You're going to be alright, Dayzee?"

"Sure, Fia. Kozy's here. Maybe I'll take a nap while you're gone. Do you need any money?"

"Oh, Dayzee, Cliff slipped me a gift card. I bet it's got a lot loaded on it."

"He slipped you something, and it was loaded up, Sis?"

"He sure did. That's funny, Sissy."

"Okay, you two, have a good time. I need a nap."

"I am reluctant to interrupt," said Kozy, "but there is still a headless dead human hopping on one leg somewhere in this building."

"God, you're right," said Dayzee. "Crazy that I can forget that so easily."

"Knives too."

"Right. Girls, how about hanging around and helping us find that dead guy thing?"

"Sure. Sissy and I will help you find it. Kozy will have to kill it, though. I'm not sure I believe what the Boss said."

"Sis is right. We knew for sure how to kill the last time this thing came back to life, which was really disgusting, by the way."

"Oh, Sissy, you enjoyed it. Remember how you and Kenzie somehow lost all your clothes when you were alone with her upstairs? I still haven't figured out why a possessed Kenzie would take her clothes off and yours, too, and she ended up sitting between your legs, and that dead guy—"

"Yep, I remember. Okay, already. Yeah, it wasn't all that bad. Then, you burned through his heart, and he should have stayed dead. This new thing, the new assassin, can somehow bring him back again."

"Maybe you'll have to get naked up there with Kozy this time, Sissy. Maybe then, you could—"

"I could do that. Yeah, I could get totally naked, and I'm sure he'd—"

"Girls! Just stop, alright? I swear, I never should have taught you about the fountain of youth. You've been like teenagers ever since. Can we just take a walk through the house now?"

"Sure, Dayzee," said Sophia. "Let's go find a dead guy with no head that's hopping around trying to scare us."

"Don't forget—he's still looking for head."

"Yeah, he probably is," said Dayzee. "Kozy, what do you suggest?"

"I have observed that the assassin might try to kill any of you. Marilyn, those knives did fly in your direction when Cliff was visiting. However, it appears to want to seduce only Dayzee."

"Seduced by a chair. That's me," said Dayzee.

"It's attention," said Sophia.

"Like a fan club?" said Marilyn.

"More like a chair club," said Sophia with a grin.

Dayzee sighed and said, "Let's just go room to room and watch out for those knives."

*　　*　　*

"I don't get it, Dayzee," said Sophia. "We looked everywhere. We started in the basement and now, we're way up here in the attic again, where that wardrobe tried to chop you up."

"Sissy's right. Where can it be?"

"Maybe it left?" said Dayzee. "Can we be sure it's still in here?"

"Good point. Maybe it's not inside the house at all," said Sophia.

"Hey, can we take the elevator down? This has been a lot of walking around in these heels."

"Sure, Mare," said Dayzee. "I think it's right down this hall."

"You don't know?"

"I get lost sometimes."

Marilyn and Sophia led the way, and Dayzee and Kozy followed. No one spoke as they walked down the long hallway lined with artwork on the walls and an occasional chair or table. All eyes watched every bit of wood as they passed.

"Just hit the button, Mare."

She did, and they waited. A long minute passed.

"What's taking so long?"

"I don't know, Fia. I remember it being quicker than this. Mare, try again."

111

Marilyn tapped the button a couple of times. They waited two more minutes.

"Oh, I don't want to believe it," said Dayzee.

"What?"

"Mare, could that thing have taken an elevator ride, hit the 'hold' button, then maybe fell over or something?"

"Yep," said Sophia. "It's not like he can see—he's not even getting his own head."

"Good one, Sissy!"

"No, I'm serious, girls. I bet that thing is camping out in my elevator."

"Now what?"

"I don't know, Mare. I guess I have to call someone."

"Not Carlos," said Sophia.

"Not Ramon either," Marilyn said with a giggle.

"I wouldn't call them even if they were still alive. We don't need a yard guy. We need a 'get the headless one-legged dead body out of the stuck elevator' guy."

"That's pretty funny, Dayzee," said Sophia. "How many guys like that can there be around here?"

"It's Beverly Hills, remember?"

*   *   *

"That's a lot of steps. This house is too big, Dayzee."

"I sometimes think that, too, Mare. Why don't you girls sit for a while before shopping? I'll mix us some drinks."

Marilyn and Sophia plopped down on the couch in the great room, and Kozy stood guard.

"That really is a hot outfit we put on Kozy, Sissy."

"Isn't it, though? Look at those chest muscles that the jacket's too small to hide. I like the hat too. Sexy."

"Look at that bulge too. I can tell we're in danger just from the sight, Sissy."

"Never gets old."

"Nope."

"Here are your drinks. Kozy, did you want one too?"

"Yes. I will try to understand your interest in the chemical mixtures you so often prepare."

"Alright. Sure, I'll get you one."

Dayzee walked back behind the bar and poured some whiskey on ice.

"Here you go."

"You were going to call somebody, weren't you, Dayzee?"

"Oh yeah, because there's a dead guy stuck in the elevator."

"Well, my drink's gone, and I think Sis and I should take a ride. You have it under control, Dayzee?"

"I think so. You girls go have some fun. Come back for dinner, and I'll order us something good, alright?"

"Sure thing. Come on, Sis."

Dayzee watched the twins exit into the garage, and a few minutes later, she heard one of her cars start up. She turned to Kozy, sighed, and took out her phone.

"Mack, it's Dayzee. Are you at the Prism? You are? Good. Can you take a break to help me out with something? No, not an alcohol delivery! It's a mechanical thing. I know you're talented like that. Alright, I guess it can wait a short while. Can you text when you're on your way? Alright, good. Thanks, Mack. See you later."

She put her phone away and sighed deeply.

"It's been quite a day, Kozy. I shouldn't be surprised I'm tired. Are you? Can you keep watch while I take a nap?"

"I am fine. Yes, I will watch over you while you sleep. Your bed is somewhat destroyed. Will you use a different bedroom?"

"There sure are a lot to choose from. God, this house sure is big. Yeah, come on, let's go get a room."

"That has another meaning on Earth, does it not?"

"Yeah, but I was just saying. Although, there *is* a lot of danger all around us, isn't there?"

"We have not found those knives, and many other objects can instantly become lethal. Yes, there is danger."

"Hmm . . . I might need you to stay close. Real close."

"I am here to serve you."

"That's exactly what I like to hear on the way to a bedroom. Alright, let's head upstairs."

*   *   *

"Ooh, I like this car, Sissy."

"Me too, Sis. You sure you can handle it?"

"The hardest part will be backing it out of the garage."

"'Hardest part.' Still thinking about Kozy, huh?"

"Yes, of course!"

"Alright, well, let's just get some new clothes. We'll get back to him soon enough."

Marilyn started the sports car's big motor and backed it out onto the driveway. She was just about to shift and turn into the circular drive to head for the exit gate when a rusty pickup truck pulled in behind them.

"Who's that?"

"I don't know, Sissy. They're getting out, so let's just wait and see what they want."

"Hey, you live here?"

Marilyn looked out of the car window at a young man in a tight black t-shirt and a black ball cap. His black skin glistened in the Beverly Hills sun, and an unlit cigarette hung from his lips.

"No, I'm just visiting. Dayzee is inside. Just knock on the door, and she can talk to you."

"I ain't in the mood for much talking. You see, I know that my foreman and his brother came here earlier. He said he'd call when he was done, and I haven't heard anything—just a weird text. Something's wrong. I can feel it."

Marilyn turned to her sister and winked. Sophia shrugged and grinned. Marilyn turned back to the young man beside the car.

"Hi, I'm Marilyn."

She held her hand out of the window. He frowned at her for a few seconds, then shook her hand.

"I'm Mattie. This,"—he tipped his head to one side—"is Runt."

"Hey, I ain't tall, but I make up for it, babe."

"Ooh, I like the sound of that. This is my twin sister, Sophia. Isn't she hot?"

The two yard guys leaned to get a look, and that look mostly landed on her bare legs.

"My Sis is even hotter," Sophia said. "Nice to meet you fellas."

They both stood up, and Mattie kept looking at Marilyn as Runt looked all around them.

"We don't see Carlos's truck, so—"

"Well, of course, you can't see it," said Marilyn, "because it's—"

"Gone. My sister's trying to say that Carlos left. We don't know where he went."

"I don't get it," said Mattie. "He started to type me a text, and he sent it before it was finished. Like he was in too much of a hurry."

"What did he say?" said Marilyn.

"He said 'Get here quick. This is fucked up.' I texted him right back, and that was it. Didn't hear anything else from him."

"That's weird. Something about the yard, maybe? You know, he was—"

"Hey, wait a minute. Where did you get that necklace? That looks just like the one Carlos wears."

Sophia spoke up.

"Oh, well, he gave it to Sis. He said he was going to do something dangerous, and he wanted her to keep it safe."

"What dangerous thing? What the hell is going on, here? Fuck this. I'm going inside."

Mattie began a determined walk toward the house with Runt close behind. Marilyn and Sophia rushed out of the car, taking short steps in their high heels, and chased after them.

"Wait, Mattie," said Sophia. "You know, I think I saw Carlos and his brother go check out the big guesthouse. I think that's where they're at, right, Sis?"

"Sissy's right. Come on, let's go look."

Each girl tugged on an arm and gave them bright smiles. The young men looked at each other and shrugged.

"Okay, lead the way," said Mattie. "Hell, nice pool too."

"We like to swim, don't we, Sissy?"

"Mostly, we like being wet," said Sophia. "I feel like getting really wet right now. Can you boys wait a second or two for us to take a dip?"

"You'll like us wet," said Marilyn.

*　　*　　*

Dayzee paused near the closed elevator door and listened for a moment.

"Nothing going bump in the night," said Dayzee.

"It is not dancing, then."

"Not you too, Kozy. Let's pick one of the bedrooms in the back. I could really use that nap."

They found an unoccupied bedroom, walked in, and Dayzee closed and locked the door.

When Kozy stared at the lock, Dayzee said, "Just to keep the dead guy out, in case he breaks out of the elevator."

"Okay, Dayzee. I will watch all the wooden items in the room while you rest."

"Fine. Stay close, though. Come with me to look out the window. I like the sight of the pool from up here."

*　　*　　*

"You boys wait right there," said Sophia. "I just need to help my darling sister out of her dress."

116

"Yes, then I'll help *my* darling sister out of her skirt and whatever might be under there."

Mattie and Runt stood still and stared.

"Which is nothing. There's nothing under there, Sis. You know that."

"Hmm . . . yes, every time I check."

"She checks all the time, boys. Here, Sis, let's unzip you in back. Good, now I'll just slide these straps off of your shoulders. Oh, and look at that—no bra! You're so luscious, Sis."

She stood behind Marilyn and pulled her hair back behind her while they both smiled at the hypnotized men.

"Isn't she luscious, boys?"

They nodded and stared.

She slid the dress down over Marilyn's hips and said, "Oh, those sure are tiny panties. They're so cute. Maybe we should just leave—"

"No, Sissy, I think they want me naked. Do you guys want me naked?"

They nodded again.

"Alright, Sis, let me help you slide those down . . . ooh, snug around your hips . . . there . . . okay, good, just kick that to our new friends."

Marilyn hooked a toe in her underwear and flung it toward Mattie, and he caught it. He never broke his gaze, but he held it close and inhaled.

"Your turn, Sissy."

Marilyn stood behind her sister and reached around to unbutton her blouse. Sophia continued to smile at the frozen men. After undoing the last button, Marilyn slipped it down over her sister's shoulders, and Sophia pulled her arms free.

"That's a very stylish bra, Sissy. Do you feel shy in front of these boys, or should we show them your boobies too?"

"Oh, for sure, Sis. Can you help me?"

"I know you could do it yourself."

"I know, but I like it so much better when you help."

Sophia looked from Mattie to Runt and back again as her sister reached around for the clasp between her breasts, with her wrists squishing her breasts up and together. She took her time, bouncing and squeezing her sister around, then she unhooked it and pulled it open, letting them drop softly and settle. Seconds later, she tossed it to Runt.

"That's a good start, Sissy. It's just that tiny little skirt now. Let's give them both big smiles, okay?"

"Oh, you know it, Sis."

Marilyn reached for the elastic band at the top and stretched it over her sister's hips.

"Oh, look—no panties."

Soon, the skirt lay bunched around Sophia's heels. She stepped out of it, and Marilyn moved to stand beside her. They held each other around their waists and gazed at the two young men beside the pool who had forgotten anything else existed anywhere.

"Now, you have two naked twins beside a pool in Beverly Hills. Can either of you guess what happens next?"

They continued to stare.

"No, Sissy," Marilyn said with a giggle. "No, they can't."

*　*　*

"It's always a nice view from up here, Kozy. At the right time, you can catch the sun—oh, what the hell is going on now?"

Kozy stood so close behind Dayzee that she could feel his reaction to the dangerous goings-on near the pool.

"Oh, it's like you're holding a pistol up against me! Kozy, is that because the beautiful twins are standing there naked? They sure are gorgeous."

"I sense you are all in danger. Marilyn and Sophia are trying to help. They are about to kill those two men."

"Ah, my beautiful twins—the Kildare Killers. Stay close, Kozy, just like that. Maybe even closer. Let's watch!"

Chapter 12 – What a Bod He Has

"They do look quite stunning after discarding their wardrobe."

"Oh, Kozy, are you attracted to that now?"

"When any of you are in perilous situations, since I am a One-Eighty, this body of Kenzie responds purely as a male of her species."

"You feel plenty male pressed into me like you are. Do you feel like a human male?"

"Yes. I am enjoying the sight of Marilyn and Sophia, though it also causes a peculiar anguish."

"Why don't you reach around and hold me, then? Go on. Hold me real tight."

He reached around with both hands on her waist and pulled her in close. She took each of his hands and placed them on her breasts.

"How do those feel, Kozy? Pretty good?"

"They feel very good, Dayzee, though I do not understand why. May I squeeze them? My male human feelings are telling me to squeeze."

"Who are we to argue with that? Yeah, of course, squeeze them and do anything else you feel like doing."

Dayzee sighed and leaned her head back onto his hard chest, and they both watched the naked twin girls about to incinerate two paralyzed yardmen as Kozy continued to squeeze and fondle.

"Wow, your voice is getting deeper too."

Dayzee reached up and back with both hands to touch his cheeks, which she found to be rough with stubble.

"Wow. Unbutton my blouse, Kozy."

* * *

Marilyn and Sophia still held each other side by side and smiled at Mattie and Runt. Something caught Sophia's eye, and she looked up at the second-floor bedroom.

"Sis, look. Dayzee's watching us."

"So is Kozy. Sissy, he's hugging and fondling Dayzee. Oh my, he's undressing her!"

They both watched as Dayzee's blouse was opened all the way, revealing that she wore no bra. Kozy's hands kept busy as they both stared down at the girls beside the pool.

"Well, that's a sight," said Sophia. "You can see even from here how strong Kozy's hands are. Just like Dayzee to make the most of that."

"Yes, Sissy. How far do you think Dayzee will go?"

"If I know Dayzee, she'll take full advantage of it."

"Right there in the window? While they're watching us?"

"Pretty exciting, huh, Sis? We better get busy too."

"Yes, it sure is better to have an audience, and look how these guys are frozen with those silly grins. This is just too easy!"

Marilyn turned to look at her sister, who turned and gave her a quick kiss on her lips.

"Let's have some fun of our own, Sis."

"Mm-hmm. You are so right, Sissy."

* * *

"Your hands are so strong, Kozy. Do I feel soft in your hands?"

"Yes. I am still guarding you, Dayzee, even though—"

"Even though you have your hands full? Help me get this shirt off."

He used one hand to help her out of her blouse, and she let it drop to the floor.

"Are you still watching those beautiful twins working down there? Look . . . they laid those guys down on chair cushions."

"Yes, I am watching. They plan to have sex with them first?"

Dayzee brushed her long blond hair off to her right and said, "That's how the Kildare Killers kill. Why don't you kiss my neck while you're watching them?"

"As you wish."

"Oh, and press me into this wall, alright? Yeah, just like that . . ."

Dayzee sighed, and they both gazed out through the second-floor bedroom window at the scene by the pool.

* * *

"No, that's perfect, Mattie. Just lie down on your cushion. You too, Runt," said Sophia.

"Oh, you're not really a runt once your pants are down. Look, Sissy—nothing runty about that."

"Hmm . . . I'll take him, Sis. You take care of Mattie."

"Oh, I plan to."

The girls stepped in closer until their heels were tight against the sides of each man's legs. They stood there a few moments looking down on them as they looked up with big, goofy smiles.

"They sure have big, um, smiles, Sis. You always get that, don't you?"

"We both do, Sissy. Earthmen don't stand a chance with us."

"Have we teased them enough yet?"

"Yes, we have. Let's give them something to remember us by."

"Until we turn up the heat, Sis?"

"Yes. Let's take our time. Remember that Dayzee and Kozy are watching."

Each girl dropped down onto their man's lap and wiggled around to get things lined up just right.

"There. I got mine, Sissy."

"Mm . . . me too."

* * *

"Oh, will you look at those gorgeous twins? Those lucky guys . . ."

"Until they burn them, you mean?"

"Yeah, Kozy, but they won't even care about getting crispy. It's like they're in a trance. I'm almost in a trance myself."

Still kissing Dayzee's neck, Kozy said, "I am having a human urge to raise your skirt. Is that an expected component of this type of human biological interaction?"

"Uh-huh. Keep talking dirty, Kozy. That One-Eighty business of yours is doing the thinking now."

"It does have some intention that I do not completely understand."

"You will. Look at those girls going so slow down there. I think they're giving us some extra time too. Hey, take your jacket off, okay?"

"As you wish."

He leaned away from her, pulled his arms free, and tossed it to the floor.

"As you were, Kozy."

He leaned back into her, reached around, and continued his curious fondling.

"Oh, that's good, Kozy, and don't forget: there's so much danger everywhere."

"I have not forgotten. Can you tell?"

"Oh, yeah. Hey, all those knives are probably right outside the door."

"That is likely."

"Ooh, even better now."

*　*　*

"This is perfect, Sis. No way can we burn down Dayzee's mansion," said Sophia.

"No, just these two and the cushions, and you know what, Sissy? They'll love it."

"They sure will. I'm in no hurry. How about you?"

122

"I only wish we had some special potion to give them," said Marilyn. "We could be having another fountain of youth."

"Yep, but this is still good. Oh, look up there now. Even Kozy lost his jacket. Oh, wow, what a bod he has."

"Kozy is some amazing kind of One-Eighty. Dayzee has all the luck. Funny how he kind of looks like Kenzie still."

"If you mean Kenzie as an exaggerated male, then yeah, sure. I hope she's alright with all this."

"Sissy, when this is all over, Kenzie might be upset, so you should plan on comforting her."

"Sure, I'll buy her a drink, Sis. You know, I can barely hold back all my heat."

"I know," said Marilyn. "It's killing me to take it slow. It's the anticipation, Sissy."

Each girl began letting out their heat, and still, the men only stared up at them with unchanging smiles.

"They're still happy, Sissy, and it feels so, so good."

"Mm-hmm. Wow, does it ever. And the smell!"

*   *   *

"Kozy, the girls are starting to burn. Now's a good time for you to see what that thing of yours is for. Here, I'll help you."

Dayzee reached down for her skirt's bottom hem, but she took her time and watched the twins ramping up their heat. She carefully began to pull the skirt up along her thighs, stretched it up and over her behind, and left it bunched up around her waist.

"You'll need to drop those pants down a little, too, Kozy. Go on. Let's see what happens."

He let go and reached for his pants with both hands. A second later, his khakis were down around his knees, and Dayzee could feel pressed against her what the One-Eighty change had brought.

"Now?" said Kozy.

"Huh? What do you—"

123

"I have determined this to be an acceptable time. Kenzie is resurfacing now."

"Wait, you mean—"

"Yes, that is what I mean. There is danger, but it is not imminent."

"You picked a wild time for this!"

"Kenzie will not be in control, and she will not remember any of it."

"How about maybe some other—"

"Oh, Dayzee, this is absolutely amazing! I've wondered what this would be like. How is this happening?"

"I have no idea, Kenzie. You're not in control, are you?"

"No, not at all. I'm just watching. Oh, and talking too!"

"Well, just enjoy it, then. Enjoy that deep voice too."

Kozy reached down with both hands and got a solid grip on Dayzee's skirt around her waist, and he pulled her hips back.

"Don't need to tell this guy twice," said Kenzie. "Damn, he's so strong!"

He let go with one hand and grabbed Dayzee's hair, pulling her head back.

"Oh my, Kenzie, he sure can be rough too!"

"Don't blame me! I'm not doing any of this!"

He let go of her hair, grabbed her hips with both hands, and backed her two steps from the window. With one hand, he pushed on her back, leaning her over until her forearms rested on the windowsill.

"Oh yeah, that's it. No arguing with you, is there, Mr. One-Eighty?"

"Mr. Who? Dayzee, who is this guy? Is he for real?"

"Oh, he's real, but don't ask me to explain it."

With one shiny black boot, Kozy nudged each of Dayzee's legs farther apart, then took her mane in one strong hand.

"Oh, you know, I think he really is going to—"

"I doubt you could stop him, Dayzee!"

They heard a door slam, and a voice yelled, "Dayzee! It's Mack! Where in this monstrous house are you?"

"Oh, shit. So close. Raincheck, Kenzie? I mean, Kozy? Whoever?"

Kozy looked at the sky and said, "I have checked, and there is no rain in this locality, Dayzee."

He released her hair and held her hips with both hands.

"That's actually kind of funny. I guess Kenzie is gone. Alright, put away that thing of yours and get your jacket back on. I need to get dressed before I call Mack up here."

"As you wish."

"Kenzie," said Dayzee, "you just wait. I'll find a way to make you remember this."

She pulled down her skirt and buttoned her blouse while watching the twins steadily toasting their guys.

*　*　*

"Look, Sissy," said Marilyn. "They're gone from the window. Something fun must be going on."

"Maybe they're just using the bed, Sis. I can barely focus on what you're saying."

"It's the heat. It's making me crazy too."

"Are you turned up all the way?" said Sophia.

"No, not yet, Sissy. I'd love to be watching Dayzee and Kozy right now."

"Next time. I promise, we'll make that happen somehow."

"Not with two more yard guys, though, right?"

"Sis, I don't think there are two more of them."

*　*　*

Dayzee walked to the bedroom door and opened it only enough to scream to Mack.

"Mack! I'm upstairs!"

The sound of Mack running up the stairs filled the quiet house.

"Down here, Mack."

125

Dayzee turned and walked back toward the window, where she saw that Kozy still hadn't stretched the jacket back on.

"Hey, get a move on. Mack is coming up."

"I believe my chest grows with increasing danger too. I find this species difficult to categorize."

"Well, those muscles sure are impressive. They're so—"

The door swung in with a loud pound, and Mack stood there staring at Kozy's bare torso.

"Hey, you said you'd text first," said Dayzee.

"Oh, right. Sorry."

He continued to stare with a big grin.

"I didn't know you had company," he said without looking at Dayzee. He glanced up and said, "Hey, Kozy. Damn, that's some serious gym time."

"We were just finding something new for Kozy to wear, that's all. It seems this jacket is a little tight."

"You think? Kozy, you do kind of resemble Kenzie, but she—"

"Kenzie will return with her expected attributes."

"Sure. Okay," he said while watching Kozy fumbling to jam his thick arms into the sleeves.

"We were also trying to figure out how to fix that damn elevator."

"It's in the bedroom?"

"No, I mean, we were looking for some kind of tool."

"I believe that has comical overtones too," said Kozy.

"You're learning fast, Kozy. Mack, it doesn't matter. Come on, the elevator is down one of the halls."

Mack looked back at her and said, "This house is incredible, Dayzee. I bet the view is good from up here too."

He started walking toward the window.

"No!" Dayzee said and blocked his path. "I mean, there's no time. We need to fix that elevator."

"What's the rush? Just a quick peek, then—"

Dayzee held his head in both hands and kissed him on the lips. Thirty seconds passed.

"Oh, wow, Dayzee. That's . . . that was—"

She kissed him again and walked forward, forcing him away from the window. She finally let him go.

"What was that for?"

"I'm just happy to see you, that's all."

"I'm feeling kind of happy now myself. I've always wondered what it would be like to kiss you. Maybe someday, you and I could—"

"Fix the elevator? Yes, let's go take a look."

Mack tipped his head and squinted at her. She took him by his hand and led him out of the room. He turned back several times to watch Kozy still struggling with his jacket. Before entering the hallway, he stopped completely.

"Just one look out the window. It'll only take a second."

"Mack . . . the elevator?"

Dayzee yanked his arm and pulled him away from the doorway.

"Maybe I need a hat like that."

*   *   *

"I can't wait any longer, Sissy," said Marilyn. "I've got a big itch to do some extreme burning."

"You might as well. Your guy looks dead already. I'm pretty sure mine is too."

"My guy isn't slowing down at all, though. He's as eager now as when he was alive."

"Let's do it at the same time, Sis."

They each laid a hand on the other's shoulder, and they began to move up and down at the same time. Marilyn brushed her blond hair back over her shoulders, and Sophia shook her black hair back. Both closed their eyes and smiled as they ramped up enough heat to incinerate the two men and the two cushions, just as each reached their peak.

"Oh, Sissy, it was hard not to scream," said Marilyn.

"There sure is a joke in there somewhere, Sis. Remind me to figure it out later."

Several minutes passed before the girls opened their eyes to see nothing but ashes beneath them.

"Oh, Sissy, that was the best."

"I feel only a little bit bad about it, Sis. I'm glad the Boss gave us permission to do it like this. We really had to, didn't we?"

"We sure did," said Marilyn. "These two would have caused more problems."

"We're killers, Sis."

"Yes, we are. We're the Kildare Killers."

*　　*　　*

"Right there, Mack. There's that blasted elevator. It seems to be hung up between floors. Think you can help?"

"Who knows, Dayzee? I can try."

"You want a drink while you're at it?"

"Sure. Straight vodka for me."

"You got it. Kozy, you want anything?"

"I will have what Mack is having."

"Sure.

"Thanks, Dayzee. I'll see if I can figure this out."

Dayzee left, and Mack hit the button a couple of times.

"For sure, that button isn't doing us any good," said Mack. "Is there a way to get into the shaft?"

"I do not know. Perhaps at a higher elevation in this structure."

"Good thinking. Damn, you look a lot like Kenzie. Except . . . well, like a guy, of course. What the hell do you do, spend all your time at the gym?"

"I am a One-Eighty. One-Eighties need not follow any specific protocol. We are strong. We respond to danger."

Mack stared for a second, then shook his head.

"I don't have a clue what you're talking about. Must be some crazy supplements you're on. Come on, let's hike up to the next floor."

Mack led Kozy, who was still struggling with his jacket, to the staircase, and they climbed up to the attic where the wardrobe had attacked Dayzee.

"Hey, this is nice up here. Lots of room. Oh, I see the elevator right over there."

Standing in front of the closed door, Mack hit the button a few more times, but nothing happened. He turned his back to lean against it.

"Seriously, how much working out do you do?"

"I am capable of working outside or inside, in any manner that is required."

"You're kind of hard to understand, you know that?"

"Yes, I have not completely grasped the vocabulary, grammar, and colloquialisms of this language."

Mack stared with his head tipped to one side and said, "Well, okay, then."

He pointed his thumb back at the elevator and said, "This is making things harder than they need to be."

"Why, have you detected danger associated with the elevator?"

"Huh?"

"Here's your drink, Mack," Dayzee said as she walked toward them across the third-floor room.

"Kozy, here, thinks there might be some kind of danger with this elevator. What's he talking about?"

"Oh, Mack, he just watches for danger everywhere, and when he does find some, then I want to be around, I mean . . . I want to be on top of it . . . right on top of it, because—"

"What the hell are *you* talking about? I don't—"

A loud pounding came from the elevator shaft. Kozy responded to the danger, and Dayzee reached over and turned him to face away from Mack.

"Oh my, Kozy," she said. "That's pretty much instant, isn't it?"

"Yes. One-Eighties respond with no need for conscious thought."

"What the hell are you two—"

"Nothing important, Mack. I'll handle it. Boy, would I love to handle it. I sure came close!"

"What does—"

More banging came through the elevator door.

"Goodness, Kozy!"

"There is increasing danger."

"Really, what are you two talking about?"

"Nothing. We'll never fix it from this level. Mack, there's a hidden passage right behind that panel,"—Dayzee pointed to her left along the wall—"just push on the right side, and it'll open. You can climb the ladder and get up above the shaft up there."

"Sure. Secret passageways. Why am I not surprised?"

"It cannot be a secret any longer since we are all aware of it."

Mack shook his head at Kozy, turned from the elevator door, and left for the secret panel, and Dayzee rotated Kozy to stay faced away from him.

"While we have a minute or two . . ."

She held on and leaned in for a quick kiss.

"I find satisfaction in that."

"Excitement too?"

"Yes. But it is distant. They are feelings of human lust and are still alien to me."

"Now that Mack's gone, maybe we should try again? Just remember . . . that dead guy will be free again. Ooh, lots of danger, Kozy."

Dayzee got a better grip, and Kozy's lips met her halfway.

Chapter 13 – Scary Wooden Thing

"Should we clean up what's left of them, Sissy?" said Marilyn.

"No, let's leave it for the yard crew."

"Sissy, we've already killed four of the crew. Who will take care of Dayzee's lawn?"

"Alright, that's a good point. We're killers, but we should stop killing Dayzee's workers, don't you think?"

"Yes, there are plenty around that are expendable. Maybe we can get those ashes later. Right now, let's go see what Dayzee and Kozy are up to. I hope we walk in on something fun!"

"Oh, that's right—they had a little something going on, didn't they? Let's go."

"Sissy, maybe we should get dressed first?"

"Sure, Sis. I suppose we should."

"It's a shame," said Marilyn. "You're absolutely stunning standing there naked like that."

"You too. That other Marilyn would be ashamed to show herself with you around."

"Aw, thanks. Same thing with you and that other Sophia. I suppose we can get ourselves dressed since there's no one around to drive crazy."

"We do drive them crazy, Sis."

"It's just too easy on Earth."

*　　*　　*

Dayzee pulled away from the kiss but didn't let go.

"Is that Kenzie doing the kissing?"

"Kenzie is only a witness. It is entirely me."

"Between the two of you . . . damn. You know, we might have time to finish what we started before. How about a quickie?"

"How would a short time interval—"

"Dayzee! I'm right behind the door, and I'm standing on the cab. I can't see why it's stuck, though."

"Damn. We don't have time," Dayzee said softly to Kozy.

"Mack, maybe try to open the door from your side? Can you do that?"

"I'll try. There has to be a way."

"Okay, we still have a minute or—"

"You really have your hands full, Dayzee," said Marilyn. "Wow, that's a sight."

"Oh, there was some danger, and I was just, you know, investigating how things—"

"Sure, Dayzee," said Sophia. "Maybe Sis and I should leave you two alone?"

Dayzee let go and tried to arrange Kozy's trousers to better conceal the One-Eighty part that had responded to danger in such a dramatic way. It took some effort, but she managed to hide it.

"It's still pretty damn obvious," said Sophia.

"Boy, is it ever," said Marilyn.

With a loud clunk, the elevator door opened. The top of the cab was just below the floor level, and Mack stood on it, looking into the room.

"Found the lever. Opened right up."

"You're a lifesaver, Mack," said Dayzee. "Look, the twins are here too."

"Hi, Marilyn. Hi, Sophia. Nice to see you again."

They waved and smiled, then Marilyn looked down at Kozy's bulge, and Sophia shook her head at the sight of Dayzee's smudged lipstick.

"Any idea why that car is stuck there, Mack?" said Dayzee. "Can you drop it down to the next floor somehow?"

"Oh, I don't know, Dayzee. What if it falls all the way? How many stories would that be?"

"Oh, right . . . all the way to the basement. We don't want to kill you, Mack. Look around—maybe there's another way?"

"Give me a minute. Let me look—"

More pounding came from the stuck elevator car as it shook around beneath Mack's feet.

"Oh, what the hell?"

"It's probably just the motor acting up, Mack. I wouldn't worry about it."

"That's crazy. How could it—"

"It's an old mansion, so anything can happen, right, girls? Aren't there always strange things going on around here?"

"Oh, yes, Dayzee," said Marilyn. "Lots of scary things."

"Scary?"

"No, Mack," said Sophia. "Sis just means unexpected things. Like that elevator motor. Go figure."

The pounding stopped, and Mack said, "Hey, here's something. It's some kind of crank wheel. Look. Watch this."

He turned the wheel to the left, and the car moved up a few inches, causing more pounding and shaking.

"No, no, no, Mack! Turn it the other way!"

"Okay, Dayzee, sure. Geez."

He turned the wheel a few times, sending the elevator down more each time.

"That should put it at the second floor," said Mack.

"Wonderful," said Dayzee. "Maybe we should—"

They all heard the elevator door open on the floor below.

"Uh-oh," said Marilyn. "Sounds like danger, Kozy."

"Mack, did you open the door?"

"No, Dayzee, I didn't do anything. Must have been automatic somehow."

They all stood and listed to the sound of heavy, unsteady pounding on the tile floor of the hallway below them.

"Who's that?" said Mack.

Sophia elbowed her sister, prompting her to say, "Oh, um, that must be my boyfriend, Cliff. Sounds like he's been drinking."

"You have a boyfriend?" said Mack. "Since when?"

"Oh, we go way back. I just don't talk about him much."

Mack climbed up out of the elevator shaft and brushed dust off of his arms and legs.

"Well, whatever. It looks like you're all fixed up, Dayzee. I should probably get back to the Prism."

"No! No, you can't! Let's just hang around up here awhile, Mack, okay?"

"I don't know. The afternoon crowd will be coming in, and the crew will need my help."

"Mack, just enjoy your drink, and maybe you can—"

"Hear that, Dayzee?" said Sophia. "Sis's boyfriend is on the steps and coming up here."

Dayzee stared, and only her mouth moved for several seconds with no words coming out.

"He's jealous! Marilyn, your boyfriend, Cliff, is one jealous son of a bitch, right?"

"Oh, Dayzee, I don't—"

Sophia elbowed her again.

"I mean, yes, he's crazy! He always carries a gun too. Mack, you need to get out of here!"

"Like how? We're on the third floor. You have a fire escape or something?"

"Out the window," said Dayzee, and they heard the footfalls landing on the stairs. "Marilyn, hurry and lock that door, alright?"

"Sure, Dayzee."

"What? I can't jump out your window, Dayzee!"

"You're right. Hey, maybe you could climb out there and wait, and one of us will set up a ladder for you."

"Do you even have a ladder, Dayzee?"

"Not a single one. Sorry, Mack."

They heard the doorknob rattling just after Marilyn had locked it.

"Look, it's either that or get shot. Go, Mack. Go wait on the roof!"

"Dammit, Dayzee, this is what I get for fixing your damn elevator?"

"We can talk about that later. Go!"

Mack had just stepped out onto the roof and swung his other leg out, and Dayzee watched the base trim begin to peel away from the wall. It started with a short length, then it kept going, forming a large coil that scraped along the floor as it moved along the wall toward them.

"Uh-oh, danger time," said Marilyn. "We're surrounded—I'm staying close to Kozy."

"How close, Sis?"

"On Kozy's lap if I can."

"Well, you can't because—"

"Girls! This isn't the time! Fia, can you go and close that window? Make sure you stay away from the scary wooden thing going on over there."

"What are we going to do about Mack? He's stuck out there, and—"

"Not now, Fia. Just close the window and draw the shades. We can't have Mack seeing any of this."

"Alright, Dayzee."

"Kozy," said Dayzee, "damn, you look stronger than ever."

"You are in much danger. I am ready."

"You sure look ready the way you're stretching those pants," said Marilyn. "But I better check to be sure that—"

"No, Mare—leave Kozy alone!"

"But I just—"

"No! We need to—"

Dayzee gasped when the trim board shot out, uncoiling itself, and wrapped around one of her ankles.

"No foreplay this time, Dayzee," said Marilyn.

"Funny, Mare. Kozy, can you help with this?"

Kozy moved so quickly that no one could see and snapped off the part wrapped around Dayzee's leg. Instantly, the broken end rewrapped itself again, and he tore that apart too.

"Kozy, maybe grab that whole mess and throw it out the window? Just don't hit Mack with it."

Kozy took hold of the wobbling end that was ready to attack again and pulled it away from Dayzee. He gathered up and crushed all of it together into a knot of twisted, squirming wood. A short walk later, he raised the window and tossed it all far into the yard.

Mack said, "Hey, what was—"

Kozy slammed the window shut. The door came alive, pulled itself off of its hinges, and began to waddle toward Dayzee. The dead man turned to fit through the doorway and wasn't far behind, hopping on one leg.

"Oh, look at that," said Marilyn. "The assassin stabbed it with a rake handle. That's how it brought the dead guy back to life."

They watched as the door and dead man approached, with an arm's length of rake handle protruding from one side of its rib cage and the tines fanned out at its other side.

"You know what?" said Dayzee. "I bet that's what happened to the elevator. The dead guy turned, and his rake hit the 'stop' button. Then he couldn't see to get the thing going again."

"Because he's still looking for head," said Marilyn.

"That's actually still pretty funny, Sis," Sophia said while grinning and shaking her head.

"Alright, Kozy," said Dayzee. "Got any ideas?"

"If the door will fit through the window, I can dispose of that first."

"I think it should fit. Alright, grab it. Quick. Get rid of that thing."

Kozy held the door with both hands as it fought to get away. He was too strong and carried it to the window, Sophia opened it, and he sent it sailing and spinning almost all the way back to the guesthouses.

"What the hell is going—"

Kozy slammed the window shut.

"Poor Mack," said Dayzee. "I'll have to buy him a drink. Oh, run, Mare! I forgot about the dead guy!"

The headless dead man swung its arms and just missed Marilyn, and she and Dayzee scurried across the room. Kozy and Sophia came back from the window, and he got it in an inescapable hug from behind and lifted it up off of its one leg.

"We still don't know how to kill it for real, do we, Kozy?"

"No, Dayzee. We can render this vessel ineffective, though."

"It's almost there already," said Marilyn. "No head. No leg. A massive piercing."

"It really is pretty pathetic," said Dayzee. "Hey, Kozy, can you carry it down to the basement and find a way to keep it there? I believe there's some old furniture down there. Maybe you can just bury that guy?"

"I will do that."

Kozy left through the open doorway that no longer had a door and began maneuvering the dead guy and his rake to travel down the several flights of stairs to the basement.

"Alright, Mare, let's let Mack back in. Fia, can you keep an eye on the woodwork? Oh, and watch out for those knives too. We still haven't found those."

"Sure, Dayzee," said Sophia.

Marilyn let Mack back in and said, "Guess what, Mack. Cliff took off. He said he just remembered he had an appointment at the gun range."

"Lucky me."

"Here's your drink, Mack. Oh, wait . . . I drank it all. Come on, I'll set you up with another."

"No thanks, Dayzee. I just want to get back to the Prism already."

He started walking toward the door, and Marilyn grabbed his arm.

"Wait, Mack. Kozy needs a head start."

"What? Why would—"

"Kozy went down to make sure Cliff left, that's all," said Sophia. "That's what Sis meant."

"Kozy went down," said Marilyn. "You know, that's kind of—"

"Alright, Mare. Later. Right now, we should be able to get Mack on his way. Come on."

*   *   *

After a cautious walk down two levels of stairs, with Mack looking only forward and the other three looking in every direction for flying knives or anything else made of wood, they reached the first floor.

"Sure I can't tempt you with a drink, Mack?" said Dayzee. "I selfishly drank your last one myself."

"No, that's okay, Dayzee. I really should get back. See you up at the bar soon?"

"Sure, Mack. We'll probably all come up there for—"

A knocking at the front door silenced Dayzee, and she stood and stared.

"Who the hell could that be?"

"No clue, Fia. You want to answer it?"

"Alright, I'll get it."

Sophia walked over and pulled the door open. Cliff stood there with a big grin.

"Hi, Dayzee," he said and waved. "I thought I'd drive over and check with you about one other thing. I hope it's not a bad time?"

"Oh, Cliff," said Dayzee.

"Look," said Mack while holding Cliff's curious stare, "I just want to leave, alright? There's nothing going on between Marilyn and me."

Cliff stared at Mack for a second, then looked to Dayzee.

"I won't stop you," Cliff said, then shrugged. "What was supposed to be going on?"

"With Marilyn, I mean. I like her, of course . . . who wouldn't? But I wasn't—"

"Oh, Mack. This is a different Cliff. Marilyn's Cliff is long gone."

"Oh, okay. That makes sense. Sorry, I thought you were somebody else. See you later, Dayzee. Girls."

He hurried out the door, requiring Cliff to turn sideways.

"What was that all about?"

"Oh, nothing, Cliff. We know him from the Prism, our favorite place to hang out. He was just helping out with some repair work."

"I see. Marilyn, you have a romantic interest named Cliff? We could use that on the show. Let's schedule a get-together with him to go over the details. I'd like to bring him in early so that—"

"Oh, I don't think so," said Marilyn. "He's not real—"

"She means he's not really the kind to get in front of a camera," said Dayzee. "We'll have to leave him out."

"He's not like us," said Sophia. "The three of us could live in front of cameras."

"In fact," said Marilyn, "I think I'm done with him. That's it. I just made up my mind. I don't ever want to see him again."

Cliff stared at Marilyn, then he looked at Sophia, who was nodding with a grin, then he turned again to look at Dayzee, who only shrugged.

"Things change pretty quick around here, but that's good for the show. You three are more perfect than—hey, where's the other one? Kozy was his name?"

"Oh, Kozy just carried some garbage to the basement for us."

"You have a basement? Can I see it? That could be an interesting place for a secret rendezvous, or it could be someplace scary that you could all talk about. Let's go. I want to see it."

Kozy walked into the foyer, and Cliff stared at his bare chest stretching open his jacket, then the thick thighs squeezed into his khakis, and he finally looked Kozy in the eye.

"There you are. We were just going to take a peek at—"

"No. No, Cliff, we don't have time right now," said Dayzee. "We need to get ready to go out soon. How about another time?"

"Sure, that would be fine, Dayzee. I only stopped by to ask if any of you have relatives that you'd like to move into the smaller of the guesthouses for the show. How about that? How interesting could that be?"

"Can we get back to you on that?" said Dayzee. "We really need to get going."

She walked over and nudged him over the threshold and onto the porch. He was about to speak.

"Have a good afternoon, Cliff. Sorry to kick you out, but it's a really busy day! Goodbye!"

She closed the door and leaned against it.

"Girls, this is exhausting."

"Exciting too," said Sophia.

"I think it's kind of fun," said Marilyn.

"You girls. Kozy, we need to kill that thing . . . that assassin. Any ideas?"

Before he could answer, Dayzee saw five knives float down the stairway in a neat arrangement. They all turned at once to point at them. One at a time, they raced through the air. Kozy was a blur, holding a thick coffee table book up as a target for each of them.

"Well, damn," said Sophia. "Thanks, Kozy."

"You are welcome. All of you."

"At least we know where the knives are," said Marilyn. "Kozy, that was sure dangerous, wasn't it? That was maybe the most—"

"Sis is right, Kozy. We're probably in more danger right now than—"

"Girls! Maybe it's you two that are exhausting?"

Chapter 14 – Liking this Planet

"Girls, we can't keep up this way."

She pointed at the book Kozy had set down. Five bloody knives were dug in deep, and their wooden handles pointed straight up.

"I agree," said Sophia. "Was the Boss right about how to kill the assassin, Kozy?"

"I do not know. It is possible he fabricated a narrative to get what he wanted from all of you."

"Oh," said Dayzec, "that makes sense. That was all BS to get him burned like he wanted."

Kozy said, "How did you learn the correct method for the previous assassin?"

"The Boss told us," said Marilyn. "He knew for sure about that one. It took some effort on our part, but we got the truth out of him. He was in too much pain to lie."

"We sure got him good, Sis," said Sophia. "We can't ask him anymore, though."

"No, Sissy, we'd have to talk to a can of ashes. We'd be asking Carlos and Ramon too. That's just weird."

"No, girls, we sure can't ask any of them. Hey, I just thought of something. Remember how we called the Boss?"

"I sure do," said Marilyn. "That was so much fun. We were just about to do that until your barstool liked what it saw."

"Good one, Sis."

Marilyn said, "Should we try that again? I know my short robe is ready to go."

"Oh, I don't know about the same thing, Mare. But we could—"

"Hey, it's my turn," said Sophia, "remember? I can put on that tiny robe again and see what happens."

"A lot would happen, Sissy—you're gorgeous!"

"So are you, Sis—we're twins. Seriously, though, it should be *my* turn. I'd be the one about to get into so, so much trouble. That would get Dayzee worried, and then—"

"You know what I think?" said Dayzee. "I think both of you would play that game whether I was there or not."

"We would," said Marilyn.

"Yep."

"My point is that maybe somebody replaced the Boss. They'd have to find someone else, wouldn't they?"

"How would the Guild know that your Boss is dead?" said Kozy.

"I think he had some kind of tracker built into him," said Dayzee. "Or maybe they'd figure since he didn't come back that he must be dead because he couldn't survive here very long. Oh, you know what else? He might have said goodbye to everyone. He knew he was about dead anyway."

"He wanted us to kill him," said Sophia.

"Yes, Sissy, because of how hot we are."

"He did want that heat."

"And our barbs. I know I dug mine in really deep."

"Girls. Focus. All I'm saying is that maybe we should hang around the portal for a while and see if anyone shows up. Besides, this mansion has become creepy as hell. It'd be good to get out of here."

"Good," said Sophia. "I could use a drink. A couple of them."

"How about that Popsicle, Sissy?"

"Oh, well, yeah . . . that too."

"Alright, we agree. Let's get ready and go. The Prism is having its famous post-Halloween party tonight. Let's rock and roll!"

* * *

Up in Dayzee's closet, which was almost as big as her bedroom, which was almost as big as her great room, Marilyn sighed loudly enough for everyone else to hear her.

"We never did make it shopping, Sissy."

"Nope, but don't you think it was worth it?"

"How was it worth it, Fia?"

"Oh, you saw out the window, Dayzee, when you and Kozy . . . when you two were, um . . ."

"Getting undressed," said Marilyn.

"Oh, that. That was like a scientific experiment, nothing more."

Marilyn giggled, and Sophia snickered.

"Until Kenzie showed up," Dayzee said with a big grin.

"What?" said Sophia. "What do you mean?"

"I mean that Kozy thought it was a good time to let Kenzie out. Kenzie was along for the ride when Kozy was about to take me right there at the window."

"Oh, no way!" said Marilyn. "Was Kozy still . . . you know . . . completely a guy, though?"

"Very much so, Mare. Kenzie seemed to like it too."

"Kenzie was with Kozy while he had that One-Eighty part all revved up? She was there to—"

"Yeah, Fia. Boy, Kozy was rough, too, then Mack showed up. Kozy was just about to give it to me good."

"That can happen again?" said Sophia. "Kozy, you can do that?"

"Yes, when elements of the situation have met necessary criteria."

"Ooh, that sounds fun!" said Marilyn.

"It sure does," said Sophia. "We liked watching you two up in the window. You saw Sis and me, didn't you?"

"Yeah, we did see you two by the pool. Who were those guys?"

"They were looking for Carlos and his brother. They were going to run in the house and look for them. We had to stop them, Dayzee."

"Sis is right. We really didn't have a choice."

"Fine, but who's going to take care of my lawn? You've killed most of the crew."

"Kildare Killers," Marilyn said with a big shrug.

"Yep. That's us."

"Still, I think there's only one or two of the crew left."

"They'll find new guys, Dayzee. Soon, I hope, because someone has to clean up all that ash by the pool."

Dayzee shook her head and stared at Sophia, then Marilyn. She let out a deep sigh.

"Look, let's just get all dressed up, and we can have some fun while we stare at that big guy statue."

"I'm starting to like that statue," said Sophia.

"I'd like to get Kozy undressed, then all dressed up again," said Marilyn.

"Same outfit?"

"Yes, Sissy, and I want things to get real scary before the dressing up again."

"I kind of do, too, Mare," said Dayzee. "Kozy, are you okay with all that attention?"

"I am acquiring an affinity for many situations here. There are human physical functions I have not yet explored."

"Oh my God," said Sophia. "Too bad we can't bring Kenzie back whenever we want."

"Sissy, that would be something. Kozy, can we do that just for fun?"

"The best I can condone is to allow Kenzie to resurface briefly. Kenzie enjoyed regaining the ability to speak earlier when my One-Eighty qualities were fully manifested and leading me in unknown, human directions."

"Aw, Kozy got itchy too?" said Marilyn.

"Yeah, Mare, he sure did."

"We need something like a switch on Kozy's back," said Marilyn. "Danger on—danger off."

"Maybe something like a special word, and we can bounce Kozy and Kenzie back and forth, Sis, then we—"

"That sounds too confusing, girls," said Dayzee. "Let's just get ourselves dressed and go. You both can play dress-up with Kozy later—after we figure out this crazy mess."

"We should hurry," said Kozy.

"Why? What's wrong?"

"Dayzee, I cannot remain on this planet much longer. I believe my predecessor had the same constraints."

"Oh no, you too? How much longer do you have?"

"There is no way to ascertain that with any confidence. When my telepathic portal is activated, I will depart immediately."

"Just wonderful," said Dayzee. "We don't have much time."

"We sure don't," said Marilyn, "so let's play dress-up before it's too late."

"Yep, and that back-and-forth Kozy Kenzie game. We should do that now because—"

"Girls, just stop. You know that we need to find a way to stop the assassin. Seriously, let's get dressed and go."

"I'm bringing my short robe again," said Sophia.

"That's really hot, Sissy."

*　*　*

"Mack, you're back to work already," said Dayzee. "How about a round to get us started?"

"Coming right up, Dayzee. Hi, Kozy. You know, I could probably loan you a t-shirt or something."

"I appreciate the quantity of thought devoted to my lack of appropriate dress, Mack. Your suggestion has merit."

Mack took off to fetch their drinks, and Marilyn said, "No, Kozy. Don't even think about it."

"Sis is right about that," said Sophia. "You just stay the way you are. No t-shirt."

"Besides," said Dayzee, "you'd probably just rip his shirt apart anyway."

145

"Here are your drinks, everyone. We're going to have quite a crowd tonight, so just yell if you need something, alright?"

"Wait and see—I'm predicting lots of yelling tonight," said Dayzee.

Mack smiled at Dayzee and walked down the bar to help other patrons.

Sophia sat on the left, with Kozy on her right. Next in line was Dayzee, and Marilyn sat on the right end. All stopped talking long enough to enjoy their drinks, and all looked over at the silent statue at least twice.

"What's the plan, Dayzee?" said Sophia. "If you don't have one, I'll just slip on my teeny tiny robe and get something started."

"No one can start stuff up like my Sissy," said Marilyn.

"Girls, how about if we just enjoy hanging out for a while and see what happens?"

"That might not be safe, Dayzee," said Kozy. "You were attacked not long ago in that very seat."

"Yeah, why was that? Shouldn't that thing just hang out at the mansion?"

"Your home is where it has settled in and where it has the most power. It will prefer to interact with you there, but it is obvious that it can make limited journeys to attack you elsewhere."

Dayzee frowned and looked down at the damaged footrest. She looked around the room and saw the broken barstool near the back door, ready to be tossed out with the trash.

"So, this seat can try to get me too?"

"Yes, which means you are safer here but not completely safe."

"Good point, Kozy."

"Kozy doesn't have points like Kenzie," said Sophia. "Remember those?"

"Sissy sure is right about that. I remember when Kenzie was up in that bedroom naked on Sissy's lap. Wow, very nice!"

"Did you notice what good shape even Kenzie was in, Sis? Even then, her legs—"

"Ugh . . . girls! Kozy's right—I'm not safe, and you know what? That thing—that assassin—might decide to go after you two again too."

Sophia leaned forward and looked past Kozy and Dayzee to see her sister.

"She's right, Sis. We need to figure this out. I'll put on my robe."

"Wait," said Dayzee. "Let's figure out something different. Enjoy your drink, and let's think this through."

"Hey," said Sophia, "maybe that's it—let's just drink, and maybe something will happen."

"I believe that could work, Sissy. Mack, another round here, please."

Before Mack returned with their drinks, Dayzee shook her head and said, "I'm in. Kozy, maybe you should ease up on the alcohol. We'll need you to protect us more than ever."

"I can drink extreme amounts, and only Kenzie will become intoxicated. You are all safe."

"That's pretty amazing," said Dayzee. "Okay, try to keep up with us."

"Here you go, ladies and Kozy."

Mack set their drinks down, and they all picked them up and emptied them.

"Another, Mack," said Sophia. "Keep them coming."

"That's what *we* do, Sissy!"

"Yep, Sis, before we kill them," she said with a smirk.

"Sometimes, even after."

"You girls aren't bad . . . not really. You just like the way it feels, right?"

"We deserve to feel good, don't we, Dayzee?"

"You sure do, Mare, and I know you two killed all those yard guys only because you had to."

"Yep, but we did enjoy it too. If we have to kill any more of them, I'm using my barbs."

"Oh, me too, Sissy!"

"What the hell, you might as well. Hey, that rhymes—Mack, another round!"

Marilyn spun her barstool around and looked at the crowd of men and women gathered around the pool table.

"Sissy, there's quite a bunch building up over at the pool table. If you don't put on that tiny robe, I think maybe—"

Marilyn found that Kozy was now sitting on her lap, holding the triangle from the pool table. It spun around his wrist a few times, then came to a rest.

"Uh-oh," said Marilyn. "I think the assassin hates me again too."

Too quickly for anyone to see, Kozy had shifted toward Sophia and held a pool ball close to the back of her head. He dropped it and held another, almost touching her back. She looked back over her shoulder as the first ball rolled across the floor.

"Me too, Sis. It hates us both again. I was wondering if that would—"

Kozy returned to Marilyn's lap and held an unused stool from one of the small tables that lined the walls.

"Oh, this is getting serious," said Dayzee. "Mare, do you always have to check Kozy's anatomy like that?"

"Oh, I just want to make sure it doesn't pop out of there."

"If you need any help, Sis, you know I'm happy to lend a hand."

"Maybe two hands, Sissy! There's certainly enough for—"

"Girls! I think you're missing something—those pool balls aren't made of wood. This new assassin is learning how to use anything."

"She is correct," said Kozy from Marilyn's lap. "That is one horrific aspect of sorsciencery: it mutates. It can rarely be predicted."

"'Dicted,'" said Marilyn as she continued to hold on. "Oh, yes!"

"That's pretty funny, Sis. Mack,"—she waved both arms above her head—"another round."

"You girls aren't taking this seriously, are you?"

"I'm serious about that next drink, Dayzee. Relax . . . Kozy's got us covered."

"I think we're better off uncovered, Sissy. When was the last time we were all naked? Oh, in your pool, Dayzee, when Bruno held his breath, and he—"

"He was holding my ass, too, Sis."

"That did feel fantastic, girls. It was way better than forcing me to be upset to get the Boss through the portal because—"

Dayzee paused and looked at the big statue wearing a big hat. He looked back in silence.

"Because what?" said Marilyn.

"I just thought of something. Mare, when you were almost naked and bent over the pool table by that gang, and—"

"I loved it!"

"Yes, we know. We know, Mare, but you were in trouble, and Bruno was strangling Fia, and—"

"I didn't like that so much."

"No, of course not, Fia, but the thing is, that gave me feelings that called out to the Boss somehow."

"Yep, it did. So?"

"Fia, don't you see? Maybe we could use other feelings to call someone."

"Oh, you're starting to make sense, Dayzee. Mack, another round here."

"Good, let's keep drinking, Fia. I think that'll help for what we have to do."

"Which is?" said Marilyn.

"All three of us need to remember how it felt with Bruno under the water and giving us all that wonderful treatment."

"Oh, I see—maybe that'll call Bruno back?"

"Exactly, Mare. Let's try it. Alright, everyone remember how it felt with Bruno going at it."

The new drinks were in front of them, and Mack had moved farther down the bar.

"A toast."

They all held up their glasses.

"To Bruno—he was right there, at just the right place, to give us just what we needed."

"He loved it," said Marilyn.

"Yeah, he sure did. Down the hatch."

They all slammed their empty glasses down.

"Okay, all of us, let's remember how that felt."

The three fell silent and closed their eyes, and Kozy continued to guard them. Several minutes later, Dayzee opened her eyes.

"Girls, it's not working."

"What else can we do?"

"Amplify the signal," said Kozy.

"Huh?"

"Move closer to the portal, Dayzee."

"Oh, that's brilliant, Kozy. Mare, Fia, come on. Let's go huddle around that big guy in the hat."

"Won't that look a little odd?" said Marilyn.

"Such a sweet kid," Dayzee said to Sophia. "No, it's Beverly Hills, remember? No one cares."

* * *

Dayzee, Marilyn, and Sophia formed a semi-circle facing the statue. Kozy faced the room and would occasionally catch a pool ball or shot glass as it whistled toward one of them.

"The assassin is exerting a steady pressure on us, but it does not launch an overwhelming attack. I must try to discern its strategy."

He reached back to show them a handful of knives and forks before tossing them into the corner with a clatter.

"Fine," said Dayzee. "You work on that, and we'll work on this."

Sophia's eyes followed the bouncing items, and she said, "No big surprise—that head got kicked into the corner. Look."

Dayzee and Marilyn turned to see, and Marilyn said, "I like it better when he's turned into the corner. It's like they gave him a timeout. I wonder if he's pouting about that? We should—"

"We need to focus," said Dayzee. "Just imagine you're in the pool again. The sun is shining, the water's a perfect temperature, and Bruno is down below, taking turns with us. Can you feel it, girls? I can."

"I feel it," said Marilyn. "He was just the right height for that."

"He loved it as much as we did," said Sophia.

They all closed their eyes again. Several minutes later, after Kozy had caught two more barstools and three liquor bottles and added them to the pile in the corner, Dayzee opened her eyes.

"It's still not working, girls."

"Oh, you know what, Dayzee? We're still dressed—maybe that's the problem?"

"You might be right, Mare. Fia, you and I are wearing short skirts, and Mare, your dress is really short, so why don't we—"

"I always wear short dresses, Dayzee. Shorter than that other Marilyn ever would. I don't think she should have even had that name. I'm much better at—"

"Mare, try to remember what we're doing, alright? Look, my point is that we should all roll our clothes up to our waists. Are either of you wearing underwear?"

"I am," said Marilyn.

"You're still asking?" said Sophia while shaking her head and grinning.

"That's my girl, Fia. Either way, let's do it. We have to."

Dayzee was the first to roll her skirt up around her waist. The girls looked down from each side at her tiny white panties.

"That's hot, Dayzee," said Marilyn. "Bruno would love that. My turn."

She rolled up her dress and said, "I know he'd want this too. Sissy, get going. Don't be shy."

"Shy? That's funny, Sis."

Sophia rolled her skirt up high and confirmed that she wore nothing under it.

"Think he'd like that?"

"Oh, yes, Sissy. Who wouldn't?"

"Alright, girls, let's concentrate. Think about Bruno under the water, just the right height to—"

"I sure was the right height," said Bruno, standing before them and dressed in the same tight t-shirt, thick jeans, heavy boots, and a ball cap that said "Liking This Planet" across the front of it. He looked from girl to girl and smiled. His face was even with all of their breasts.

Dayzee said, "Bruno, you've grown!"

"Yes, I have. The longer I'm away from that planet with the crushing gravity, the more I'm returning to my normal height."

"You're still at a pretty good height for us," said Marilyn.

"Oh, he sure is, Sis. I could use some of that."

They all rolled down their clothes and smiled at the much-taller-than-before Bruno.

"There will be time for that later," said Dayzee, "but right now, we need to—"

"No, there won't be time. I can't stay. Tell me what you need quickly before I poof out of here again."

"You're still doing that poofing thing?" said Sophia.

"No one poofs like Bruno, Sissy."

"Girls, we have to hurry. Bruno, how do we kill this assassin thing once and for all?"

"I can tell you, but I don't think you're going to like it."

"I think you can do both at the same time," Sophia said as she began to unbutton her blouse. "How does that sound, tough guy?"

Bruno nodded and grinned while his eyes darted left and right over and over at what Sophia was revealing.

Chapter 15 – Keep Talking Sexy

"And just like that, he's gone," said Dayzee.

"He did say he could poof out of here at any time," said Sophia.

"I can't believe what he just told us about how that thing can be killed."

"Neither can I, Mare," said Dayzee, "but I can't imagine Bruno lying to us. He risked coming back here just to tell us that."

"Huh. I think he came back for me," said Sophia.

"Who wouldn't, Sissy? You're absolutely gorgeous."

"So are you—we're twins. Maybe he came back for you or for Dayzee?"

"I think he might have come back for all of us, girls. Did you see his new hat? I'm glad he found time in between giving us such sweet attention to tell us what we needed to know."

"But it's disgusting," said Sophia. "I'm not sure any of us would be able to do that."

"Well," said Dayzee, "we might not have a choice. We should get going."

"I'm in no hurry to put my dress back up and hide these again," Marilyn said as she squeezed them together.

"You never are, Sis."

"Girls, wasn't Bruno something else again?" said Dayzee. "He gave us all a couple of turns at his new height, and then—"

"He reminded us of how much he liked being shorter—I mean, less tall—I mean, a different height."

"Yeah, he gave us all a couple of turns there too. Ah . . . I feel a lot better now," said Dayzee.

She turned to look at Kozy, who still faced away from them and kept a wary view of the danger all around them.

"Now that we know how to kill that thing—even though I'm not sure any of us could actually do it—shouldn't we get back to the mansion?"

"Kozy," said Marilyn, "can you still catch tables and chairs lying on your back?"

"Oh, Mare . . ."

"I'm just asking, Dayzee. This place is so crowded no one would even notice. Right here by the statue. Oh, and Sissy, you could put on that robe and get in some trouble at the pool table. I'd love to watch you while I test out Kozy!"

"Girls! No, there's no time."

Kozy snapped around and held a high-top table that had rocketed across the room.

"This is getting absurd," said Dayzee. "We need to get out of here before the entire room tries to swallow us up."

"Swallow," said Marilyn. "You sure there isn't time, Dayzee?"

"No, Mare, not this time. Let's see if we can make it out to the limo."

"After another drink, you mean?"

"Sure, Fia, why the hell not? Let's all stay close to Kozy and make it quick."

"Shouldn't we get dressed back up like normal earthwomen, Dayzee?"

"Yeah, you're right. Let's cover up."

After they'd smoothed down clothes and buttoned blouses and pulled straps of a white dress back up, Kozy led the way back to the bar. Mack had another round waiting for them and said, "I saved your seats for you. Where did you all go anyway?"

"To talk to the statue guy," said Marilyn.

"We didn't really talk to it, Mack," said Sophia. "You know that."

"Who put that here?" said Dayzee.

"Who knows? It's been here a long time. That's all I know."
"Did you ever notice anything strange about it?" said Dayzee.
"Just the hat. That's a big hat."

*   *   *

"So, Dayzee," said Sophia, "that assassin isn't just using wood anymore?"
"Apparently not."
"Anything can try to kill us?"
"Yeah, Mare. We just need to kill it first. Please, take us home, Kozy."
Dayzee sat up front on the passenger side, and Marilyn and Sophia shared the back seat. Kozy started the engine and cut off traffic to make a wide U-turn on Sunset Boulevard to the sounds of honking horns and screeching tires.
"Whoa, Kozy. What was that all about?" said Sophia.
"I am still agitated from all the danger. I am at a high state of aggression in order to defend all of you."
"Aw, poor Kozy," said Marilyn. "When we get home, we should give him some special attention. That would help, wouldn't it?"
"Yes, it would. Thank you, Marilyn."
"Well, I haven't done anything yet. I'm sure thinking about it, though."
The short ride in the fading evening sunlight down Sunset remained mostly quiet until Kozy turned onto Dayzee's street and immediately slammed on the brakes.
"You gotta be kidding me," said Dayzee.
Marilyn and Sophia sat up, and they all stared through the windshield. Several houses down the street, between the entrance and exit gates of Dayzee's mansion, sat Mattie's truck. Its engine was rumbling, but they didn't see anyone driving it until the headless guy leaned out of the open window, then back in.
"Did that headless thing just look at us?" said Marilyn.

"You know what it's still looking for, Sis."

"That'll always be funny, Sissy."

"How is this even possible, Kozy?" said Dayzee. "I thought you buried that thing in the basement?"

"I did, but that was when the assassin could move only much smaller objects. I believe it has freed the dead body."

"And then taught it how to drive," said Marilyn.

"A guy's gotta at least have a car to get some head, Sis."

"So true, Sissy. You're on a roll."

"Girls, please. Kozy, what do you recommend?"

"If you three exit this vehicle, I can ram the threat we face. That would disable the opposing—"

"I'm not getting that far from you," said Sophia. "You're the only one that can protect us."

"Sissy's right. I'm not going anywhere."

"Okay, me neither," said Dayzee. "What's Plan B?"

"I back away slowly, and perhaps it will not pursue. But . . ."

"But what?" said Marilyn.

"I am so agitated I can barely concentrate. It is a feeling of imminent explosion."

"Aw, poor Kozy," said Marilyn.

She reached over the back of the seat with both hands, resting her chin on his right shoulder, and got a comfortable hold.

"Mare, you're shameless. I hope that helps, though. Kozy, does that help?"

"It provides hope for relief even as it escalates the impending eruption. Yes, it mostly helps."

"Quite a way with words," said Dayzee.

"It's quite a sight back here, Sis, with your dress riding up. Here, let me just get it back up around your waist."

Sophia reached over and began working her sister's dress higher.

"Why, Fia? Is that really necessary?"

"Nope, Dayzee, not at all—I just like it. Sis is gorgeous."

"I like it, too, Dayzee," said Marilyn with a giggle. "If I could, I'd sit on Kozy's lap."

"Oh, don't even try," said Dayzee. "Well, this is quite a scene we have here. Alright, Kozy, try backing away."

He shifted the limo into reverse and gave it some gas. The long car backed away slowly, and the truck crept forward, maintaining the same distance.

"You've been working out, Sis?"

"If you call burning up yard guys 'exercise,' then yeah."

"Wow, you are magnificent. Here, let me help."

Sophia scooched over to sit beneath her sister, who was then able to sit back on the edge of Sophia's lap.

"Oh, that's much better. Can you get my dress up a little higher, Sissy? My hands are full."

"Yep. Kozy's keeping you busy, Sis?"

"I think I'm keeping him busy!"

"Maybe you should get in the front seat, then you could—"

"Stop, you two! God, you're sex-crazed teenage human females!"

"Uh-huh. Yep. So?"

"Fia, try to take this seriously. We need to get back inside the mansion. We can't let some headless guy driving the truck of a burned-up lawn guy boss us around!"

"Sure, Dayzee. I'll just sit here with my hot sister on my lap. Hey, maybe you could help Sis out with that?"

"I think one of us should keep an eye on the dead guy, don't you? Kozy, can you do a tight U-turn if you're spinning the tires?"

"The physics would suggest that I can."

"Keep talking sexy like that," said Marilyn.

Dayzee rolled her eyes and shook her head.

"Go ahead, Kozy, try—"

"Head," said Marilyn. "That's what Kozy needs. Hey, so does the headless guy!"

"This is just too weird, Sis."

"Kozy, ignore them, and spin this car around. If you can get the dead guy to chase us around the block, maybe we can sneak back in and close the gate. What do you think?"

"I will attempt the procedure you suggest."

He angled the limo to one side of the street until it was scraping along the curb. A quick shift into drive, followed by flooring the gas and turning the wheel, sent the car into a tight, screaming turn. He kept the tires spinning, and the limo shot down Dayzee's street with the dead guy trucking close behind.

"Nice job—you're a hell of a driver!" said Dayzee.

"I liked how Sis was shaking all around from that. Good thing I was holding onto her."

"I did slide around on your lap, Sissy, but I never let go of him."

"Oh, you two. Kozy, keep going all the way around the block. Ignore traffic. Hit anyone that gets in your way."

The squealing limo tires dug in, and their speed ramped up.

"Don't slow down! Turn right on Sunset!"

He never let up, and the rear end slid across the pavement for a short ride on Sunset, then a quick right on the next street.

"He's right behind us, Kozy, so pick it up a little, alright? Go!"

The pickup remained a short distance behind them as the limo rocketed south. As they approached Elevado Avenue, Dayzee screamed out.

"You're going too fast! Don't try to turn here!"

The limo raced through the intersection with the pickup close behind.

"Oh, Sis, you're really flexing trying to stay up there. You have some serious tone going on back here."

"Aw, thanks for holding onto my hips, Sissy. I just don't want to let go of Kozy yet!"

"She has not let go," said Kozy. "The danger is extreme."

"Turn here," Dayzee yelled. "Here! Turn on Carmelita!"

"We might be traveling too quickly, Dayzee."

"We have to try. Maybe we'll lose that headless loser behind us."

Kozy fishtailed the limo into the intersection, dodged several oncoming vehicles on Carmelita Avenue, and quickly turned back onto Dayzee's street.

"Kozy, you lost him!" said Dayzee.

"I haven't lost anything," said Marilyn.

"You kind of lost your dress there, Sis."

"Here, Kozy—turn in right here."

Dayzee got out her phone and typed all but one number. Right after the limo roared through the gate, she finished the code, and the gate swung shut. She hurried to close the exit gate too. The pickup came to a screeching stop just outside the entrance gate. They all looked out the limo's back window.

"Look, he's just watching us," said Marilyn.

"That doesn't make any sense, Sis."

They watched the headless guy open the door and get out of the truck. He hopped around the front end and approached the gate.

"Oh, look at that: he broke the rake handle off at his left side so he could sit behind the wheel. Pretty smart," said Sophia.

"Human men don't think with that head that's missing anyway, Sissy."

"Girls, the dead guy's not doing anything. It's dead. It's the assassin."

The headless guy reached out for the gate with both hands, but before he could get a hold on it, he collapsed.

"Did he just get too tired? Does that thing—that assassin—get tired, Kozy?"

"It appears so, Dayzee. It will surely strike again, though."

"Well, before anything else happens, we should—"

Dayzee's phone chimed, and she took it out and received the call.

"Hello, this is Dayzee. Who? Oh, the manager, of course. No, I haven't seen Carlos. His brother is missing too? Two other guys? Maybe you have a mutiny on your hands. No, of course, it's not funny. It's just that now's not really a good time—we can talk about that some other day. No, do not come over right now. You'll have to—"

Dayzee held her phone away and stared at it with a frown.

"That doesn't sound good, Dayzee," said Sophia.

"He hung up on me. He said he'd be here in a few minutes."

"Hey, can you ask him to get that body out of here already? How many times has that thing attacked us?"

"Oh, Mare, no, we need to get rid of that before he gets here."

"It would help if it could walk—"

"Hop, Sis."

"Right, if it could hop, we could let it chase us into the garage and close the door."

"I can place it in the vehicle's rear storage compartment, Dayzee."

"Again?" said Dayzee. "How many times has that thing been in and out of the trunk?"

"I'm losing track," said Sophia. "Is that even the same guy? Sheesh . . . so many corpses."

"Does it matter which one it is, Sissy? It's all kind of thrilling."

A loud tap on the windshield silenced their deliberations, and they turned to look.

"What was that?"

"A bird, Dayzee?" said Marilyn.

"Sis, birds don't fly into—"

A piece of wood the size of a golf ball struck the windshield. It stuck there for a moment, then it retreated from the glass before striking it again. Another one joined it. Then, ten more, all pounding against the glass.

"What the hell?"

"It's my bark mulch, Sophia," said Dayzee. "The assassin got bored with the dead guy."

"This is actually kind of funny," said Marilyn. "Look, there are even more of them now—the windshield is almost covered."

"What a day. Alright, we still need that body," said Dayzee. "Kozy, will you be alright out there?"

"I believe so. It is not programmed to harm Earth dwellers controlled by a One-Eighty."

"This sure does get complicated," said Dayzee.

"Yes."

He put the car in reverse and backed up as far as possible to still allow the gate to swing in.

"Oh, another thing," said Dayzee. "We need to move that truck too."

"I can relocate that," said Kozy.

"Wonderful. We need to hurry too."

The noisy pounding on the windshield had spread to every other window and the roof. There were countless pieces of bark chattering loudly on every surface of the limo.

"Yes, Dayzee. Can you open the gate?"

"What?"

"The gate," said Kozy.

"Who's Kate?"

Kozy pointed toward the back window.

"Oh, the gate!"

Dayzee hit the code, and the gate opened. Kozy rushed out and slammed the door, but one piece of bark flew inside. It pounded into the windshield and bounced down onto the dash, where Dayzee grabbed it.

"Pesky little thing," Sophia said.

"For sure," said Dayzee as she powered her window down just far enough to fling it back outside.

Marilyn sat all the way back on her sister's lap and said, "Oh, well hello there."

Sophia wrapped her arms around her sister's waist and said, "That's a good place for you, Sis. Hey, this would be good for when Dayzee's picture guy is hanging out with us."

"Yes, you are so right. Or even if he isn't," she said with a giggle.

The car bounced, the trunk slammed shut, and Kozy quickly climbed back in.

"Well, that's a good start. Kozy, can you see enough to get the limo into the garage?"

"Yes, I believe I can."

"Good. Then, can you move that pickup? There won't be any room in the garage, so can you get it out of sight around the side of the house with Carlos's?"

"As you wish. I must disclose that I am still agitated."

"I can hold on," said Marilyn. "At least until we get to the garage."

She leaned forward and rose up to get her hands back in place on Kozy's lap.

"Oh, what the hell," said Sophia as she pulled her sister's dress up around her waist. "It just never gets old, Sis."

"Not for me either."

Safely parked in the garage, Kozy switched off the engine. The car was completely covered with chunks of wood, all bouncing and flying around, trying to get inside.

"How can we get in the house, Dayzee?" said Marilyn. "We'll get beat up by all that bark."

"Oh, I have no idea. Kozy, what do you think?"

"It is a plan with a low probability of success, but I will suggest it anyway. I believe the assassin would rather switch back to the deceased human in the trunk. I will remove it and place it near the door to your house. The assassin will know that it will be more challenging for you to avoid its attacks."

"That's brilliant," said Marilyn. "Let's do it."

"I think you kind of are doing it, Sis."

"Getting close, I think, Sissy."

"Still looking good back here too."

"Girls. Alright, Kozy, let's try that plan."

He rushed out, dragged the body out of the trunk, and placed it near the doorway. All of the mulch stopped moving at once, and most of the pieces slid off of the car and onto the concrete floor.

"The yard guys are cleaning this up," said Dayzee.

"I don't think there are any left," said Sophia.

"Just the one that's coming to visit," said Dayzee. "Look, our favorite dead guy is alive again. So predictable."

"Kozy just ran out to get the pickup," said Marilyn, again sitting back on her sister's lap. "You should probably close the garage door, Dayzee."

"Okay, Mare. And you . . . you can get off your sister's lap."

"Do I have to?"

"She doesn't want to," said Sophia.

"I totally understand, but we still have to get going. Let's try to get past that thing and into the house."

They all got out and got closer but still out of its reach. Its arms swung around frantically as it hopped around.

"You know, this is kind of easy," Sophia said as she grabbed the rake sticking out of its ribs on its right side. She guided the hopping guy around behind them and kicked him once, sending him to the concrete.

"Sheesh . . . my heel stabbed it."

"Go, girls! Run inside!"

Before they got too far, the mulch pieces came to life, and all of them floated up at the same time.

"Run! The bark is back!"

Dayzee had just closed the door when every piece of mulch banged into it over and over.

"Weird stuff, Dayzee," said Marilyn. "Even for the Hills. Is Kozy going to be okay?"

"I sure hope so. Let's go get ready to open the back door. Hey, does he know where the back door is?"

"I don't know, Dayzee," said Sophia. "How about if we each take a door? We'll be ready no matter where he goes."

"Wait. You hear that?" said Dayzee. "He's at the front door. Come on."

Sophia got there first and opened it up, and Kozy rushed in. A second later, thousands of pieces of mulch flung themselves against the door.

"Home, sweet home," said Dayzee.

"More like home, sweet giant mansion," said Sophia.

"Yes, and it's gone crazy," said Marilyn.

Chapter 16 – Just Like That

"Now that all that excitement is behind us," said Marilyn, "I'm starting to feel a little drunk."

"Hey, Sis," said Sophia with a big grin, "don't talk about Bruno like that."

"That's funny, Sissy. We could get him liquored up, and—"

"Did you say licked up, Sis?"

"You really are on a roll!"

"Girls, this is probably a bad idea, but I'm getting a round of doubles for all of us."

"Sounds good to me," said Sophia. "No ice. I need to watch my figure."

"Funny, Sissy. Ice. Everyone always watches your figure because it's unbelievable."

"Yours too, Sis."

"What about my figure?" said Kozy.

"Well, technically, yours is called a physique," said Sophia. "You definitely added some muscle."

"Something else too," said Marilyn.

Dayzee returned with the drinks and passed them out.

"Before anything else starts attacking us, why don't we all have a seat in the great room? I could get that fireplace working, and we could—"

"I would not advise that," said Kozy. "The assassin would probably like to send flaming wood flying around your mansion."

"Flaming wood," said Sophia with a snort. "There's a joke in there somewhere, but I'm too drunk."

"Yes, but we're not done drinking yet, Sissy. If I'm going to get murdered by a corpse, I'd like to at least be drunk."

"No one is getting murdered," said Dayzee. "We know what we have to do. We just don't like it."

"Does it have to be all of us or just one?" said Marilyn.

"Bruno didn't say for sure. I think he meant just one of us."

"How do we pick?" said Sophia.

"You must let the assassin choose," said Kozy.

"How does that happen?" said Dayzee.

"I believe we will know. We must wait until it reveals its intentions."

"I expect it to bring me a drink, then I'll know it's me," said Sophia.

"If it's me, I think it should do some extravagant courting," said Marilyn.

"You think everyone should, Sis."

"Girls, we're not waiting for someone to ask us out on a date. This is serious. That thing wants to kill us."

"It wants more from you than that," said Kozy. "Recall your bedposts this morning. The chair in the living room. The barstool."

"It wants to have sex with me, is that what you're saying?"

"Yes, Dayzee. It probably wants that with any or all of you."

Dayzee frowned and said, "Creepiest orgy ever."

"Where's that photographer friend of yours, Dayzee?" said Sophia. "I have a feeling it's going to be a wild scene."

"It's the only way, girls. We'll have to let it—"

A pounding on the door made them all turn and look.

"I didn't even notice, but the bark must be bark again," said Sophia.

"Yes, and maybe that's one giant piece."

"No, Mare, it's probably just the manager. What am I supposed to tell him? That his entire yard crew is dead?"

"It's just him now, Dayzee?"

"Yeah, just him. There's no way he'll be able to take care of this property."

"I'll help him interview new guys," said Sophia.

"Why not girls, too, Sissy?"

"Alright, we can interview girls too," said Sophia. "How will we know if they're good at lawn stuff?"

"Do we care? As long as they're hot and fun and—"

"Enough!"

Dayzee rose and walked to the front door. She peeked through the peephole then opened it just enough to speak.

"Oh, good. It's just you."

"Were you expecting someone else?"

She opened the door and let in a tall, thin man with a shaved head, a neat gray beard, and very dark skin. He held his ball cap in his hand.

"No, just you, Mr. Barkus. Are you sure this can't wait?"

Marilyn whispered to her sister, "Barkus? Did I hear that right?"

Sophia whispered back, "Yep, how weird is that? We were being attacked by bark!"

"It's kind of urgent, Dayzee, and please, just call me Rake. That's my nickname."

Marilyn whispered again, "Rake? Like stuck in the dead guy? What the hell?"

"This just gets weirder all the time, Sis," Sophia whispered back.

"No, Dayzee," said Rake, "this can't wait. My entire crew is missing. There's something going on in this mansion of yours," he said as he frowned and looked all around the spacious foyer and through the doorways.

"Why, whatever do you mean?"

"You're not a killer, Dayzee, are you? Tell me you didn't kill those boys."

While Dayzee answered, Rake walked over and stood in the open doorway to her office, craning his neck to look all around.

"Oh, you think they're dead? Hey, of course, I'm not a killer!"

She glanced at the twins. Marilyn had a hand over her mouth to contain her giggling, and Sophia grinned and pointed to her sister and herself several times while mouthing the words, "We are!"

"I hate to think of you as a killer. I can't imagine why you'd be involved in something so diabolical."

He walked over and peered into the living room. His eyes rested on the busted-up chair, the one that had violated and attacked Dayzee, and he frowned and walked up to it.

"What happened here? What the hell is this? Something bad happened here."

"No, Rake, that's just an old chair that finally wore out. It's been around since—"

"Like hell, this wore out, Dayzee."

He reached out and pulled at the shattered wood.

"What the hell is going on?"

The twins had walked over and stood beside Dayzee.

"It really is just an old chair," said Sophia. "Mr. Bark."

Marilyn fought to hide a giggle that was about to erupt.

"It's Barkus," he said before turning to look at them. "And who the hell are you two? I've never seen you around here before."

"Oh, these are my good friends from Ireland," said Dayzee. "They're staying with me for a while. This is Marilyn, and this is Sophia."

Rake looked at Kozy, wearing khaki pants and boots, a uniform jacket open over his bare chest, and a fashionable cap.

"And you," he said, "what are you all dressed up for?"

"I am here to help Dayzee and Marilyn and Sophia."

"Oh, like hired help? Whatever. Look, all of you, I know my guys are in trouble, and I know they all came here."

"You're welcome to look around," said Dayzee. "Those boys aren't anywhere around here."

"Look in any room you want," said Marilyn. "It's a big mansion, though, so that'll take a while."

"Just don't look in the can," said Sophia.

Marilyn elbowed her, causing a soft giggle.

Rake walked back over and stood in front of Dayzee, close enough to smack her. He stayed silent as he looked into the eyes of Kozy on the left, then Dayzee, then Marilyn, then Sophia.

"Don't mind them, Rake," said Dayzee. "She meant the restroom, of course. They're trying to pick up slang in the good old U.S. of A. Look in the restrooms too. I'm telling you, there's no—"

"You think I'm a hick because I take care of people's lawns, is that it?"

"I don't know what—"

"Save it, Dayzee. All my trucks are on G.P.S. I know they were both here."

"Well, they might have visited, you know, just to check on the grounds, which are pretty messed up right now."

"Yes, there's bark everywhere," said Marilyn.

"I think she means 'mulch,'" said Sophia.

"Whatever it's called," said Dayzee, "when you find those lost boys of yours, get them a rake or something, and—"

"Rake!" Marilyn yelled before her sister elbowed her.

"She just thinks tools are funny things," said Sophia. "Something from her childhood, maybe?"

"Listen! The point is, I know where those trucks are."

"And where exactly do you think the trucks are?" said Dayzee.

"On the side of your house, where no one can see them. No one except for the goddamn satellites!" he said with squinting eyes and one finger pointing up.

Rake slapped his cap onto his bald head and stood with his arms crossed, frowning at each of them in turn. A barely noticeable cracking sound from behind him caused Dayzee to look past him, but only while his eyes were on one of the other three. She saw that the wood trim around the doorway in which Rake stood had split at its midpoint above the doorway, and it was quietly pulling away from the walls.

"Rake, that's a very unusual thing that you speak of," Dayzee said slowly as she held his gaze. "I simply can't imagine why your crew would park their trucks there and just leave."

She glanced away quickly to see the two free ends of the trim boards snaking toward Rake.

"They're such good employees, and you must know that I'm always satisfied with their professionalism and hard work."

The boards kept pulling away from the wall, and the ends were coming up behind Rake.

"Why, just the other day, Carlos, I think it was, finished trimming around my bushes, and—"

"Trimming bushes!" said Marilyn, and Sophia elbowed her.

"—and he looked thirsty, so—"

The boards were just about to touch Rake's upper arms.

"—I said, 'Hey, Carlos, how about some cold lemonade?' And he said—"

The boards raced in unison to coil around Rake's large biceps and lifted him off of the floor.

"What the hell is this?"

"Oh, this mansion has turned into a maniac, Rake, and not a second too soon. I was running out of steam with that stupid lemonade story."

"Put me down! Dayzee?"

Another board broke loose along the floor and quickly wound around his head, covering his mouth. Rake made only muffled sounds.

"That's better," said Sophia. "Who the hell is he to accuse us of stuff?"

"Exactly, Sissy. Rake Bark, if that is his real name, which I'm starting to doubt, was getting very annoying."

"Kozy, what's going on this time?"

"The assassin is evolving. It is learning to protect you too."

"Why the hell would it do that? Its whole point is to kill us!"

Rake's feet kicked high above the floor, and he twisted and fought, but the trim was too strong. He tried to scream, too, but he barely made a sound.

"It also has the objective of seducing you. It wishes you to continue to live, at least until it can kill you itself."

"That is one hell of a complicated assassin, Kozy."

"Sorsciencery is a difficult practice to master with any reliability. It is likely the lab has no idea what a chaotic mess it has created."

"Well, what now?" said Sophia.

"Ooh, I think I know," said Marilyn.

"Oh, you're right. Is there room in the can, Sis?"

Dayzee looked at the wide-open eyes of the man high above the floor and said, "You *should* be worried. She really doesn't mean the restroom, Rake."

Marilyn pulled the straps of her dress down over her shoulders and freed her arms. She left it bunched around her waist, and the struggling man's eyes moved to her breasts.

"Why, Sis?"

"Look. It calmed him down. He likes them."

"Oh, who wouldn't, Sis? They're stunning."

"Yours are, too, Sissy—show him."

Sophia unbuttoned her blouse, then unfastened her black lacy bra and stretched it all apart. Rake's eyes went from one pair to another. His thrashing stopped, but his legs still kicked a little.

"Oh, what the hell," said Dayzee as she unbuttoned her blouse too. "Kozy, you're part of this gang now. Show this big angry piece of bark what you have going on, in case he likes that too."

Soon, Rake was taking turns staring from his choice of three pairs of bare breasts and one chest packed with muscle. He stopped kicking, and only his eyes moved.

"Aw, I think he likes us," said Marilyn.

"Earth," said Sophia. "It's almost too easy."

"We all know where this is ending up," said Dayzee. "Kozy, is there any way to command the assassin to command the trim to—"

"It will probably know what to do. Look, it is beginning to make arrangements for you."

The trim lowered Rake until his feet touched the floor, then it snapped him like a tablecloth, sending his feet out and quickly laying him on his back on the smooth tile floor.

"Who gets the honor, Dayzee?" said Sophia.

"My mansion, my monsters."

"She's right, Sissy. You and I have already had our fun."

"It's never enough, Sis. You know that."

"We should go clean up all that bark out there while Dayzee cleans up the Bark in here."

"Wood outside and wood inside? That's pretty clever, Sis. Nice one."

"Thanks, Sissy. Come on, let's go. Kozy, maybe you should stay and make sure Dayzee is okay?"

"Yes, I will watch closely."

"I sure would," said Marilyn.

"Me too."

"Girls, just go ahead and leave me to this. Oh, I'm ready to heat things up again."

"Remember the fireplace, Dayzee?" said Marilyn. "You're making that fire in your foyer now."

"Good one, Sis," said Sophia. "Dayzee's burning up some wood."

"Wood . . . bark . . ." said Dayzee, "it all goes up in smoke."

*   *   *

The twins walked out onto Dayzee's porch and closed the front door. They stood side by side and looked around at all the bark mulch lying everywhere, covering everything.

"We should probably get dressed again, Sis."

"Oh, okay, Sissy."

They got their clothing back in order and scanned the mess all over the porch and walk.

"Sis, I'm not cleaning this up. That's what yard guys are for."

"Only when they're alive, Sissy. Hey, if that assassin really wants to help, too, maybe it'll get that headless guy out here to pick all of this up."

"Think about it, Sis. It doesn't have a head, and it has only one leg. How the hell would it pick up all this crap?"

Marilyn thought for a few seconds, then a big smile lit up her face.

"He already has a rake, Sissy. Remember? He could use that!"

"Oh, you know, that would make a hilarious video. We could ask Dayzee to talk to that assassin—maybe she could sweet-talk it into that."

*   *   *

"Look at him, Kozy, all tied up and helpless on the floor. He's not even struggling—he's just staring at my legs."

"Other attractive things, too, Dayzee. He is studying many of your physical attributes."

"He deserves a better look," she said as she unbuttoned her blouse all the way, slipped it off, and dropped it on the floor.

While looking him in the eye, she took her time wiggling out of her skirt until that fell to the floor, too, where she kicked it aside. She hooked her thumbs in the thin elastic circling her trim waist.

"Only this little thing now, Mr. Bark. Can I call you Mr. Bark? Of course, I can. I can do anything with you now. Isn't that right?"

He nodded and grinned, and Dayzee turned to Kozy to say, "Earthmen are so easy!"

"It is because you are more attractive than any woman from Earth."

"The twins too. We just take our pick, and right now, I pick this big guy. Can you help out, Kozy, and get him ready?"

"Yes."

Kozy stood over the man, facing him with boots tight against his thighs, and reached down for his belt.

"Wait a second. Why don't you turn the other way? Just for fun?"

"There is much danger, Dayzee. You still place a priority on amusement?"

"Always. Rock and roll, Kozy."

"As you wish."

Kozy rotated and stood with shiny black boots on each side of the foreman's chest, then reached down and got him ready for Dayzee. Before Kozy could step away, Dayzee said, "No, no, no. Just stay there, alright?"

"As you wish."

"I do wish."

Dayzee straddled Rake and didn't hesitate to lower herself down onto him.

"Oh, there we go, Big Bad Bark. Just a little bit of fun before we heat you up."

She reached up to hold Kozy's thighs.

"I'm just trying to help you balance yourself, that's all."

"You are quite selfless, Dayzee. I did not know I was at risk of toppling."

"Oh, this is perfect. Alright, time for some heat! Kozy, don't you even think of moving."

"I did think of moving my pantaloons."

"Pants. No one talks like that."

"Thank you. Pants. I feel strangely compelled. In the vehicle, Marilyn did not finish something that I felt necessary for my biological equilibrium."

"By all means. Yeah, let's get those trousers down and out of the way."

"Like this?"

"Yeah, exactly like that. Oh, hello!"

*   *   *

"I know Dayzee deserves some fun, too, Sis, but I wish it was me," said Sophia.

"Or me? We could have taken turns."

"Do you think she'll use her barbs too?

"I sure would," said Marilyn. "That feels so good that I don't really mind being a killer."

"Well, next time for us, Sis. We still need to figure out all this mulch. There's no way Dayzee will get a crew out here quick enough."

"Yes, Sissy, that's the last of the yard guys crew in there. He sure isn't going to do it."

"Nope. A pile of ashes could never—"

The front door opened, and Dayzee poked her head out.

"The mulch can wait, girls. Grab that can, okay? Oh, and a broom and dustpan too."

"Rake will never bark again, Dayzee?"

"My God, Sis, you're not just gorgeous—you are way more clever than I ever knew!"

Chapter 17 – Unsuspecting Human Males

Back inside and standing in the foyer, they all stared at the pile of ashes in the shape of a man. His ball cap remained on the floor to one side.

"How was it, Dayzee?" said Marilyn. "I thought maybe you'd take your time with him."

"It's always a sweet ecstasy, but you already know that. The only thing better is——"

"Using our barbs," said Sophia. "God, that's good."

"Kozy was a big help, too, girls. Kozy really kept an eye on things."

"Wait," said Sophia. "Just how 'big' of a help was Kozy?"

"Oh, it was really dangerous, Fia. Those trim boards were sharp and could have attacked me at any time."

"So, Kozy was a 'big' help? That's what you mean?"

"Yeah, Mare. A really large, irresistible help," Dayzee said with a grin.

"To keep an eye on things, Kozy had to stand real close?"

"Really close, Fia."

Marilyn looked up at Kozy and said, "Hey, is that a smile? I don't think I've seen you smile before."

"That's a smile, Sis."

Marilyn said, "Kozy, are you still agitated from all the crazy danger?"

Kozy grinned and said, "Nope."

"Hey, you never use slang like that," said Sophia. "You seem a lot more mellow."

"Kozy stood really, really close, girls. You could say it was a team effort."

"Kozy helped burn Rake Bark?" said Marilyn.

"Nope," said Kozy.

"There you go again! Oh, I know what happened, Sis."

"I think I do, too, Sissy. Dayzee, did you—"

"Yeah, girls. Kozy was sent to help us, remember? Hmm . . . that really helped."

"I think you helped yourself!" said Marilyn.

"Another good one, Sis."

"Anyway, girls, that doesn't matter now. We need to—"

"It sure matters to Kozy," said Sophia. "Look at that grin."

"Kozy, did you just sigh?" said Marilyn.

"Girls, forget that. Leave Kozy be. We need to get things cleaned up around here."

"We can't pick up all that bark, Dayzee. Maybe we could get that headless guy to—"

"No, I don't care about the mulch. That's for the yard crew. We need to—"

"You don't have a yard crew—we were too hot for all of them."

"Yeah, you're right about that, Mare. I'm talking about their trucks. We have three pickup trucks to get rid of."

"Oh, that's right," said Marilyn.

"How big is your yard?" said Sophia. "Can we bury them somewhere?"

"Fia, how could we ever dig—"

"No, Dayzee," said Marilyn, "we'll make the headless guy do it."

"It's not like he's our personal slave! Anyway, how's a one-legged headless man supposed to dig a big hole?"

"She's right, Sis," said Sophia. "Alright, Dayzee, what do you suggest?"

"You girls remember Bruno and how he was supposed to take all those dead gang guys out to a canyon and dump them?"

"He never did, though. He lost them all because he was thinking about us without our clothes."

"Sis is right. Then, they all came back here to attack us."

"That's not the point, girls. The thing is, we can drive all those trucks out of town and leave them. Just push them off the road somewhere."

"You want each of us to drive a truck out of Beverly Hills?" said Marilyn.

"Yeah, and Kozy can follow in the limo. What do you two think?"

Marilyn and Sophia looked at each other, then back at Dayzee.

"Why not?" said Sophia. "Taking care of that and cleaning up all the ashes should just about—"

"Sissy, there's still a headless guy in the garage."

"Sis is right, Dayzee. What about him?"

"Let's put him in one of the trucks. It'll look like that all happened to him from the accident."

"Won't the cops wonder where his head ended up?" said Marilyn.

"More guys looking for head, Sis. Guys with uniforms and guns and badges, this time."

"Girls, they'll just think a mountain lion ripped it loose and ran off with it. Let's just do it and hope for the best. We should leave right away."

"Damn lions," Kozy said with a big grin.

Dayzee smiled and pointed at Kozy. He grinned back.

"I don't want to get pelted with chunks of bark," said Sophia.

Dayzee nodded and paused while looking at Rake's ashes on the floor.

"Alright, I hate to ask this of you, Kozy, but I'm going to. Can you pull the trucks into the garage one by one, and each of us will drive one back out and wait?"

"I can do that. What you just did for me was so—"

"We don't need to actually discuss that in any detail, Kozy. Alright, that's our plan, then. We'll—"

"Someone without a head is still hopping around in the garage," said Sophia, causing her sister to giggle.

"Oh, that's right. Kozy, can you tie that thing up in the back of the first truck?"

"I can. You have already done so—"

"Yeah, I know. I was there. We still don't need to talk about that."

"I want to talk about it," said Marilyn.

"I'm with Sis. Let's hear all about it."

"While Dayzee was burning up Rake, the manager, I stood in front of Dayzee and pulled down—"

"Whoa! Let's try to focus, all three of you, alright? Let's get going and deal with that ash pile when we get back."

*　*　*

A half an hour later, the procession was lined up around Dayzee's circular drive leading to the exit gate of her estate. Dayzee sat in one pickup in the lead with Sophia behind her. Marilyn was next, and Kozy followed them all in the limo. Dayzee honked her horn twice, and the parade crawled toward the gate.

Once through, Dayzee turned right onto her street and pulled over to wait for the rest. They all exited and lined up behind her, then she hit the code on her phone to close the gate.

Before starting on their journey out of Beverly Hills, Dayzee turned and looked through the back window. She returned Marilyn's wave, then glanced down at the wrapped and writhing body squirming around in the truck bed. She sighed and shook her head just as a loud bang shattered the windshield and deflected up through the roof of the cab, letting in a thin ray of sunlight.

She turned to look, and through the cracked glass, saw a figure standing far down the street and holding what appeared to be a rifle.

"Oh, you gotta be kidding me," she said out loud. "I forgot all about you!"

She jammed the truck into drive and made a squealing turn to the left, into a neighbor's driveway. She glanced out through the passenger window and saw the man fumbling with the rifle, trying to move the stuck bolt.

"Holy crap!"

She backed out and screeched her tires until she was even with Marilyn's open window.

"Get out of here, Mare! Turn around and follow me! Make it snappy!"

"We have that shooter after us now?"

"No time to talk! Go!"

Marilyn burned her tires into the driveway across the street and was soon following Dayzee away from the gunman. Sophia did the same. Kozy revved the engine of the limo and rocketed straight toward the lone person attempting to assassinate Dayzee.

The limo roared down the street, tons of metal fishtailing as the rear tires fought for traction. Dayzee turned to watch. Sophia poked her head out of her window to see Kozy attacking, and Marilyn leaned over her steering wheel and covered her head.

The unidentified killer finally got the next round loaded and began to raise the rifle. It was almost up enough to send a volley toward Kozy, but the limo's heavy front bumper struck first. Dayzee and Sophia both watched as the shooter and rifle took separate paths high into the air.

Kozy hit the brakes and backed the limo up, running over the limp body lying in the street. A quick turn in one of the driveways allowed him to pull up next to Dayzee at the head of the line.

"It was not the assassin animating wooden items and dead bodies without heads."

"No, it sure as hell wasn't. I wonder who it was."

"There is no longer any way for you to recognize. It is now what is called 'roadkill.'"

"Well, sure, because you killed it in the road. Nice work, Kozy."

"I am here to assist you. Besides, what you just did for me back at your mansion was so—"

"Alright, already! Look, we really need to quit talking about that, you know? Just follow behind the three of us. We still need to get rid of these trucks."

"What about that roadkill body?"

"What about it? Someone will scrape it up to keep the neighborhood looking good."

*   *   *

Dayzee led them down her street and turned right on Elevado. They traveled a few blocks and took a left. She pulled into a driveway unblocked by a gate and parked up close to the garage. Everyone drove in behind her and shut off their motors.

After slamming her door, Dayzee walked back to Marilyn's truck.

"Marilyn, come on out of there. Take the keys."

She walked on and told Sophia the same thing.

"Kozy, keep the motor running. We're getting out of here."

"We're just leaving these trucks here, Dayzee?"

"Yeah, Mare. I know these people, and I don't really like them. The matriarch gave me a bad review once. More importantly, they're gone for the season."

"This is good, Dayzee," said Sophia. "It'll look like a yard crew is here working. No one will know the difference."

"Sure, until the real lawn guys show up, Sissy. Then what?"

"They'll call and have the trucks towed away, that's all," said Dayzee. She laughed and added, "Heck, they'll probably end up where we would have dumped them anyway."

"What about the almost dead guy?"

"We can't worry about every little detail, Mare. Things happen in the Hills—everyone accepts that. Someone will take it away."

"Is it still alive-ish?"

"Good question, Mare. Let me take a look."

Dayzee walked back to her truck and peeked into the bed. Nothing was moving. She shoved it and waited, but it still didn't move.

"It's back to being dead, girls. Come on, Kozy's ready to—"

"Kozy was really ready when you burned that bark man, I bet," said Marilyn.

"Really, really ready, Sis."

"Maybe I will tell you about that someday, girls. Over a bottle of my best whiskey. We really should go."

*   *   *

Dayzee tapped out the garage door code, and Kozy drove the limo in and shut off the engine.

"It's good to be home. You know, I'm actually getting a little tired," said Dayzee.

"Maybe you need another fountain of youth?"

"You might be right about that, Mare. That always perks me up."

"Sis and I only did it that one time, but wow, I still feel it," said Sophia.

"Me too, Sissy. Hey, when Dayzee gets a new batch of yard guys, you and I can pick two of them and—"

"No! Come on, you two, I do need someone to take care of this place. The Kildare Killers can go prowl for their own guys to use."

"Fine. How about that whiskey, then?"

"Sure, Fia. Let's go in."

They all exited the limo and slammed their doors shut. One by one, they filed in and down the hallway to the kitchen. Dayzee continued on toward the bar in the great room, and the other three sat at her kitchen table.

"I'm just waiting for a leg of this table to grab *my* leg, Sis."

"Kozy's here to protect us. Isn't that right, Kozy?"

"Yes, of course, but I believe the assassin has mutated to the point where it only wants sex with you three now."

"That just sounds obscene," said Sophia. "I can't believe what Bruno told us we have to do to kill it."

"When the time comes, you will—"

181

"When the time comes, Sissy. Maybe it's more like when the table—"

"Sheesh, Sis. That's gross. Besides, there's no way that can happen."

"Do not underestimate a product of sorsciencery. It is learning new methods as time goes on."

"Sheesh again, Kozy. Really gross."

Dayzee returned with a bottle and four glasses.

"What are you all talking about?"

"We were discussing the evolving abilities of the assassin to create conditions and manipulate inanimate objects and materials to mimic a common human sexual outcome."

They all stared at each other for several seconds before Sophia laughed and said, "You know what? I'll leave that to Dayzee. Dayzee, I nominate you for the honor."

"Why me?"

"Your mansion . . . your monsters."

"Sissy makes a lot of sense, Dayzee."

She looked from one twin to the other several times before speaking.

"Fine. When the time is right, I'll—"

"She means 'when the kitchen table is feeling romantic,' Sissy."

"Or maybe a dresser, Sis? Talk about getting into someone's drawers."

"That was a good one. How about the mantle from the fireplace?"

"Which one, Sis? This place is huge. There's so much wood—"

"Girls! I swear, no more fountains for either of you."

She uncapped the bottle, filled the four glasses, and passed them out.

"Cheers to all of you," Dayzee said with a smile and held up her glass.

The other three raised their glasses, then they all took a drink.

"I think we mostly have things back under control," said Dayzee. "The yard guys are cleaned up, and their trucks are gone. Mack got the dead guy out of the elevator, and now the dead guy is gone too. Kozy's here to help us out, and we know that when he has to leave, we'll have Kenzie back."

"You could pick right up where you left off, Sissy."

"I don't know about that. I do miss her, though. She's nice."

"Uh-huh. Sure."

"We figured out how to get Bruno back any time we need him too," said Dayzee.

"We could bring him back just for fun," said Marilyn.

"Sis is right. We could put him to work and kick his ass back through the portal when we've had enough."

"Sound a little selfish, Fia."

"Yep, it sure is."

"It was good to see Bruno again, but I'm not thrilled with what we have to do to—"

"What *you* have to do," said Marilyn. "You promised."

"I didn't promise! Oh, alright. Yeah, I'll do it."

"I want to watch," said Sophia. "We didn't see that fun little thing that happened in the foyer. You owe us."

"Sissy's right, Dayzee. I want to watch too."

"You two. I swear. Fine, you can watch. Besides that, what am I missing? Things are good, right?"

"Except for the blood and guts all over the limo," said Sophia.

"It's Beverly Hills, remember?" said Dayzee. "No one will even notice, and the next rain will clean it right up. What else?"

"I haven't seen those five knives in a while," said Marilyn. "That's kind of scary."

"Kozy will handle it, won't you, Kozy?"

"Yes, I am watching, even now."

"Good. Oh, and the crackpot that's been taking shots at me is smeared all over the street. That should be the end of that."

"Unless there are more than one after you," said Kozy.

"God, I didn't even think of that. You think there's a whole bunch of them out to get me?"

"You are pretty hot, Dayzee."

"No, Mare, I didn't mean *get* me. I meant *kill* me."

"Oh, yes. Well, how many wives have you pissed off?"

Dayzee started counting with the fingers on her left hand, then she looked at her right and continued. She went back to the left for more, then the right again, then—

"Dayzee! Okay, we get it—it's a lot. You've been busy in the Hills."

"I love it here, Fia. Yeah, there could be a whole army coming to kill me."

"Well, at least they're just humans," said Sophia, "but that should do it. We're sitting pretty good."

"I bet Dayzee was sitting pretty good on that old piece of bark, Sissy. I wish I could have watched."

"Yeah," Dayzee said with a laugh before she took another drink, "I bet that was a sight."

"Especially because Kozy was all agitated and—"

"And nothing! Focus, Mare. What else is going on that we have to worry about?"

Kozy spoke up. "Much of your mansion is damaged, and Cliff will likely return soon."

"Oh, dammit, that's right. We need a carpenter, or a furniture guy, or something."

"Let's get one of each," said Sophia.

"Young ones, Dayzee," said Marilyn.

"I can't even fight you two anymore. Fine, we'll get some unsuspecting human males in here to help clean the place up, but please, don't kill them until they finish, alright?"

"No guarantees," said Marilyn.

"I just want to enjoy life and be surrounded by people I like," said Sophia.

"Yeah, until you kill them," said Dayzee.

"Yes, because it's what Sissy and I are made to do," said Marilyn.

Chapter 18 – Things Happen, That's All

Still sitting around Dayzee's kitchen table, but with an empty whiskey bottle, Dayzee had an announcement.

"Alright, all of you. I say we take a break."

She picked her glass up high and tipped it above her open mouth with only two drops falling.

"Damn. What was I saying?"

"Breaking stuff?"

"Oh, I know, Mare—we should take a break. Think of all the crap we've been through today."

"It sure has been a busy day," said Sophia. "Even Kozy got busy."

"Maybe Kozy would get busy on finding another bottle of this stuff?"

"As you wish, Dayzee."

He picked up the bottle to check the label, then left for the bar.

"Remember to swagger," Sophia said with a snicker.

"There you go!" Marilyn said two seconds later.

"There's no rush to fix this place up. We probably won't see that Cliff character until—"

Dayzee stopped at the sound of her phone vibrating on the table. She picked it up, looked at it, and shook her head with a grin. She hit a button.

"Cliff. We were just talking about you. How the hell are you?"

She listened and held her glass up for Kozy to fill.

"Tomorrow? Cliff, that's too—"

She took a big sip while listening.

"Fine. No, it's alright. See you at 9:00."

Dayzee ended the call and set the phone down. She showed no trace of a smile as she picked up her glass of whiskey and finished it. After setting the empty glass on the table, she stared at it for a few seconds as everyone watched her and waited. She finally looked up.

"I don't believe it. He wants to bring a film crew in tomorrow to look everything over. He said they need to check lighting and stuff like that. Girls, we have work to do."

"No, we have people to hire," said Sophia. "We don't really work. You know that, Dayzee."

"Sissy's right. We can't fix anything in your mansion. We can sure look good for the cameras, though."

"There's no time to waste, girls. Remember my bed? That has to be replaced. Remember the trim up on the third floor? The door too? Kozy threw that all out the window."

"Don't forget the chair in your living room," said Sophia. "That thing was sure having some fun with you until Kozy destroyed it."

"Right, we need to replace that, too, and the trim in the foyer where it helped me take care of Rake."

"Rake Bark," Marilyn said with a giggle. "That's just silly. Oh, and we have to clean up pieces of Mr. Bark in the front yard."

"It's not pieces of Mr. Bark, Sis."

"I know, but it's fun to say so. Anyway, all that mulchy bark stuff has to be cleaned up. Oh, is there still a head stuck in a bush somewhere?"

"That's funny, Sis. The dead guy was looking for head, but the whole time, it had already found a bush."

Dayzee shook her own head and said, "Girls, that really is funny, but we have to get going on all of this."

"Let me know if I can be of service," said Kozy.

"Hey, maybe you can find those five knives now?"

"Fia's right, Kozy. Can you find those and lock them up somewhere?"

"Yes, I can. I will need to be more vigilant with guests in the house."

"What do you mean?" said Dayzee.

"Recall how the assassin helped you eliminate the yard crew manager. It wants you all to itself."

"That's creepy," said Marilyn. "You think it'll try to kill even the furniture delivery guys?"

"Yes. It does not want anyone else in the house now."

"How about by the pool?" said Sophia. "If you can keep them alive while they're inside, Sis and I can have some fun by the pool."

"I do not know."

"Girls, can't you just let these human men do their jobs and leave?"

"Oh, Dayzee," Marilyn said with a pleasant smile, "you know we can't do that."

"Nope. Like Sis says."

Dayzee sighed, then saluted Kozy.

"We'll scream if we need anything. Oh, can you get what's left of Rake cleaned up too?"

"Yes, Dayzee."

He stood, straightened his jacket, and arranged his hat before beginning the search.

"I can order furniture from a place I know in L.A., and for the right price, they'll deliver it really quick."

"How do you know that?" said Marilyn.

"Oh, such a sweet kid," Dayzee said while grinning at Sophia before turning back to Marilyn. "Mare, it's not the first time things have gotten rough here. First, I need to call a carpenter. He'll have to get here soon and get started."

Sophia stared at her glass as she tapped it on the table.

"What?" said Dayzee.

"I'm counting. That's one guy with a hammer and two to deliver the new furniture."

"One for each of us, Sissy."

"Mare, that's not—hey, you know, maybe you're right. Why not? We can each—"

"What about Kozy?" said Sophia. "Shouldn't we line someone up for him too?"

"Do we even know what a One-Eighty prefers?" said Marilyn.

"I sure do," said Dayzee. "He knew exactly what he wanted while we watched you two fry those yard guys."

"Alright, so why don't we let him take his pick?" said Sophia.

"I like that idea!" said Marilyn. "He can just jump in wherever he wants."

"You're right, Sis," said Sophia. "I know I'm going to put on a good show because I want him—"

"Girls! Try to remember that we really do need Kozy to protect us too. He's not here just for our amusement."

"Hey," said Marilyn, "how about if Sissy watches for knives and dead guys while I'm enjoying Kozy, then I'll watch for bad things while Sissy—"

"No! Look, you two, let's just worry about getting this place fixed up first, alright? Then, after we finally kill the assassin, we'll put that One-Eighty of ours to work on *all* of us!"

*   *   *

"Yes?"

"I'm the carpenter you called. Name's Kenny. See the truck?"

Dayzee looked past him at the pickup he'd left near her front door on the circular drive. A faded magnetic sign on the door read, "Kenny and his Tools."

"Wonderful. Another pickup."

His big eyes peered out from under the brim of a white cap covering bushy orange hair. Worn work boots, khaki shorts, and a baggy tank top completed his attire.

"What?"

"Nothing. I've just seen enough pickups for a lifetime. Got your tools, Kenny?"

"Yes, ma'am. Can you show me what you need done?"

"Oh, careful with your questions, Kenny. I just might be a little too honest for you."

Kenny looked away from Dayzee's eyes and focused on her breasts, which were barely covered by her tight white blouse. She brushed her long blond hair back over her shoulders. He kept going, looking all the way past the hem of her short black skirt, all the way down her shapely legs covered in fishnet, until he smiled at her short black boots with high heels.

"I think we could work something out, ma'am."

"Please, call me Dayzee."

"Sure thing, Dayzee. Maybe I should start with the carpentry you mentioned?"

"I guess that does make sense, doesn't it? Alright, come on in. The first project is right here in the foyer."

He walked in, and Dayzee closed the door. She was about to point out how the trim boards had somehow twisted away from the wall in several places, but the sound of a large truck rolling down the driveway caused her to reopen the door.

"Oh, good. The furniture is here already. Why don't you have a seat in the living room—but not on that busted up chair—and I'll get these furniture guys going."

"Sure thing, Dayzee."

He went to take a seat just as Marilyn and Sophia came down the stairs wearing only their short white robes.

"Girls . . . really?"

"It's either here or at the Prism," said Sophia.

"Maybe both, Sissy."

Dayzee sighed and said, "Well, you both do look really hot like that. You're just in time. Can you help the furniture guys find the right places for everything?"

"Everything except the furniture," said Marilyn.

"Sis makes a lot of sense," said Sophia.

"Alright, I know I can't control you two. Just don't burn down the house, alright?"

"No guarantees."

"Sis is joking. We probably won't even burn them."

"'Probably,' Sissy?"

"*Maybe* we won't burn them."

"Girls, be careful—we do want to have that reality show here, remember?"

"Oh, she's right, Sissy. Okay, Dayzee, we'll be good."

Dayzee nodded and turned toward the front door just as two young men were walking up the steps onto the porch.

"We have the furniture you ordered."

"Thanks for such good service. I can't believe how quickly you got here. I'm Dayzee."

"Hi. I'm Joey, and this is Arden."

Each wore baggy uniform pants and white polo shirts. Joey had black hair, and Arden's was a dirty blond.

"Arden . . . I like that name. Arden sounds familiar for some reason."

The delivery guys looked at each other for a second, then they both turned to look at the street. Joey said, "Oh, boy," and Arden laughed before they both turned back to Dayzee.

She opened the door wider and stepped out of the way. Joey and Arden stared into the foyer at the gorgeous blond and brunette twins, both dressed only in short robes and heels. Their mouths hung open, and they didn't blink.

"Uh . . . hi. I'm—"

"We heard. I'm Sophia, and this is my twin sister, Marilyn. Isn't she the hottest thing ever?"

"Oh yeah, she sure is," said Joey. "She . . . she's so—"

"I think maybe *you* are the hottest thing ever," Arden said while looking Sophia up and down.

"Why, thank you. I hear you boys brought a bed. Sis and I want to try it out."

"We do," said Marilyn. "We do everything together too."

Joey and Arden stared.

Dayzee said, "Girls, they have a job to do. Can you fellas take the bed upstairs? We need the chair right here,"—she pointed to the living room—"to replace that broken one. If you bring the wardrobe door inside, we'll take it up to the third floor."

They still stared at the twins in their short robes.

"Work first, alright, boys? After that, you're on your own. Good luck with those two."

Dayzee turned and walked into the living room.

*   *   *

"Hey, boys," said Sophia, "why don't you start with the chair—that's the easiest. Just bring inside the new door for the wardrobe. Let's save the bed for last."

"Sure, Sophia. That's a good plan," said Arden. "We'll get right to it."

"Is there an elevator in this mansion?" said Joey while looking around.

"Yes, but it's too small for the bed. You'll have to use the stairs. We'll be right ahead of you, showing you the way."

"Our robes are really short too," said Sophia. "That should be fun, don't you think?"

"Can't wait," said Joey.

"Yeah, let's do this!" said Arden.

*   *   *

"So, Kenny, we should probably—"

"I located only two of the knives so far, Dayzee."

Kenny turned to see Kozy standing near in boots, stretched khakis, showing a bare chest under a uniform jacket, and wearing a hat.

"Hey, you remind me of someone. Oh . . . Kenzie. You look a lot like this barmaid I know."

"I am an entity distinct and separate from Kenzie, but Kenzie is still—"

"On vacation. Kenzie is still on vacation. This is her brother, Kozy. I see the resemblance too."

"What? Kenzie has a brother?"

"Yeah, she sure does, Kenny," said Dayzee. "Except, Kozy is much more into fitness, which I see you've noticed. Look at those abs."

"Yeah, you ain't kidding."

"There are still three knives with unknown whereabouts. I suspect they are moving around to avoid detection."

"Three?" Dayzee said as she looked at Kenny, then she looked into the foyer at the two men carrying in the new chair and door for the wardrobe.

"Three. Yeah, that's the right number—that's all they'll need. I'm glad you're fast, Kozy."

"I might not be fast enough."

"What are you two talking about?"

"Oh, nothing, Kenny. Come on. Let's look at the work in the foyer first."

Dayzee got up with Kenny, and they both followed Kozy out of the living room, passing Joey and Arden carrying a chair as they brought it in to replace the broken one. Marilyn and Sophia were waiting.

"Do you girls have the furniture guys under control?"

"Ooh, that sounds good, Dayzee," said Marilyn.

"That's not what she meant, Sis. We'll wait until they're done delivering the stuff, Dayzee."

"Alright, good. I'll show Kenny all the things that need to be fixed up."

"They're bringing your new bed in last," said Sophia. "That's where we'll be."

"Trying it out for you, Dayzee."

"You're such a big help, Mare."

Dayzee shook her head and pointed at the broken and twisted trim boards.

"See how messed up that trim is, Kenny?"

"What the hell happened to it?"

"Who knows? Things happen, that's all. Come on, let's check the upstairs."

They walked together and began up the stairs, with Dayzee smiling at the view as Kozy led the way.

*   *   *

At the landing, where the kitchen stairway changed directions on the way to the second floor, Kozy waved a hand to stop Dayzee and Kenny. He leaned over to peek around the post, causing his hat to tip until he straightened it out.

"That hat sure adds a certain something, doesn't it, Kenny?"

"Sure. I guess."

Kozy turned around and said, "It appears to be safe and free of knives."

"Why do you two keep talking about knives?" said Kenny.

"He's like a bodyguard for me and the girls, that's all. Kind of overprotective."

"I'll say. Obsessed with knives too."

"Go ahead, Kozy, lead the way."

He stepped around the post, took three steps up, then looked all the way up to the second floor, and so did Dayzee. Kenny only looked across at Dayzee's cleavage, and he didn't see that one knife was floating directly in their path, the blade pointed down the stairs toward them.

"Kozy, that's—"

The knife raced out of sight to the left.

"I will be vigilant."

"I know you will, Kozy. Alright, let's show Kenny the damage upstairs."

Kozy continued to lead them up the next stairway to the third floor. The stairs led to a small landing and a doorway without a door, and beyond that, they found the quiet upstairs room.

Before allowing Dayzee and Kenny to enter, Kozy peeked in both directions, didn't see any knives, and stepped aside to let them in.

Chapter 19 – More Dead Bodies

"Sissy, it's too big! They'll never get that thing up there!"

Marilyn and Sophia stood on the first landing, wearing their tiny robes and high heels, and looked down on the struggling delivery guys.

"Nonsense, Sis," said Sophia. "Hey, you two, break time is over. Let's give it another try."

"Man, you don't understand," said Joey. "This son of a bitch is heavy."

"Can't even get a good hold on it," said Arden.

The twins turned to each other and grinned before looking back down the stairs.

"Maybe you can get a good hold on me, instead?" Marilyn said as she ran her palms up and down her thighs.

"We're twins, you know," said Sophia. "Double trouble for you boys if you can finish your job first."

They both stared up the stairs at the beautiful twins standing only a few steps above them. They grinned before looking at each other, and Joey said, "Let's do this."

Arden whispered, "Let's do *them*!"

"I heard that!" said Marilyn.

"We didn't mean any disrespect. We were just—"

"Thinking about what's waiting for you?" said Sophia. "Better get moving, then."

* * *

"The third floor has the rest of the damage. See that door? No? That's because it's gone. We'll need a new one. That trim along the floor is all messed up too."

"What the hell happened up here, if you don't mind me asking?"

Dayzee walked up to Kenny, causing him to try to back away, but Kozy was standing right behind him. Dayzee stood inches away and said, "All kinds of fun things happen in this house. You've seen enough of the boring woodwork stuff."

She started unbuttoning her blouse and said, "Maybe you need to see something fun, not stupid wood things?"

"I . . . um . . ." he said as he stared at her cleavage.

Kozy said, "I must remind you, Dayzee, that you have scheduling constraints."

"Have you heard Mare talk about getting itchy? Fia too? Well, add me to that list."

She looked into Kenny's eyes.

"There's something that needs much more attention than carpentry that I want to show you."

Dayzee kept working her buttons loose and glanced up at Kozy, who was staring past her, so she turned to look. One of the lost knives hovered near the end of the room, its point holding still while the handle spun in slow circles.

"Kozy?"

"He is in danger, not you. I believe it will save you for later."

"Well, that doesn't sound too good either. Is it coming after us?"

"No. It is only watching."

"It's doing what?"

"Nothing. I meant that it is pointing at us."

"Alright, then, keep your eyes on it. This boy has his eyes on me. You're not afraid of that knife, are you, Kenny?"

He kept staring at her breasts and said, "Nope. Don't care. You are . . . you're so . . . hot."

"Earth, Kozy. So easy."

Dayzee had popped all of her buttons and pulled her blouse open, giving the smiling carpenter a good sight.

"Not bad, huh?"

"God, they're magnificent."

"You can touch them all you want, you know."

He still stared with a silly grin.

"That wasn't a request, Kenny."

Just as he began reaching out, Kozy gently tipped Dayzee's head to the side and caught a knife whose pointy end just barely touched Kenny's cheek, causing a small bead of blood to appear.

"Whew, that was close. Nice work, Kozy."

"There is still danger."

"Good, I like what that does to you. You don't mind that little knife distraction, do you, Kenny?"

He looked away from the knife as Kozy lowered it, and he focused again on Dayzee's opened blouse.

"What distraction? All I want is—"

Two soft squishy thumps rang out in the quiet attic, and Kenny screamed and slumped to the floor unconscious. A knife protruded from each of his calves.

"Why, those little shits!" said Dayzee. "One faked us out, and the other two ambushed him from behind?"

"It is learning strategy."

"Their aim sucks, though."

"Yes, that is true, Dayzee. At least, we have recovered all of the knives, so we can—"

The two knives wiggled around, eased back out of Kenny's legs, and quickly fled to the far side of the room, leaving strings of red drops to mark their path.

"They will surely strike again."

"Yeah, I bet, but you're watching them this time. You *are* watching them, right?"

"Yes, and the third knife is still in my hand."

Dayzee kept her eyes on the knives and said, "Kozy, do you think you could carry Kenny? He's not going to be walking anytime soon."

"I can easily carry him if you wish. Where shall I place the body?"

"Body? He just passed out—he's not dead! Oh God, I don't know. We don't want the furniture guys to see him. Hey, how about tossing him in the elevator? We could get rid of those other two then come back to help him."

"The elevator can offer some level of containment should he become possessed. That is a good choice."

"Perfect. Hoist him up, and let's go."

Dayzee followed Kozy carrying Kenny through the open doorway and said, "I wish he would have replaced the door first. There's no way to lock those knives up here."

"At least, I have one of them. I will be ready if they attack again."

"Two knives and two furniture guys. Oh, that math isn't good. I'm guessing two more dead guys coming up."

*   *   *

"I think they need more encouragement, Sissy," Marilyn said as she untied her belt and opened her robe. "Look at what I'm going to show them."

"Sis, they're already trying. I think you're just doing that for yourself. You like being naked too much."

"Yes, I really do. Why don't you do the same?"

"Oh, you'd like that, wouldn't you?"

"You know I would, Sissy—yours are stunning."

"So are yours, Sis. Alright, you talked me into it."

Sophia loosened her belt and pulled her robe open and off of her shoulders. She held it around her waist and shook back her long black hair. Marilyn laid her head on her sister's shoulder, and they both smiled down at the two young men.

"Hurry, boys. We're waiting," said Marilyn.

"You like twins? Get that stupid bed up here already."

198

Joey and Arden pushed against the bulky, heavy headboard, straining to pick it up one more step. The girls heard something whizzing past their heads just as the movers lost their grip. They stumbled, slipped back down a step, and the large wooden cargo tipped and covered them, just as the two knives struck and stuck.

"Oh, that was lucky, Sis."

"Look at the knives, Sissy. They're twitching around and trying to get back out."

Kozy rushed between the twins, spinning them around and causing Sophia to lose her robe altogether, and grabbed the handles of both knives.

Dayzee came up behind them and said, "That was close, girls. Looks like Kozy has things in hand."

"We will soon, too, Dayzee," said Sophia. "I say we leave that thing where it is and let these boys take a rest."

"Sissy's right. They've worked so hard, and they deserve a treat."

"We're the treats," said her sister.

"What about me, girls? I want some fun too."

"You have your own guy. Hey, where is he anyway?"

"Gone."

"He left?"

"Um . . . no, Mare."

"Oh. Something happened to him?"

Dayzee nodded, looked away, and said, "Never mind those knives, you guys. Let's get that thing upstairs already."

"Before it's too late," Marilyn whispered to her sister. "Earth guys are so easy. They don't even care that knives are flying around on their own and trying to kill them."

"Sometimes, I kind of like Earth, Sis."

Sophia picked up her robe and slipped it back on. She and her sister both left their robes untied, and Dayzee's blouse was still unbuttoned. Kozy held three bloody knives, and Joey and Arden managed to bring the headboard up to the landing.

"Good job, Joey," said Marilyn. "You're my hero."

"Arden, too, Sis. I think we should all show them how much we appreciate them."

"Dayzee too?"

They both looked at Dayzee, who nodded quickly with a big grin.

"I'm in," said Dayzee. "But Kozy, find someplace safe for those knives, alright?"

"I will."

He squeezed back up the stairs between the twins and disappeared down a long hallway.

"Alright, guys," said Dayzee, "this is the last item. How about if we get it into the bedroom and set it up?"

"Sure thing. Come on, Arden, we got this."

Within a few minutes, they'd set up the bed, including the mattress. Before even adding a sheet, Marilyn threw Joey down onto it on his back.

"Hey, I don't know. There are a lot of people—"

"Don't be shy," Marilyn said as she climbed up to sit on his lap. "Help me out of this robe, please."

With the mattress bouncing from Sophia pushing Arden down next to him, Joey stared at Marilyn's breasts, pulled her robe down over her shoulders, and let it fall behind her.

"I'm already naked, Sis," Sophia said as she sat on Arden and put her arm around her sister's waist.

"Aw, look, Sissy," said Marilyn. "Two more hypnotized human men. It's not even a challenge."

"I really do like Earth sometimes."

They each reached for their guy's belt as the bedroom door slammed shut with Kozy on the inside and leaning against it.

"What's wrong?" said Dayzee. "Oh, it's obvious something bad is happening."

"Yes, I am certainly reacting to the adversity. The knives began spinning in my hands, and I was forced to let them go."

There were three loud splintering sounds, and the points of the knives poked into the room in a pattern around Kozy's head.

Both Marilyn and Sophia turned to look.

"That's not good," Dayzee said and looked at his growing muscles and a noticeable bulge. "Except for that. That's kind of good."

"He has things under control, Sissy," Marilyn said as she turned back to Joey and reached for his belt.

"Yep, he's amazing, Sis."

Both girls began unbuckling, then they heard scraping sounds, turned around again, and saw the knives wiggling back out from the door.

"Good, they gave up, Sis. Let's give these guys a treat already."

"Yes, Sissy, I think they're ready for us."

"Kozy's ready for some attention, too, girls," said Dayzee. "Maybe I'll get going on him, and—"

Dust and bits of plaster above the bed began raining down on Joey and Arden, but their eyes never left the naked twin girls sitting on them. Every other pair of eyes looked up at the ceiling, where the points of two knives were slowly twisting through and protruding farther with every second.

"Uh-oh, Sissy. That's not good. Kozy? A little help here?"

Kozy sprinted over, his hat falling to the floor behind him, and reached around the twins, trying to grab the speedy knives dropping from the ceiling, but it was too late. A sharp blade planted itself in each furniture mover's chest before Kozy could get a grip on their handles. Both men still stared at the naked women on their laps, but when the girls waved their hands over their faces, they didn't move.

"Here we go again, Sissy. More dead bodies."

"This mansion seems to always be full of them, Sis."

"You know what else, girls?" said Dayzee. "Now, we have a furniture truck to get rid of too."

With Kozy squeezing them together, the twins turned to face each other only inches apart, both resting their heads back onto Kozy's hard chest.

"Oh, hi there, Sis."

"I kind of like Kozy holding us like this, Sissy. This would make a fantastic photo."

"Maybe like this?" Sophia said before she turned her head and looked up into his eyes.

"Ooh, I like that. Me too."

Both twins were cheek to cheek between Kozy's arms, their faces pressed against his bare chest and gazing up with smiles.

"Now, that's a photo I'd hang on the wall," said Dayzee.

"Hey, Dayzee," said Sophia. "Where's that photo guy of yours?"

"Girls, we have bigger problems to deal with. That assassin is probably going to take control of those two now."

"Not if I remove the knives," Kozy said before sloshing the knives out of their chests, holding them up above them, and letting them drip.

"Now, that's a good shot too," said Dayzee. "Two gorgeous, naked girls pushed up against each other by the remarkable Kozy, who's so obviously reacting to the danger. Oh, and the dead guys make it kind of interesting too. Only one thing would make it better."

"I know," said Marilyn. "If I gave Sissy a kiss."

"Exactly, but there's no time. Kozy, can you lock up those two knives? Keep a lookout for the last one too. It's still roaming these hallways somewhere."

Kozy backed off of the bed and walked to the door with the knives, and Marilyn said, "There's time," and gave her sister a quick kiss.

"You're sweet, Sis," Sophia said and gave Marilyn a kiss right back.

"Girls, there's really no time for that, even though I could watch that all day. Kozy, we have to—"

Dayzee froze at the sight of dead Joey and Arden sitting up with glazed-over eyes. The twins scurried down from the bed and ran toward the door, where they slipped their robes back on.

"That didn't take long," said Marilyn. "What are we going to do?"

"That assassin is back to taking over dead guys, and it doesn't need to stick something wooden into them," said Dayzee. "Kozy, can you toss them somewhere?"

"Yes, of course, Dayzee. How about in the elevator?"

"No, the stabbed carpenter guy is in there, remember? Maybe put them in the back of their truck?"

"That is a practical and effective utilization of available resources."

"I love when Kozy talks like that," said Marilyn.

The dead men had crawled off of the bed and were staggering toward the twins, Dayzee, and Kozy. He rushed over and picked them up, holding each of them tight over a shoulder, while their arms and legs kicked in every direction, and while he held two bloody blades in one hand.

"God, Dayzee," said Sophia. "The bizarre things that happen in your mansion."

"Yeah, I know. Never a dull moment."

Dayzee opened the door to let Kozy through with the heavy cargo, and they all hiked down the stairs to the first floor, where he left through the front door. He tossed the squirming dead men into the back, rolled the door down, and latched it. A second later, he opened the door just enough to toss the two knives inside and locked the door again.

Back inside, he closed the mansion's front door and locked it.

"Are they jumping around in there, Kozy?" said Dayzee.

"No. They stopped moving once they were confined inside the vehicle."

"So, the assassin left them. Everyone be careful of anything made of wood or anything else."

"We will, Dayzee," said Marilyn. "I still can't believe what you'll have to do to kill that thing."

"I'm not looking forward to it, you know."

"Maybe you have to," said Sophia. "You know, maybe just try to enjoy it?"

"Oh, you'd like that, wouldn't you? You all want to watch, I bet."

"Yes, we sure do. Why don't you call that Jiffy guy of yours to video the whole thing?"

"His name is Jiff, and I don't think I want that recorded, whatever it turns out to be. Besides, we still have work to do. Those knives kind of messed up the carpenter. Kozy trapped him in the elevator."

"I can relocate him to the truck too," said Kozy.

"No, he's not even dead."

"He might be by now, Dayzee."

"Yeah, he just might. Let's go take a look. Everyone watch out for the last knife too."

"If he's still alive, I know what I want to do," said Marilyn. "I'm even itchier now since Sissy and I almost had those guys."

"Sis is right. We can take turns with him."

"Fine. Count me in," said Dayzee. "Maybe we can help Kozy out too. All this perilous stuff!"

"I'll do it," said Marilyn. "I will definitely help him out."

"Well, this is shaping up to be quite the party. Come on, girls, let's—"

The front door shook with the rapid pounding from someone on the porch. Dayzee and the twins and Kozy all looked at each other before Dayzee unlocked the door and swung it in.

"Oh, Cliff! What are you doing here?"

Chapter 20 – A Really Hard Bargain

Dayzee took a step back from the doorway, and Cliff looked past her to see Marilyn and Sophia wearing only short white robes and heels and Kozy in a uniform that was disheveled and spotted with wet blood.

He smiled and said, "Girls, you look lovely. You too, Dayzee," then he turned for a quick peek at her before studying Kozy. "Kozy, you do have a striking appearance, even if you're still playing with knives and fake blood."

"The knives do not participate in any form of recreation, and the blood is not—"

"What he means," said Dayzee, "is that we had a messy accident cleaning up the Halloween stuff, that's all. So, Cliff, what brings you here?"

"Sorry to arrive unannounced, but I'd really like to see more than just the first floor. Any chance I could take a quick walk through the upper levels?"

"Why, sure, Cliff," said Dayzee. "Come on in."

Cliff stepped inside, and Dayzee closed the door.

"You're sure this isn't a bad time? I did notice that you're taking some deliveries, and it looks like you've put a carpenter to work. I could always—"

"No, it's a good enough time. The carpenter and delivery guys are on break."

"Well, if they're in the kitchen, I don't need to disturb—"

"They're not even in the house. I think they walked somewhere to get tacos."

"Oh. Why didn't they just drive?"

"Who knows, Cliff? It's the Hills. Should we be surprised by anything people do?"

"No, I don't suppose so."

She took Cliff's arm and turned to look at the twins.

"Girls, would you like to lead the way?"

"Of course," Marilyn said before she took her sister's hand. "Come on, Sissy."

They led the way up the stairs, followed by Dayzee and Cliff with Kozy close behind. Dayzee remained silent and glanced over to see Cliff studying the long, exposed legs of the twins, plus a little bit more that their short robes didn't hide. When his stare turned into a grin, Dayzee laughed.

"How's that for a sight, Cliff? Are they gorgeous, or what?"

"My goodness. I'm speechless. I'd greedily spend an eternity stomping on this staircase."

"Sadly, the stairs do end, but you should get used to sights like that if you're going to be around us a lot."

Marilyn giggled and turned to look quickly at Cliff, then she looked back up the stairs and put her arm around Sophia's waist. Sophia did the same to her sister.

"Twins, huh?" Dayzee said with her own giggle. "Oh, the things that happen around here. You'd be shocked, Cliff."

"As long as we get it all on video, I'll be happy. We're about to have the most popular show ever."

"I certainly hope so. Don't forget that Kozy is quite a specimen too."

Cliff looked back, shook his head with a smile, and said, "Specimen is right."

He turned back to Dayzee.

"My, oh my, and then there's you. Please, please don't ask me to pick between you or either one of these twins. I believe it would be whichever of you I happen to be hypnotized by at the moment."

Marilyn giggled and said, "He said he was hypnotized, Sissy."

"That's pretty funny, Sis. Earthmen."

"What about the men of this planet?" said Cliff.

After the twins stopped and looked at each other, the rest of them stopped too. They didn't turn around, but Marilyn shrugged, and Sophia shook her head before they continued the procession up the steps.

They all paused in the roomy lounge area at the top of the stairs, which had a long hallway leading off of it in each direction.

"Pick a lane, Cliff," said Dayzee, "and we'll show you everything."

"You're teasing me. I know you are, and I love it."

"Who's teasing," said Marilyn. "Not me. Not Sissy either. These little robes can just—"

"Okay, girls, settle down. Cliff, why don't we start with this wing?" Dayzee said and pointed to her right.

"Excellent, as long as Marilyn and Sophia lead the way. I do believe I'd happily follow them across a burning field of broken glass overrun with giant, hissing, diseased scorpions. Barefoot."

"Aw, that's sweet!" said Marilyn.

"Yep," said Sophia, "he's a sweet talker, alright."

"Oh," said Cliff, "that looks like an elevator on the right. You even have an elevator, Dayzee?"

"Yeah, that's one of them, but it's not working at the moment."

"Can I help?" he said and approached the door with a hand outstretched to hit the button.

Marilyn and Sophia pushed him up against the wall and pressed into him, each thrusting a naked knee between his legs, and Dayzee said, "Don't do that! I think it might be an electricity thing, and you might get zapped."

"Oh, okay. I must say, though, I like being pushed around like this and restrained too."

Cliff smiled at each of the sisters as they let him go and took a step back. He cocked his head to one side and leaned his ear closer to the closed elevator door.

"Hey, I think I heard something."

"I didn't hear anything," said Dayzee. "Girls, did you hear anything?"

"Nope," said Sophia, and Marilyn shook her head.

"It was barely above the lower limits of your auditory senses," said Kozy. "It sounded like—"

"Oh, you're just being silly, Kozy," said Dayzee. "This house is as quiet as—"

"Help me!" came from inside the elevator car.

"I know you heard that," Cliff said with a big grin. "Is someone hiding out in there?"

"Oh, that might be the carpenter or one of the delivery guys. He must have gotten stuck in there."

"Let's get him out, then."

"No, Cliff, he'll be fine. You need to see the rest of the—"

"I'm really bleeding in here. Please. There's blood everywhere."

"He's bleeding? What happened to him?"

"Oh, I know what's going on," said Sophia. "We talked to him about all of our Halloween pranks, and he's just being funny."

"He's a really funny guy," said Marilyn.

"He certainly is," said Dayzee. "Girls, why don't you take dear Cliff around to some of the rooms? Kozy and I will straighten out that joker in the elevator, won't we, Kozy?"

"Yes. We can dispose of—"

"Discuss with him! No, Kozy, you mean we can discuss with him how he's not so amusing."

Cliff stared at Kozy, and Dayzee broke the silence, saying, "Kozy's pretty funny too. Go on, the three of you. We'll catch up in a few minutes."

Each of the twins took an arm and coaxed Cliff away and down the hall. He smiled at one, then the other, and Sophia turned back to wink at Dayzee. When they'd disappeared into the nearest bedroom, Dayzee turned to Kozy.

"Look, we can't leave him in there. If he starts screaming or something, we're going to be—"

"He has become silent. He is likely deceased now."

"No, he can't be. Really? Just from two knives poking him like that?"

"Earthmen have a tenuous hold on life and expire rather easily. We will soon learn of his condition."

Kozy hit the button, and the door slid open. Kenny lay slumped against the back wall in a large puddle of blood. Before Dayzee could comment, the last rogue knife whistled between them and embedded itself in Kenny's chest.

"Oh, that's not good," Dayzee said as Kenny's eyes opened, and he sat up. "Now, it's just stabbing dead bodies for the thrill of it."

Kenny began to snarl.

"Kozy, can you—"

"Great, you got the thing opened up," Cliff said as he approached them in the hallway.

"Stop! Go look at another bedroom!"

"Sure, Dayzee. You seem kind of agitated. Is everything okay?"

"Yeah, Cliff. It's just that I've had so many problems with this elevator."

Kozy stepped past her and held dead Kenny by his throat as his arms swung around and his fists pounded on the walls.

"What the hell?"

"Come on, Cliff," said Marilyn. "Sissy and I will give you a special tour."

"Sis is right. Maybe you should pick out your favorite bedroom in case you stay overnight?"

"Give him a really memorable tour, girls, alright?" Dayzee said while nodding to each of the twins.

"We definitely will," said Marilyn.

They led him away, and Dayzee leaned back to see inside the elevator, where Kozy had managed to pull the knife out of Kenny's chest. He'd flopped back to the floor, and Kozy held the dripping knife out to show Dayzee.

"Good, that's the last one. What did you do with the other two?"

Kozy looked at the ceiling with a smile before shrugging and turning back to Dayzee and saying, "I threw them into the truck with the bodies."

"You did what?"

"I placed them inside the furniture transport vehicle."

"Why would you do that? Won't they just stick themselves back in one or both of those dead guys?"

"The assassin might do that, but it no longer needs to."

"Well, maybe the dead guys will come hunting us with those knives, then?"

"Oh. Your prediction is likely correct. I should have considered the ramifications of—"

"What's going on with you, Kozy? You don't make mistakes like that."

"I am not sure. My self-perceptions are somewhat humorous."

"Huh?"

"Oh, I believe the correct phrase is that 'I am feeling funny.'"

"Are you sick?"

"No. I understand what is happening. I am losing my hold on this earthgirl named Kenzie."

"Oh, that happened to Bruno too. He got poofed out of here right when we needed him most. He said he had a mobile portal built into him."

"I am not a strictly physical being. That is why my portal is telepathic in nature. My grip is fading."

"What will happen? Are you going to disappear or something?"

Kozy's eyes blinked slowly, and a shaking hand reached the knife out toward Dayzee. Just as Dayzee took the knife from him, he fell to the floor with eyes rolled up high.

"Wonderful," Dayzee said as the bloody blade began to twist and squirm in her hand.

"Even better," she said with a laugh.

"What's so funny?"

"Oh, thank God, Kozy. I'm glad you're—"

"What did you call me? Don't you remember my name, Dayzee?"

"Kenzie? I mean, yeah, of course. Kenzie. How are you feeling?"

Dayzee saw that Kenzie had truly returned: her features, her lack of facial hair . . . even her bare breasts only partially covered by the uniform jacket.

"Exhausted! Hey, where are we? What's with the knife?"

Kenzie looked down at her long, slender legs lost in the stretched khakis and the rest of her uniform and said, "What is this? Where did these clothes come from? Where's my shirt?"

"It's a long story," Dayzee said and extended a hand to help her up.

Kenzie stood and looked down at her jacket as she started to button it, causing her hat to tip and fall off.

"A hat too? Is this some kind of joke?"

Dayzee retrieved the hat and placed it back on Kenzie's head.

"It's a really long story, Kenzie. We're at my house, and this is one of the elevators. Marilyn and Sophia are here, and we—"

"Is that a dead guy? Is that his blood on that knife? What the hell is—

"No, no, no. This is all a bunch of stupid Halloween stuff we've been trying to clean up. Yeah, that's it—you're wearing your costume. It's pretty damn hot too."

Kenzie finished buttoning her jacket while squinting and staring at Dayzee. Just as she began reaching for her hat, Dayzee watched as her legs swelled up with new muscle, including a large bulge right where Dayzee was staring. The jacket stretched, popping all of the buttons and sending them bouncing around on the elevator floor, and Kozy's muscular chest pushed the jacket open.

"Kenzie, you're—"

"I am Kozy. I cannot stay. I have only moments remaining before I will permanently depart. I will follow your instructions to help with the earthgirl's return. She will likely not believe any memories of the experiences which we have shared. What would you have me do?"

"Oh God, Kozy . . . I don't know. Hey, I know: let's put you in one of the beds. I'll get you all tucked in, and when you're gone, Kenzie will think it was all a crazy dream!"

"We should hurry. I am sorry I must leave while you are in danger."

"Mm . . . you sure are reacting to that danger, aren't you? It'd be a shame to let that go to waste."

"I recommend we hurry with your plan. The quantity of time remaining before my exit is unpredictable."

"Unpredictable. You just said a mouthful."

"I do not understand the nuances of words as well as I should."

"That's okay—I'll show you," Dayzee said as she joined Kozy in the elevator and hit the button to close the door. "You just hold still and think about all the danger all around us. There's a whole lot of danger, Kozy."

*　　*　　*

"This is my favorite bedroom," Marilyn said as she climbed up on the king-sized bed and sat back on her heels.

"Me too," Sophia said as she joined her sister and sat behind her, close enough that she could reach around her waist.

"Oh, my goodness," said Cliff. "That's a real sight, right there. Already, this is my favorite bedroom too."

"It gets better," said Sophia, and she started to untie the belt of her sister's robe.

"Uh-oh. Sissy's undressing me."

"God, she really is, isn't she?" said Cliff, and he walked up to the foot of the bed and faced them.

"She likes to undress me. Don't you, Sissy?"

"Oh, yeah. It usually starts like this,"—she opened Marilyn's robe and pulled it down over her shoulders—"just because she's so stunning. Aren't they scrumptious, Cliff?"

"God yeah," he said as he stared without a smile.

"I always end up naked too," said Sophia. "Isn't that right, Sis?"

"Mm-hmm. Sissy's gorgeous without any clothes, Cliff. It always happens this way: Sissy undresses me first,"—Sophia tossed her sister's robe to the floor— "because she can never wait to get me naked. Isn't that right, Sissy?"

"Oh yeah," Sophia said with a grin as she opened her own robe, removed it, and tossed it over the edge with the other robe. "And just like that, we're both naked."

Sophia placed her arms back around her sister's waist.

"My God, you're both absolutely perfect."

"I'm most definitely a human woman, and I always enjoy it," said Marilyn.

"You're a what?" said Cliff, still not looking up into her eyes.

"Sis is just being silly again."

"Yes, I am. Why don't you climb up here and stand real close?" said Marilyn. "I like how Sissy is hugging me so tight."

Cliff stared down at Marilyn's breasts as her sister's hands started moving up from her belly until she found a way to keep them occupied. He hurried up onto the bed and stood to one side of the twins.

"We accept the deal you offered us, Cliff," said Sophia. "You drive a really hard bargain."

"Sissy has a way with words, doesn't she, Cliff?"

"Sis sometimes talks too much," said Sophia. "There's only one reliable way to stop that, Cliff."

He stepped in closer.

"I . . . I'm not sure I should—"

"I need your help to keep Sis nice and quiet, Cliff. Go on. I'm holding her still for you."

Cliff took another step on the bed and had no room to take another. Marilyn reached up for his belt. Within seconds, Cliff had accepted Sophia's recommendation.

"Oh, there we go. Perfect, Cliff. Sometimes that's the only way. See how quiet she is now?"

"Oh, she really is. My God . . ."

After a minute, Sophia said, "I tend to talk too much myself, sometimes, just like my sister. Why don't you see what you can do about that?"

"Yeah. Yeah, you really do."

"See, Cliff?" said Marilyn. "Now, Sissy is nice and quiet. She's really holding me tight too."

"My God . . ."

"It's so delightful that we can all have such a nice, quiet time together, Cliff. You and me and Sissy."

*   *   *

Dayzee stood and said, "Wow, Kozy. You're still so . . . so . . . that's still—"

"I do not tire as long as there is any risk at all."

"No, you sure don't. Just keep thinking about all that danger, alright?"

"As you wish."

"Because, you know, I'm sure not done with you yet."

Dayzee worked at pulling Kozy's pants down farther and watched as the obvious effects of the hazards they still faced faded and disappeared altogether.

"What's going on now, Dayzee?"

"Oh, Kenzie! I was just tidying you up a little."

"By pulling down my pants?"

She grabbed Kenzie's pants, pulled them up as far as she could, and zipped.

"No, I was just straightening things out. There you go. All better."

"Right. My Halloween costume. I must have blacked out for a second, but that helped—I feel so much more relaxed now. For some reason, I wish I had my cigarettes."

Dayzee coughed and said, "Well, you look absolutely lovely in this costume. Come on, let's leave this mess to clean up later."

She took Kenzie's hand and led her into the hall, where Kenzie took the knife from her and tossed it into the elevator car.

"No, Kenzie, we can't leave that in there!"

"Nonsense, Dayzee," she said and hit the button, causing the door to slide shut. "We can pick that all up some other time."

"Oh, I don't know about that. Alright, let's go find Mare and Fia."

"I'm glad they're here too. Where are they?"

"One of these bedrooms, I think."

They walked down the hall, and just as they arrived at a closed bedroom door, it opened, and the twins stepped out into the hallway.

"Girls, Kenzie finally woke up."

Dayzee paused to hold the gaze of each of the twins.

"Kenzie?" said Sophia. "It's good to see you again!"

"What, because I took a nap? Must have been some kind of party."

"What party?" said Marilyn.

"The Halloween party, silly," said Dayzee. "Look, Kenzie is still wearing her costume."

"That's one hell of a costume," Sophia said as she looked Kenzie up and down. "You should wear that all the time."

Kenzie looked down at herself and said, "Hey, what happened to the buttons? Shouldn't there be buttons?"

"It was a wild party," said Sophia. "Besides, it looks just fine the way it is."

Kenzie held her jacket tightly closed and said, "Yeah, well, that robe of yours looks good too."

"I bet Sissy will wear that all the time now," said Marilyn.

"Hey, what did you do with Cliff?" said Dayzee.

"We kept him busy awhile," said Marilyn. "He kind of dozed off."

"I'm kind of sleepy too," said Kenzie. "Maybe I should take a nap, if you don't mind, Dayzee."

"Alright by me. Maybe Fia could get you tucked in."

"Sissy could sure do that."

"Yep, come on, Kenzie. A nap is a good idea."

She took Kenzie's hand and turned with her to walk down the hall.

"Sissy, you probably need a nap too," Marilyn said with a giggle.

Her sister only turned to flash a grin, and they continued toward one of the many bedrooms in Dayzee's mansion. The bedroom door next to Dayzee swung in, and Cliff stood there smiling with his eyes half-closed.

"Wow, hell of a tour."

"I told you, Cliff," said Dayzee. "All kinds of amazing things happen in this house. Have you seen enough yet?"

He turned his head to look at Marilyn's smile, then he studied her all the way down along her legs and back up again.

"Sure. For now. What happened to Sophia? And Kozy?"

"Kozy got tired, so Sophia is helping to find someplace to take a nap. Marilyn and I can walk you out. It was good of you to stop by. It's been a fun visit."

"I'll say. Okay, lead the way. Maybe that elevator is—"

"No! I mean, it's still not working right. We'll have to take the stairs."

"Fine. I have an appointment I need to get to, so I better move along. I have a feeling that if I stayed much longer, I'd never want to leave."

"This house is funny like that," said Dayzee. "Come on. Let's get you on your way."

They all turned to look down the hall, where Sophia stood alone looking into a bedroom. A hand reached out, and Sophia accepted it. Her arm got pulled out, and she followed the coaxing and disappeared into the bedroom. The door closed behind her.

"Aw, they're both sleepy," said Marilyn. "I think Sissy really missed—"

"Kozy," said Dayzee. "Even though Kozy has been here the whole time, right, Mare?"

"Oh, right. Yes."

She hooked her arm around Cliff's and said, "Come on, Cliff. I'll tell Sissy you said goodbye."

Chapter 21 – Some Serious Wood

"Oh, Sissy, I didn't think we'd see you for a while."

Dayzee and Marilyn had just closed the mansion's front door after Cliff walked out to get in his car and leave. They stood in the foyer and watched Sophia come down the grand staircase wearing her short skirt, heels, and a tight red blouse.

"Why is that, Sis? Oh, you thought—"

"Yes, I sure did. Dayzee did, too, I bet."

"Yeah, I thought for sure you'd—"

"No, I only tucked Kenzie in and got dressed."

"So, Kenzie is all cozy again. That's kind of funny because Kenzie isn't Kozy anymore, she's just cozy, not—"

"Yes, that certainly is funny, Mare. I don't know about you girls, but I'm starving. We could order something, I suppose, because all I have in there now is ice cream, maybe some cookies, and I think some TV dinners."

"That all sounds good," said Sophia. "I've worked up an appetite."

"Yes, Sissy, you, me, and Cliff too."

"So did Kozy and I," said Dayzee.

"Oh, you didn't. Did you?"

"It was my last chance, Mare. Kozy was fading away, kind of like how Bruno couldn't stay here forever either. It was then or never. I got my last thrill with Kozy, and then just like that, Kenzie was back."

"So, Kenzie doesn't remember any of that?"

"I don't think so, Fia. She might wonder why she doesn't remember anything about the Halloween party."

"I don't either," said Marilyn.

"Well, Mare, there wasn't any party. I just told her that. Think of how confused she must be."

"We'll be real nice to her, then. I know Sissy will."

"Sis, all I did was tuck her in. She was really exhausted, and—"

"And if she wasn't, Sissy, then I bet—"

"No, Sis, I was just acting when we brought her back from the Prism, remember?"

"Uh-huh. Sure, Sissy. I saw how you smiled—"

"Girls! You two should be calmed down after your little romp with Cliff."

"I'm never calmed down," said Marilyn. "I'm just so itchy all the time!"

"Sis is right. Me too."

"Yeah, I get it—I'm more itchy now than before having fun with Kozy in the elevator," said Dayzee. "All that did was get me more worked up."

"You didn't get a chance to, you know, get Kozy to—"

"No, Mare. Dammit. We were just about to, then Kozy turned back into Kenzie."

"You still could have—"

"Oh, Mare, not what I had in mind. I needed Kozy for that. Hey, maybe we should all go wake up Kenzie. She looks even better in that uniform than Kozy did."

"Except for one very important thing," said Marilyn.

"Oh, yeah. Hey, I just heard another car door. Maybe Cliff came back."

Dayzee opened the door a crack and saw Jiff Roberts walking up the few steps onto the porch. She pulled the door in all the way.

"Jiff! Girls, this is Jiff, the photographer friend I told you about. Jiff, that's Marilyn in the tiny robe . . ."

Marilyn giggled and waved.

". . . and that's her twin sister, Sophia."

Sophia nodded and looked him up and down. His long, wavy brown hair bunched up on his shoulders, and he wore jeans and a blue t-shirt.

"Dayzee said she had gorgeous friends, but I had no idea how much. Nice to meet you both."

"You just decided to drop by, Jiff?"

"Is it a bad time? It looks like you have a lot going on."

"No, I'm glad you're here. We've been talking about you a lot the last few days. There were so many times we all thought it'd be fun to have a pro taking photos of us because we sure get into some fun situations."

"Like right now," said Marilyn. "See this silly little robe I'm wearing? It doesn't hide much, does it?"

"Hell no. That's fantastic wardrobe for a shoot."

"Sis likes taking her clothes off and then posing."

"Sissy's right, but usually what happens is *she* takes my clothes off for me. Then, I get to—"

"Then, she takes *my* clothes off. Do you have your camera, Jiff? We'd be happy to—"

"Girls, settle down. We still have some business to take care of, remember?"

"You mean Kenzie?" said Sophia. "Yep, that's some business that needs some attention."

"I knew you liked her, Sissy."

"What's not to like, Sis?"

"She does have very nice legs."

"And everything else, Sis. Especially in that cute little uniform of hers. Why, I think maybe—"

"Hey, you two. Let's get ourselves a drink, and we can show Jiff—"

"Let's show him Kenzie!" said Marilyn.

"Yep, Sis is right—we can get some photos too. Jiff, you have your camera?"

He glanced at Dayzee, then turned toward Sophia and said, "Well, yeah, out in the car."

"The girls might be onto something, Jiff. Why don't you run out and get your gear?"

"Sure thing, Dayzee."

He opened the door and stepped out onto the porch, where he stopped and tilted his head.

"Hey, is that your delivery guys? I think they're in their truck. Hear that?"

The sound of slow pounding on the truck's walls stopped, then started again.

"Oh, those guys," said Dayzee. "I guess they didn't go for tacos after all."

"Are they alright? Maybe we should check on them."

"Never mind them, Jiff. Just grab your stuff, and we'll all take a hike upstairs."

"To wake up Kenzie," Marilyn said as she poked her elbow into her sister.

"Or we could sneak in and have some fun while we let her sleep, Sis."

"That could be fun too."

"Fine, I'll grab a camera," Jiff said before walking away toward his car parked behind the delivery van. He watched it closely as the soft pounding continued while he walked past it.

Dayzee closed the door and leaned her back against it.

"Let's do some quick thinking, girls. We have a living dead guy in the elevator and two in the—"

She stopped at the sound of wood splintering. She looked to her right, then quickly to her left, and saw the molding around the door prying itself loose from the wall. Before she could say another word, the board on her left snaked across her waistline, pinning her against the door with her arms at her sides. The one on her right laid itself on her forehead, holding her head in place.

"Girls! Get this assassin garbage off of me!"

They'd just started reaching for the trim boards when they stopped to watch the door begin to crack from the bottom to the top on each side of Dayzee. Her restraints raised her up until her heels no longer touched the floor, then the center section of the door broke itself free. As soon as it had pivoted twice along the tile floor, the trim snapped free from the wall and circled around behind the door.

"Mare! Fia!"

"What can we do, Dayzee?" said Marilyn.

The door slab continued to rock on its bottom corners, carrying Dayzee toward the stairway.

"I don't know! Do something!"

"Like what?" said Sophia.

"Anything! Hey, we can't let Jiff see this!"

Jiff poked his head through the wide opening in the door and said, "Too late. What the hell is this? Special effects?"

"Yep, that's it," said Sophia. "Get to work, alright? Get some photos of this."

Jiff uncapped his camera and pointed it as the door section made it to the base of the stairs, where it hopped up onto the first one.

"God, girls! Someone, help me!"

"Oh, you know what?" Sophia said as Jiff snapped a few photos. "We shouldn't help you at all. This is what you have to do, right?"

"I changed my mind!" Dayzee screamed and put her boots three steps up and tried to push herself back.

The handrail started popping loose near the second floor and snapped its way down until it was completely free. It gently coiled itself around the door and Dayzee's thighs and began to squeeze, and soon, even her legs were held tight.

"It isn't taking no for an answer, Dayzee," said Marilyn. "Hey, Sissy, that thing is going to undress her, right? Let's help it."

"Oh, Sis, you can't be serious."

"I sure am. I'm itching to undress Dayzee."

The door leaned to one side and spun around so that Dayzee faced toward the approaching twins.

"Aw, look, Sissy, it heard us. It wants us to help."

"No! No, it doesn't, Mare! Get me out of this thing!"

Marilyn reached up and began unbuttoning Dayzee's blouse.

"Get you out of your blouse? Okay!"

"Stop it, Mare! Don't you dare!"

Marilyn froze with her hands still on Dayzee's blouse.

"What am I doing, Dayzee? Hey, can that assassin control me too?"

"Oh, I don't know," Dayzee said before the door hopped up one step, pulling her blouse free of Marilyn's grasp.

"I think you're right, Sis," said Sophia, "because I feel like undressing Dayzee too."

"Me too," said Jiff. "But hell, I always do. Count me in."

"You guys are no help at all!"

The door hopped up another step. Jiff rushed to the stairs, shoving the twins to each side. He grabbed the door piece in both hands and tried to hold it still. It shook rapidly, then hopped up another step, and he screamed.

"Damn," he said, looking at his hands, "that thing gave me slivers in each hand!"

"It can do worse," said Marilyn. "Have you seen the flying knives yet?"

"No, I sure haven't. What's that all about?"

"I guess you already figured out that none of this is normal, right, Jiff?" said Sophia. "How well do you know Dayzee?"

"I've seen her eyes shining. Yeah, she's not really normal, is she? I mean—"

"Hey! Somebody, help me!"

The door hopped up another step.

"How?" said Marilyn. "We can't stop that thing."

The door leaned backwards, chasing all three back down as Dayzee screamed, then it tipped back up and jumped two steps closer to the second floor.

"Damn, this is some weird shit," said Jiff. "Can someone please tell me what's going on?"

"No time, Mr. Jiff," said Marilyn. "Dayzee has a hot date with some serious wood."

"That's pretty funny, Sis."

"I don't get it," said Jiff. "What the hell is going on?"

"Short story," said Sophia, "is that something was sent to kill Dayzee and Sis and me. Along the way, it picked up a little thing for Dayzee, and it wants to, you know, consummate their relationship."

The door with Dayzee trapped against it leaned backwards again, causing Marilyn to scream, and they all took a step back. It righted itself and tipped first to the left, then to the right, then hopped up another step.

"'Consummate.' That's a big word, Sissy. I'm impressed."

"Well, we did do some studying, remember? We're not just a couple of pretty faces."

"No, we're much more than that. Jiff, here, is seeing some of that with this tiny robe I have on, aren't you, Jiff?"

Jiff stopped to look first at Marilyn, then at her sister, and said, "Oh, hell yeah. I never thought of twins having different hair like you two, but now that I'm looking at you, that's really—"

"Hey! What about me? I,"—Dayzee stopped as the door took another jump—"don't want to do this!"

"There's no other way," said Sophia. "Kozy said so, remember?"

"Yeah, but—"

She fell silent at the sight of dead Kenny at the top of the stairs with a knife embedded in his chest.

"Oh God, this just keeps getting better," said Sophia. "I forgot about him. I bet he never got around to his work either. Slacker."

"What the hell?" said Jiff. "He's got a knife in him?"

"Oh yeah, well, he's dead."

"That doesn't stop them," said Marilyn. "There was even a dead guy walking around looking for head. You remember that, Sissy?"

"I sure do. That was—"

"Girls! Focus, okay? Don't let Kenny get me too!"

"I don't think he wants you, Dayzee," said Sophia. "I think he's mostly going to go after our new buddy, Jiff."

"What? Why me?"

"You're an outsider. Maybe it sees you as competition?"

"I think Sissy is right about that."

Dayzee screamed as the slab of wood turned to the right, balancing on its left corner and facing her toward the wall. It took a few short hops toward the wall until her breasts pressed against the drywall, and Kenny began stumbling down the steps. The piece of door began sliding back and forth, rubbing Dayzee's blouse against the textured wall and within seconds, buttons danced down the staircase as the thin cloth got peeled to each side.

"Oh, this is getting ridiculous!" Dayzee said, but no one listened.

"Uh-oh, Sissy, here he comes."

"Can a dead guy do that, Sis?"

"With us, I bet he can!"

"We are pretty hot. Hey, that's it. One of us needs to burn this guy."

"Oh, Sissy, that won't kill the assassin. We already tried—"

"No, Sis, of course not, but this dead Kenny body might not work anymore, right?"

"Yes, probably! Okay, how should we do it?"

Kenny had passed the trapped Dayzee, and the other three backed down the stairs.

"Jiff, you'll have to hold him. Can you do that?"

"What? Are you crazy?"

"No, just really itchy, but that doesn't matter right now. Just hold the guy, and don't be surprised by what happens, alright?"

"I, uh, I don't—"

Kenny moved quickly and tried to strangle Jiff, who turned his back to the wall and grabbed both wrists. Kenny's blank eyes stared above Jiff's head, and his hands opened and closed, trying to find Jiff's throat.

"That's good! Hold him, Jiff!" said Marilyn.

"Girls!" Dayzee screamed as her door spun and jumped up another step.

"Just a sec, Dayzee," said Marilyn. "Sissy's got some cooking to do."

Sophia moved closer and placed her left palm on Kenny's back. Instantly, smoke started to cloud up the stairway, and the smell of burning cloth and flesh filled the air.

"Do it, Sissy!"

"What the hell?" said Jiff.

"She's really hot," said Marilyn.

A second later, Sophia's hand emerged from a smoldering hole in Kenny's chest, and his body slumped and rolled to the bottom of the staircase where it lay smoking.

"What just happened?" said Jiff. "How . . . how can—"

"Oh, we can do more than that, Jiff. Maybe we'll show you sometime. Whatcha think?"

"I think I'm scared as hell!"

Sophia stood in front of him on the same step and said, "But we do look good, don't we, Jiff?"

He let out a deep sigh and said, "God yeah. You're both so . . . you're just—"

"Like no other women you've ever met?"

"Yeah, like that."

"Not scared anymore, are you?" Marilyn said with a giggle.

She stood a step above him, and when he turned, his eyes were even with her breasts. She reached for the robe, played with it some, and pulled it open more than it already was.

He stared and mumbled, "No. I mean, how could I be?"

"Good," said Sophia. "You're part of the team now. Hey, keep taking photos, alright?"

"Sure. Yeah, that's a great idea. Dayzee would probably want me—"

"Hey, all of you! Don't talk about me like I'm not here!"

The door hopped up another step.

"Oh, Dayzee," said Marilyn. "We haven't forgotten about you. Just so you know, I still feel like ripping your clothes off."

"Sis is right. So do I."

"Me too. Just for the photos, I mean. Sorry, Dayzee."

"Look, you're all too late for that," said Dayzee. "I give up. You girls are right. I have to go through with this."

"What's she talking about?"

"It's the only way to kill the assassin," said Sophia. "We have to catch it when it's having its evil, wooden way with Dayzee."

"Yes, and she has to be enjoying it," said Marilyn. "Like, really enjoying it."

"And right then, Sis and I have to burn it up. It's the only way."

"Kozy said so, Sissy."

"Oh, I forgot all about Kenzie—she's still upstairs."

"I bet she's really cozy, too, Sissy."

"Yep, she probably wiggled her way out of that—"

The sound of splintering wood interrupted them, and Jiff and the twins turned to see dead Joey and dead Arden fighting their way through the hole in the door, each with a knife in his dead hand. Dayzee's door hopped up another step.

"Oh, yeah," said Sophia. "Those two."

"They broke out of the truck," said Marilyn. "Jiff, you have to help us again."

"Sure, I'd do anything for you two."

Marilyn grinned at her sister and said, "Earthmen!"

"Maybe this planet isn't so bad, Sis."

Jiff hopped to the floor with the twins close behind. He grabbed Joey near his elbows and spun them both around.

Marilyn yelled, "My turn!" and placed her right hand on Joey's chest. Smoke and the stench of burning delivery guy flesh struck them all.

Jiff looked back over his shoulder just in time to see Arden raising his knife high for a stab. He leaned to one side, and the point found its way into Joey's head, who dropped to the floor and continued to smolder. Arden let go of the knife to grab Jiff's neck.

"Hey, that other guy is trying to choke me!"

Jiff couldn't say any more as Arden's hands found a good grip and began to squeeze.

"Hold on, there, Jiff," said Sophia.

She hurried to his right side, slipped her right hand between him and the guy choking him, and placed it over his heart. Her hand heated all the way up, and Jiff's eyes teared as he made gurgling sounds while Sophia finished off the last of the dead delivery guys. Within seconds, she'd burned clear through, and Arden collapsed onto Joey to make a bloody, sizzling heap.

"Quick, Sissy, grab that knife!"

They each grabbed the knife handles and ripped them away from the bodies on the floor. Sophia turned back toward the stairs to see the knife in Kenny's chest twisting around.

"Yikes, Sis. Look."

All three watched as the blade squished out, rose up and hesitated, then sailed up the stairs, over Dayzee's door, and disappeared around the corner to the right.

"Well, we're still doing pretty well, Sissy. All the dead guys are dead again, and we have all but one of the knives."

"Yep, and Jiff is still alive. Altogether, I guess we're doing okay."

"I'm glad I could help you two gorgeous girls. I know that was all kind of weird, but—"

"Hey! I changed my mind!" Dayzee screamed.

They all looked up to see the door hopping toward the left with Dayzee's face frozen in a silent scream.

"Okay, I changed my mind too," said Jiff. "This is some pretty weird shit."

Marilyn giggled, and Sophia shrugged, then they each gave him a kiss on the cheek at the same time.

"You don't really mean that, do you, Jiff?" Sophia said in his ear.

"Feel like taking some photos?" Marilyn cooed in his other ear. "For us?"

He let out a deep sigh and looked from one to the other.

"I'll do whatever you want."

The girls leaned back enough to look at each other with a smile.

"Hey!" they heard from far down the hallway on the second floor.

Each girl kissed Jiff's cheeks, let him go, and they started up the stairs.

Chapter 22 – It Wants All of Us!

Before taking the last step up, Marilyn, Sophia, and Jiff leaned forward and peeked around the corner to look in each direction.

"Dayzee went that way," Sophia said and pointed to the left.

"Yes, Sissy, but the knife went that way," Marilyn said and pointed to the right.

"I'd be more worried by all this craziness if you two weren't so damn hot."

"Aw, thanks, Jiff," said Marilyn. "We'll never ask you to pick because—"

"Because we do everything together," said Sophia.

"Sissy has a tiny white robe just like mine. Maybe we should tell her to go put it on."

"Sis, he might like it better if he could watch you help me slip on that robe."

"Oh, yes, Sissy. I bet he would."

"God yeah, I really would. Which way is—"

"Hey, you guys! It's taking me up to—"

They heard the elevator door slide shut.

"Uh-oh, Sissy. Dayzee's going all the way up."

"Last time she was in that elevator, I think she went all the way down."

"Oh, you're right! With Kozy! Kozy was all worked up from the danger, and I'm sure Dayzee—"

"Who's Kozy?"

"Kenzie's cousin. I mean brother. Sort of," said Sophia.

"They kind of look alike, except for a bunch of muscles and one other big difference."

"You really liked that, didn't you, Sis?"

"Just like you like Kenzie, Sissy."

"I don't, really. Not like that. I was just acting, remember? I never would have—"

"Wait," said Jiff. "I think I heard Dayzee screaming. Maybe we should go help her?"

"You're probably right," Sophia said as she took a step up and turned to the left. "Come on, there's another stairway down that way."

"Just how big is this mansion?"

"We still don't know," Marilyn said with a shrug. "I don't think even Dayzee knows for sure."

"Damn."

Marilyn and Sophia each grabbed a hand, and they led him down the hallway to the left. He kept turning around to glance behind them and said, "Aren't you two worried about that knife that can fly around on its own?"

"No, silly," said Marilyn. "You're the only one it wants to kill."

"Yep, and then it'll wake you back up just for fun."

"Damn, that's crazy."

"Earth is a funny place," said Marilyn.

"Huh?"

"Sis just means funny things happen, that's all. Come on. Let's go see what Dayzee's up to."

At the top of the stairs, they took a few steps and peered through the doorway with no door at the large room with windows at each end. Dayzee was still attached to the jagged piece of the front door, and it had laid itself flat in the middle of the floor. She turned her head toward them and tried to smile.

"Dayzee, are you okay?"

"Yeah, Mare. This is just creepy as hell, you know?"

"Better you than us," Sophia said with a chuckle. "What's next?"

"No, Sissy, this isn't the right way."

She took a step closer to Dayzee and looked down on her.

"You better start enjoying this, Dayzee," she said. "It's the only way, remember?"

"Sis is right," said Sophia. "Hey, just remember how you felt in the elevator with Kozy when you . . . got busy."

Dayzee closed her eyes and took a deep breath. Seconds later, she began to smile until the sounds of wood cracking and splintering caused them all to look to the far end of the room, where a closet door was ripping itself from its hinges while swinging open and shut.

"Oh no, Dayzee," said Marilyn. "I think that's your date."

"It's a door date," said Sophia. "That's kind of funny."

"Maybe for you two," Dayzee said. "But I'm not so sure—"

A loud crack rang out through the room as the handrail pinning Dayzee's legs to the door snapped midway between her thighs.

"Uh-oh," said Marilyn. "Now what?"

Each broken end creaked as they curled down into smooth hooks that lowered and waited just above Dayzee's thighs.

"Oh, Dayzee," said Marilyn, "remember that you're supposed to want this. You can't just get forced into it all."

"What do you mean? What am I supposed to—"

"See those wooden hand things by your legs?" said Sophia. "Don't make them do all the work."

Dayzee shook her head and snarled at the twins, then looked at the ceiling. Marilyn and Sophia and Jiff watched as Dayzee slowly spread her legs wide apart.

"Yoga," Sophia said with a smirk.

Jiff stared with his jaw hanging loose and said, "That's some sexy undies you have there, Dayzee."

"Gee, thanks, Jiff."

"Good thing you put that on," said Marilyn.

"Yep, but that isn't going to stop Mr. Wood Door guy," said Sophia.

They watched in silence as Dayzee's legs waited wide open with her skirt looped up around her waist.

"Hey, Jiff," said Marilyn, "why not take some photos? This should be quite a show."

"Mare, please. This is already pretty humiliating, even without having a permanent record of it."

"Aw, come on, Dayzee," said Sophia. "Be a good sport. Let him snap a few shots."

"You wouldn't think it was so,"—Dayzee groaned as the wood, which had formed into hands, stretched her legs farther apart and clamped them there—"funny if it was you that had to do this."

"She does have a point, Sissy," Marilyn said as she looked away from Dayzee and toward her sister. "I hope Mr. Door is gentle with her."

"Yep, me too. Even though Dayzee likes it rough. I bet not this time, though. Smooth. Let's hope this door thing is smooth."

"Does Mr. Door Guy know how to treat a lady?"

"Probably, Sis. Think about how much sex has probably happened up here, and all that time, that door was probably wishing it could join in. Well, it's finally getting its shot at the big time, and I bet it's more than ready to—"

"Girls! Just get ready to finish this thing off, alright?"

"Oh, okay. You know we have to wait for just the right time, Dayzee," said Marilyn.

"Yep, like when you're really getting into it."

"Believe me, I'm about to set a record for getting there quick. Just get over here and be ready. Jiff, you—oh, what the hell—take all the photos you want, but promise me you will NOT take them out of this house."

"Sure, Dayzee. We'll figure it out. Just what the hell is going on, though?"

Dayzee paused to watch the door shuffling across the floor toward her, all the while changing its shape into a cut-out version of a man.

"Oh, will you look at that?" said Marilyn.

"Cute," said Sophia. "I bet it isn't done getting its shape right. Needs more detail."

"Dayzee? What the hell is this?"

"I don't have time for the long story, Jiff, so listen up. This is all coming from an assassin that was sent to kill all three of us. It can possess anything made of wood. Other stuff, too, but it seems to like wood the best. Somewhere along the way, though, it started getting turned on by all of us."

"Mostly you, Dayzee," said Marilyn. "You're the big star!"

"Right. Anyway, we learned there's only one way to kill it. I have to let it—"

"It wants to take her, Jiff," said Sophia. "I bet Mr. Door is about to sprout some *real* wood."

"Wooden wood!" said Marilyn.

"Yeah, she's right. I have to enjoy it too. I mean, I have to *really* enjoy it. Then, right at that time, one of the girls has to burn the shit out of it."

"Like with a blowtorch? Wait, you mean with your hands again?"

"Oh, that's funny," said Sophia. "He thinks that's all we can do."

"Sissy, he doesn't know about us. Hey, Jiff, maybe you'll get lucky sometime."

Jiff scratched his head and looked from one twin to the other, while they both gave him big smiles, then they all watched the approaching door. It had given itself a shape with two legs, two arms, and a head with a big smile. The room behind it could be seen through its open mouth.

"Okay, that's just creepy as hell," said Dayzee.

"At least it doesn't have a tongue," said Marilyn.

"Yet," Sophia said with a smirk.

While Jiff's camera clicked away, the twins knelt on each side of Dayzee, close enough to strike at the right time. Dayzee gasped when the wooden fingers against her legs creaked and pulled her legs farther apart.

Marilyn looked down with a grin and said, "Thank God for yoga, Dayzee—you've been preparing for this for years."

"That's pretty funny, Sis."

"This isn't funny, girls! This thing is tearing me apart!"

"Aw, Dayzee, it just likes you."

"Sure, Mare. Uh-huh."

"Oh, will you look at that?" said Sophia.

The man-shaped door sprung out another appendage as it began walking instead of rocking from side to side. Its smile stretched out into a narrow slit that still showed light from behind it.

"It really means business! Look!" said Marilyn.

"Oh my God . . ." said Dayzee.

Jiff took more photos and said, "Dayzee, you're really going to let that guy—"

"Guy!" Marilyn said with a loud laugh.

"That door thing, I mean. You're really going to—"

"I have to, Jiff. It's the only way."

"We're here to help her, Jiff. Don't worry," said Sophia.

With a series of loud cracks and snaps, the floor planks began curling up, prying nails loose and twisting around like snakes. Before Marilyn could jump up from her knees, one board coiled around her neck and pulled her down onto her back. The boards beneath her arms and legs stretched up into loops just high enough to snag her limbs, then they squeezed back down into their slots and held her in place. She tried to squirm herself free, but the floorboards had her pinned down at her neck, both wrists, and both ankles.

"Sissy!"

"There's something really hot about that, Sis. I should have thought of that myself because we are so going to set you up like that when we—whoa!"

The boards quickly trapped Sophia the same way, and she struggled to say, "Sis, this wasn't supposed to happen!"

Dayzee fought against all of the boards pinning her to the door on her back, without any success, and said, "Jiff! Jiff!"

He reached for the board covering Marilyn's left arm and tried to pull it up, but another board screeched up from the floor and gave him a quick slap, sending him falling back. When he stood again, he saw both hands of both twins, palms up and glowing hot.

"No, you'll burn down Dayzee's house!"

"Sissy, I can't reach!"

"Neither can I, Sis! That thing must know all about us!"

"Jiff," screamed Dayzee, "do something!"

He stood paralyzed and staring as another thin strip of wood snaked away from the wall and toward Marilyn. It carefully tugged at her robe and laid it wide open. She kept writhing, raising her hips up off of the floor and shaking her breasts around.

"Well, damn," Jiff said with a grin. "Hello, hot naked blond."

The board raced over to Sophia, where it snapped open all of her buttons, then slid inside the clasp of her bra and ripped it open, then traveled down to pull her skirt up high. She began to struggle the same way as Marilyn, thrusting her hips around and bouncing her breasts.

"Good God! Hello, hot naked brunette too!" Jiff said as the girls screamed and Dayzee cussed. "It's like some kind of demented paradise up here!"

"Girls, it wants all of us! We have no choice!"

"Dayzee, that door is going to do all of us? This is too creepy!" said Marilyn.

Sophia fought against the smooth floorboards holding her wrists and ankles to the floor and said, "If I could just get one hand free . . ."

"Jiff," screamed Dayzee, "try again! Just get one of Fia's hands free!"

He stared at Marilyn, then Sophia and said, "Who's Fia?"

"Jiff! It's Sophia! Come on already!"

He set his camera on the floor and lay face down, where he started to shimmy closer to Sophia, whose legs were being spread apart by the wooden loops over her ankles. The door guy had reached Dayzee, and it knelt between her legs. They all stopped to watch, including Dayzee.

"Oh, I don't know, girls. Look at the size of that thing!"

"We can't help you, Dayzee," Marilyn said as she started to sob.

"If I could just get one hand loose," Sophia said before she grunted and pulled more at her restraints.

When Dayzee let out a loud gasp, all eyes turned to watch. The wooden man had found his target, and Dayzee tipped her head back and quit struggling.

"Dayzee, are you okay?" said Marilyn.

"Oh, you know, this isn't such a bad idea, I think."

"You still want us to save you, right?" said Sophia.

"In a while. We did have a,"—she paused to gasp again—"plan. Remember?"

"Oh, I see," said Marilyn. "You're starting to enjoy that a little bit, aren't you?"

"Is that so bad, Mare?"

"No, not at all. I wonder if Sissy and I would—"

Marilyn caught sight of the board that had stripped her and her sister hovering above her, transforming itself into a familiar shape.

"I was kidding! It was a joke! I didn't mean I'd really—"

The board rapidly fell and found a good spot, causing a loud groan from her.

"Sis! Sis, are you alright?"

"Oh, I think . . . maybe . . . you know . . ."

Sophia shook her head and tipped it back to look at Jiff.

"Jiff, as much as I want photos of all of this, you have to try to get me loose."

"Before that thing gets busy with you too?"

"God, I'm glad Kenzie isn't seeing this," Sophia said as she strained against the boards holding her wrists to the floor.

"Sissy . . . she might accept it . . . maybe she . . . she might—"

"I might what?" Kenzie said from the doorway before she saw everything and screamed. Only Sophia and Jiff turned to see her. "What the hell is this? What kind of weird party are you all having?"

"Oh, Kenzie! I was just thinking about you!" said Sophia.

"What the hell are you doing?"

"No time to explain. Help Jiff, alright? Just try to get one of my hands free. It's our only hope!"

Jiff had crawled close enough to grab the board holding Sophia's left wrist. Kenzie rushed over and knelt beside her and tried to help Jiff pry the board up.

"Thanks, Kenzie. You too, Jiff." She turned toward her sister and said, "Are you alright, Sis?"

"I'm actually doing pretty . . . damn good . . . Sissy."

"Huh. Wow. You really were getting itchy, weren't you?"

"Mm-hmm."

"Dayzee, are you still okay?"

"Oh, Fia, I can barely think straight. This guy really—"

"Guy! She said 'guy,' again!" Marilyn said before giggling and saying, "Ooh . . ." and allowing her head to clunk back down on the floor.

"Anyway, he really knows how to treat a girl," said Dayzee. "Better than most."

"I can't get any leverage this way, Jiff," said Kenzie.

She swung her left leg over Sophia's bare body and sat back on her hips. She placed her left hand beside Sophia's head and grabbed at the wood plank with her right.

"Oh, well, hello there," said Sophia.

"Oh, sorry, Sophia, just trying to help."

"Oh, by all means. Do carry on."

"I can't budge this thing," said Jiff. "It's like it's possessed."

"You think?" Dayzee said with a laugh.

"I can't move mine either," said Kenzie, although she kept trying.

"Girls, I think . . . maybe . . ."

"Sissy, Dayzee's trying to tell us something."

Dayzee fell silent as her door date kept at it to the sound of creaking and cracking.

Sophia fought back tears and said, "I have to get loose. I'm the only one that can kill that thing now!"

With tears trickling down her cheeks, Kenzie said, "I'm so sorry, Sophia. I'm no help at all."

She leaned forward until her forehead touched Sophia's, while Jiff kept fighting with the board over her wrist.

"Girls, and Jiff, I think I'm . . . I'm about to . . ."

"Sissy," Marilyn said between quick breaths, "I think now would be the time because Dayzee . . . she's just about . . ."

"Sis?"

"Oh, me too, Sissy. Wow . . ."

Sophia's tears broke loose and trickled down over her cheeks. Kenzie backed away just a bit and looked down on her with a frown. Jiff stopped fighting with the wooden clamp and stared at Sophia's bare chest heaving as she sobbed. Then, he looked over at Marilyn, who had closed her eyes and remained motionless as her amorous trim piece continued its efforts. He gave a quick glance at Dayzee, also with her eyes closed and smiling, then he looked up at the grinning face of the wooden door guy. Somehow, the door guy had turned to face him and winked, and Jiff said, "Damn."

No one moved when the window at the end of the room shattered, followed quickly by a loud report. Jiff looked up at the wooden guy, whose smile had turned upside-down and who now sported a clean, perfectly round hole through his forehead.

He fell to the floor off to one side of Dayzee and lay across her thigh. All of the boards holding Dayzee and the twins relaxed, and the one giving its best attention to Marilyn made one last effort before flopping down between her thighs.

Sophia pulled her arms and legs free and coaxed Kenzie off to the side. She looked first at her sister, who lay still, not trying to free herself. Then, she saw Dayzee doing the same before she looked at the dead door man with a hole in his head.

"Seriously?" she said. "That's all it took? Hell, one of us could have shot him ourselves!"

"She said 'him,'" Marilyn said before she sighed and lay there smiling.

"Thank God some whacko is still trying to shoot me," said Dayzee.

"That whacko could have waited another two minutes," Marilyn said with a deep sigh.

Jiff jumped to his feet and snatched up his camera. He circled Dayzee and the twins and Kenzie, taking photos of them and the unmoving boards from every direction. Kenzie knelt close by Sophia and smiled down on her.

"I don't think I'm even going to ask. It's this house, right? Things happen in this mansion?"

"Yeah, it goes kind of crazy sometimes. Blame it on the Hills, too, Kenzie. It's good to have you back."

"Where did I go?"

"Oh, nowhere. Nowhere at all," she said and smiled back up at her.

Marilyn had recovered enough to turn and see her sister smiling up at Kenzie, and she said, "Aw, a happy ending."

"No, Mare," said Dayzee. "I just had the happy ending. I don't think even the bullet would have killed it if I didn't enjoy the hell out of it."

"You really did, didn't you?"

"Mm-hmm. Oh, yeah."

Another bullet raced through the broken window and exploded the camera out of Jiff's hands. Pieces flew in every direction and clattered to the floor. He laid himself flat and put his hands over his head.

"So much for the photos," said Jiff.

"You'll need a new camera," said Dayzee.

"You'll need another carpenter too," said Marilyn.

"This house sure has some crazy attitude. Kenzie and I need a drink, so we're going back to the Prism. Who's coming?"

"I just did," said Dayzee.

"I was just about to," said Marilyn.

"I think," said Jiff, "maybe I . . . I mean—"

"Ew," said Sophia. "Let's just go."

Chapter 23 – Science and Sorcery

"Hey, Kenzie," said Mack, "I missed you. Glad you're back. How about helping me out back here?"

"Why does everyone keep acting like I've been gone?"

"Well, because when Kozy was around, we never saw—"

"Who the hell is Kozy? I keep hearing that name, but I've never seen—"

"That's kind of like our Halloween joke," said Dayzee. "Kozy's not a real person. It all started the first time you took a nap and got all cozy."

"Oh, no," said Mack, "Kozy sure was—"

"Fun to talk about! That's right!" Dayzee said quickly and gave him a look before turning to Kenzie. "Kenzie, we'd love seeing you on the other side of the bar again."

"Huh. I might never figure all this out. Especially your house, Dayzee. Sure, Mack, I can give you a hand."

While Kenzie walked around the bar to join Mack, Sophia took a barstool with Dayzee to her right, and Marilyn sat on the other side of Dayzee.

"Just like old times, huh, Sissy? Way back before you and Kenzie started—"

"I keep telling you, Sis, nothing ever happened."

"Oh, I know, but that was still a bunch of fun. You and Kenzie seemed to always have your clothes off, and you were in and out of beds, and how many times did you two kiss? I can count at least—"

"Girls, we survived. Isn't that the main thing?"

"You're right, Dayzee," said Sophia. "It's been an insane couple of days. I just want things to settle down for a while."

"I agree, Sissy. Just one day off, then we can all find our next fountains of youth."

"Did you mean that, Fia? About settling down?"

Before Sophia could answer, Kenzie returned with three drinks and set them on the bar, and Mack stood close behind her wiping his hands with a washcloth.

"Here you go, ladies. The night is still young—I'll keep them coming."

She gave them a smile, turned, and walked one way, and Mack walked the other way.

"You mean, like really settling down, Fia?"

"Yeah, Dayzee. I just mean someday. How about you?"

"I guess. My life has been mostly about fun, though. I'm not sure I'm ready to slow down."

"I think about it sometimes too," Marilyn said as she looked past the other two at Mack.

"Probably, we all could," said Sophia. "Maybe."

"Oh, I do think about it, girls. I hate to admit this, but for a while, I even thought maybe the Boss and I could, you know, if things were different, then—"

"You would have made a nice couple," said Marilyn. "Kind of too late for that, though, since we burned him all up."

"Yeah, too late for him, but it still sounds like a good idea. You know . . . eventually. And really, Mare, we both see you staring at Mack. Maybe he's the one for you? That is, if you're ever ready for that."

"I always thought I'd end up with some big star, Dayzee. But you're right, Mack is a pretty good catch too. I can see someday settling down with a bartender."

"You have plenty of money, so you wouldn't need someone rich," said Dayzee. "How about you, Fia? Could you see yourself with a bartender?"

"Sissy could see herself with a barmaid, I bet."

Sophia looked past her sister at Kenzie serving drinks at the other end of the bar and didn't answer.

"She's thinking about it, Mare. Look, we've all had lots of thrills here on Earth, but that doesn't mean we have to keep going like that. We could probably settle down, don't you think?"

"Oh, Dayzee," said Marilyn, "how about Cliff? He's probably only human, but still."

"Sis makes a good point," said Sophia. "Have you ever thought about that?"

"Well, yeah, I've been thinking about it. He sure is charming."

"And good looking," said Sophia.

"And rich!" said Marilyn.

"You know what, girls? Let's see how 'Kildare in the Hills' goes. We'll be spending a lot of time together. Maybe all of us will settle down."

"I don't think I'm ready for that," said Sophia. "I'm not about to slow down. How about you, Sis?"

"Not today, Sissy. I can't give up on ever using my heat and barbs again. Can you?"

"No. No way, Sis. Dayzee, can you?"

"That's part of why I thought the Boss could be the one—he could take all of that, over and over. God, that could have worked out great. Cliff could never survive it, though."

"For sure," said Marilyn. "Bruno could have taken it, too, but he's probably never coming back here, and we can't ever go back either."

"I still think about the fun we had in the pool," said Sophia. "Wasn't that something?"

"Oh, yes, Sissy, that was splendid."

"There's not much better than that," said Dayzee. "I'm getting turned on just thinking about it."

"Me too," said Marilyn. "How about you, Sissy?"

"Yep, I sure am. That time by the statue, too, when he'd grown some more. I could go for some more of that."

"Some more of what, Lady Sophia?"

Bruno stood with his beefy arms crossed and a big smile across his face. His beard was still bushy, and he still wore thick jeans, heavy black boots, and a black t-shirt. This time, "Surprise, Surprise" was written on his ball cap.

Marilyn and Sophia snapped their heads around to see, and Dayzee spun her stool all the way around.

"Bruno? How did . . . how could you—"

"I escaped. Twice. They caught me the first time, and they took me to—"

"Well, look at you!" said Dayzee. "How tall are you now?"

She jumped off of her stool, and even wearing high heels, she had to look high up to see him.

"Oh, I need to check this out too," said Sophia, and she soon stood beside Dayzee, both peering up at a smiling Bruno.

"Miss Marilyn? Your turn."

Marilyn grinned and took her place next to Dayzee. All three stared up at him with big smiles.

"Bruno, you're what . . . seven feet tall?"

"Almost. But this is it—I'm back where I started. What do you think, ladies?"

"I am shocked, Bruno," said Dayzee. "How did you come back to Earth, though? We were just thinking about you."

"That's what drew me back through the portal. I was just thinking about all three of you, and it must have been at the exact same time. That was enough power to yank me through."

"You were thinking about us?" said Marilyn.

"Yes, Miss Marilyn. It started when I remembered all that fun in Dayzee's pool. We sure had some good times, didn't we? Then, something struck me: that all of you accepted me, even though I'd been compressed by that horrible gravity planet. You never belittled me."

He stared at each of them with a twinkle in his eyes.

"Okay, now you're being funny," said Marilyn.

"And clever," Sophia said with a big grin.

"That must be what did it," said Dayzee. "We all had some powerful, real feelings, on each side of the portal, and that—"

"Poofed me right back. I won't be able to poof back through either. They can't make me because I dug that mobile portal out of me. That wasn't fun, believe me, but it's gone now."

Dayzee looked up at his hat and said, "Yeah, this sure is a surprise. We never thought—"

"No, that's not what the hat is all about. I started to tell you that I escaped once, and they caught me. Well, they took me to one of their nutty labs. You know what I'm talking about."

"Yes, the ones with all the strange science," said Marilyn.

"Oh, and sorcery too," said Sophia. "They mix that all up together, don't they?"

"Yes, Lady Sophia. They did things to me. I'm kind of unpredictable now."

"What, like you say off-the-wall things, sometimes?" said Marilyn.

"No, Miss Marilyn."

"Oh, I know: sometimes you punch people for no reason?" said Sophia.

"That's not right either, Lady Sophia."

"I know," said Dayzee, "it's because you can poof around Earth all you want, right? You can just show up in someone's bedroom when they're—"

"No. None of you are even close. It's me that's the surprise. Just me. It's not fun."

He wiped at his eyes while looking at the floor. Marilyn settled onto the seat at her right and tapped on the one that she'd just left.

"Come on, Bravo Bruno. Have a seat and tell us all about it."

"Sis is right," said Sophia. "Join us. Mack, a beer for Bruno."

By the time Bruno sat, Mack had placed the beer in front of him. Sophia's eyes no longer followed Kenzie, and Marilyn seemed to have forgotten about Mack. Dayzee spun around to face the bar, and all three waited for Bruno to continue.

"They injected me with some kind of science stuff. It was laced with little pieces of sorcery that I think they wanted to get rid of because they were scared of it. They pumped it all into me.

"There were a dozen of them in the lab, and when I'd regained consciousness, one of them explained their plan: to transform me into some kind of super soldier. He said they had no idea if they had that kind of control, though. He said most likely I'd change into something that no one could predict or contain.

"He was right. All I remember about what followed was the taste of blood on fangs, ripping out throats and hearts and lungs. I remember razor-sharp claws, long and pointy, swatting every living thing close enough. I howled too. I howled like a son of a bitch.

"There was nothing left of them but puddles and slimy chunks."

They each picked up their cocktail and downed it, slammed their glasses down, and studied Bruno closely.

"So," said Marilyn, "you must have changed back to Bruno again?"

"No, not right away. My next memory was of being really small and fluffy, and I had floppy ears that bounced around as I hopped out of the lab."

"You turned into a bunny?" said Dayzee. "Why would you do that?"

"That's just it—I didn't. It just happened. I never know what I'm going to shift into next."

"Oh, I get it," said Sophia. "That's why it says 'surprise' on your hat?"

"Yes, Lady Sophia. I never know when . . . um . . . I, uh . . . I feel kind of strange . . ."

Bruno set his beer down, stared straight ahead, and began shaking.

"Uh-oh," said Marilyn.

He snapped his head straight up and forced all of his breath out through his nose.

"Here we go," said Dayzee.

Bruno's arms began to shrivel back on themselves and disappeared inside his shirt. His neck started stretching, and his features began to smooth out while his skin became textured and shiny.

"Sheesh," said Sophia.

Bruno had become a long, thick, purple snake, which tried to coil up on the barstool but dumped off the side and onto the floor next to his clothes. His head remained where it had been, and he calmly looked from one pair of staring eyes to the other. His tongue flicked out repeatedly.

"It's still me, though, so don't be scared. I won't hurt anyone."

"He can still talk!" said Marilyn.

"And drink," said Bruno. "Dayzee, how about some help?"

"Oh, sure. How can you talk? You're a snake."

"Sorcery. Nasty stuff."

Dayzee picked up Bruno's beer bottle and poured it into his mouth, which was open wide and hissing, causing the beer to bubble around before he swallowed it.

"Well, this is weird as hell," said Sophia.

"Maybe we should cover him up or something?" said Marilyn. "What will people think?"

Dayzee turned to Sophia, grinned and shook her head, and said, "She still doesn't get it. Such a sweet kid."

She turned back to Bruno and said, "How do we change you back?"

"I can't just decide to switch to Bruno or anything else, Dayzee."

"What are we supposed to do with you now?"

"Dayzee, I really need someplace to stay, at least until I can figure this out. I'm not sure this switching stuff will keep up forever."

"Not a problem. There's plenty of room back at the house. What are you going to do in the meantime?"

"All I can do is make the most of it, you know?"

"Like how?"

"For one thing, how about a thrill like you've probably never had before?"

Dayzee looked at Marilyn, who nodded rapidly and grinned. She turned around to see Sophia, who only shrugged, smirked, and whistled for another drink.

"Sure, Bruno. I'm always ready for a thrill."

Kenzie brought Sophia's drink, set it down, and stared at the giant snake between Dayzee and Marilyn.

"That's a new one."

"Eh, just go with it, Kenzie. He's an old friend."

Bruno continued to stare into Dayzee's eyes while his split tongue waved all around. Dayzee felt something touching her right ankle, then winding around it and up her calf. She looked down and saw the end of his tail between her knees.

"Oh, Bruno, the end of your tail, it looks just like a—"

"I know. Ain't that crazy? I tell you, no one should *ever* mix science and sorcery."

"Yes," said Marilyn, "and then inject it into someone."

"Right, and portal him to Earth," said Sophia.

"In my bar," said Kenzie.

"You girls sure are hot," said Mack.

"Earth!" Marilyn said to her sister.

Dayzee watched with unblinking eyes as Bruno's snake tail rubbed its way up between her thighs and under her skirt until she let out a loud squeal.

"Oh my, Bruno," she said with a giggle. "That's some kind of tail you got there."

Marilyn and Sophia both stared at the commotion beneath Dayzee's skirt.

"Wow, Bruno, that tail of yours knows what it's doing!"

Bruno seemed to smile and said, "You once told me that these earthmen rarely satisfy you. You remember that?"

"Well, yeah," she said and picked up a menu to fan her face. "They try, but they just don't have . . . enough."

"Right, so let me start coiling up for you."

"Oh, you sure are bunching up in there! Oh my God, girls!"

"Hey, I want some of that too," said Sophia.

"Me too! Dayzee shouldn't have all the fun!"

"Hey, ladies, as long as I'm still a snake, I got plenty for all of you. Dayzee still hasn't found out the best thing yet."

"Oh," said Dayzee, "I can barely breathe already! What is this best thing you're talking about?"

Bruno twisted his head around to look over the bar and said, "Mack, how about a cigarette?"

Mack jabbed one into the snake's mouth and lit it. He shook his head, smiled, shrugged, and resumed looking from one twin to the other.

"After all that he's seen, huh, Sis?"

"Yes, Sissy. Nothing's going to phase Mack anymore. Kenzie, though?"

"She's catching on. The more she sees, the more she—"

"Girls, hold up. I need to hear about that best thing Bruno was talking about."

"Oh, right. Hey, Bruno, Dayzee wants to know what else you got?"

"Hey, how about my hat too?" he said.

Marilyn picked it up off of the floor and put it on his snake head.

"What else do I have?" he said as he looked at her from under the brim of his hat. He let out a thick cloud of smoke and said, "Dayzee, I'm a rattlesnake."

A soft buzzing began, and Dayzee cackled and held onto the bar with both hands.

"Oh, girls, forget about rocking and rolling. Rattling is where it's at!"

Her phone rang, and when she didn't move to answer it, Sophia picked it up, listened briefly, then put it on speaker.

"Dayzee, it's Cliff. We're in a bind with some other schedules, and we need to start your Kildare show right away."

"Oh, Cliff, that's . . . I mean, um . . . if we—"

"Dayzee, are you okay? You sound kind of funny."

"Oh, no, I'm fine. We need to get started on the show, you said?"

"Yeah, like right away. Your gate was open, so the whole crew is waiting on your driveway. When can you get here?"

Dayzee took quick, short breaths and stared up at the ceiling, so Sophia answered.

"Hey, don't worry," she said with a smirk. "We'll slither right over there."

"'Slither!' That's what Sissy said!" said Marilyn.

"Marilyn, is that you? Okay, we'll hang tight. Can't wait to get started in this monstrous mansion."

"It's so big," said Marilyn, "that we'll all be rattling around in there!"

"Good one, Sis."

"Are you girls okay?"

"They're fine, Cliff," said Dayzee. "We're coming. *Real* soon."

Sophia laughed, Marilyn giggled, and Kenzie stared silently while Mack continued to smile at the Kildare Killers. Bruno flicked his tongue all around, chuckled while puffing his cigarette, and bobbed his purple snake head in time with the jukebox.

Dayzee grinned at the twins, picked up her drink, and said, "God, only in Beverly Hills!"

Enjoy the Story?

Thank you for reading! Please consider leaving a review and/or a rating at your favorite bookseller or with your favorite book club. Help your fellow readers meet Dayzee Dazzle!

For more about Edward Allen Karr and his books, visit:

www.LakesideLetters.com

What's Next for Dayzee Dazzle?

Dayzee Dazzle and the On-Set Onslaught
Thrills N Kills in the Hills Book Three

The time has come to begin shooting the reality show, "Kildare in the Hills," in Dayzee Dazzle's mansion in the Beverly Hills Flats. Dayzee and her best friends, Marilyn and Sophia, a.k.a. the Kildare Killers, are sure to become even bigger stars. What could possibly go wrong? Well, for one thing, their friend Bruno is having a little trouble with the science and sorcery experiments performed on him by the Guild. At any time, he can find himself transformed into any type of creature, indigenous or off-worldly or imaginary, and of course, Dayzee is bringing him home. What else? Well, her house might just have a few dark secrets of its own. Lights . . . camera . . . bedlam!

Have You Met Lin Finity?

She's the powerful star of her own series titled the Fringes Of Infinity. In the beginning, she's forced to learn how to control the unstoppable, magical power she earned at age fifteen. After killing her abusive uncle with her deadly new ability, she locked it away inside herself. Now, she's in her forties, and it's back. She calls it *Mayhem*. And it's done waiting.

Book One and the Novella are free in e-book format. Just visit
www.LakesideLetters.com

Lin Finity and her Mayhem Rising
Lin Finity in Holding On

About the Author

Edward Allen Karr was born, raised, and continues to reside in Ohio, USA. His adult life has followed a meandering path, ranging from working an automotive assembly line to designing space flight hardware. And through all of it, he's seen that life is a captivating and ultimately unexplainable endeavor. His writing seeks to add a splash of wonder to a world already awash in it.

* * *

For more information, please visit:

www.LakesideLetters.com